Praise for *A Sho...*

"Nearly everything about Kate Walbert's new novel is wickedly smart, starting with the title. . . . Her writing wears both its intelligence and its ideology lightly. . . . No manifesto, this is a gorgeously wrought and ultimately wrenching work of art. . . . It is Walbert's conceit that while the oldest and youngest generations never meet, they share a legacy of echoes: objects and phrases that repeat mysteriously, and with increasing significance, across the decades. This spare novel manages, improbably, to live up to its title. . . . Each chapter is like a slice of exquisite cake. . . . I found myself going back time and again to reread whole paragraphs, not because they'd been obscure, but in the way one might press a finger to the crumbs littering an otherwise cleaned plate: out of a desire to savor every morsel. . . ."

—Leah Hager Cohen, *The New York Times Book Review* (cover review)

"Ambitious and impressive . . . Reminiscent of a host of innovative writers from Virginia Woolf to Muriel Spark to Pat Barker . . . A witty and assured testament to the women's movement and women writers, obscure and renowned."

—*The Washington Post*

"An engrossing tale."

—*Marie Claire*

"In her luminous new novel, Kate Walbert weaves the strands of five beautifully particular lives into a tapestry made from key moments in modern history. The result is a subtle and profound book, as thought provoking as it is moving."

—Ann Packer

"Remarkable . . . Walbert doesn't indulge in melodrama, nor does she sentimentalize women's solidarity. . . . Walbert's characterizations are astute, and she captures complex, often contradictory emotions with lapidary precision."

—*Bookforum*

"Ambitious . . . Walbert . . . is a gifted writer . . . Intelligent, admirable."

—*The Dallas Morning News*

"Insightful and moving . . . Perhaps 'The Woman Question,' as one Victorian lecturer in the book calls it, will never be fully answered. Walbert, however, raises and illustrates it beautifully through the lives of Dorothy and her descendants."

—*Hartford Courant*

"Wise, engrossing . . . With restraint, perception, and gentle humor, [Walbert] goes way beyond sexual politics to human nature itself and its eternal verities: the longing of people for connection, be it man and woman or parent and child; to emerge from the protective cage; to experience the sky, trees, and air of freedom and self-realization."

—*Winston-Salem Journal*

"Vivid."

—*Elle*

"The lives of the Townsend women intersect with larger events in twentieth-century history—VJ Day, 1970s consciousness-raising sessions, the aforementioned 9/11—and Walbert beautifully evokes the moods of those various times with a few spare sentences."

—*Fresh Air* on NPR

"Quietly, steadily, Kate Walbert has over the years built an impressive literary reputation as a modern-day Virginia Woolf. . . . Walbert writes with a taut lyricism rarely found in contemporary fiction. . . . Walbert's style is wholly original. Peppered with fine observations, it is, for all its influences and elasticity, still very much her own."

—Philadelphia City Paper

"A Short History of Women . . . is for any woman who has ever struggled to find her own voice; to make sense of being a mother, wife, daughter, and lover. But it is not only for women. . . . Walbert's writing is rich. It reflects each period with such vividness, the reader is transported back. It never feels cliché or unreal. It brings the reader into the character's world and mind-set."

—Associated Press

"I'll read anything written by Kate Walbert. . . . She's one of the most amazing writers."

—Dan Barber, Time magazine

"A Short History of Women is an accomplished, absorbing, and ferociously graceful work. . . . The novel's technical grace is remarkable, Walbert's prose masterful. . . . Walbert resists drawing easy parallels between the lives of her women; rather, the chapters, all centering around crucial moments in the characters' lives, create a perfect interlocking, a luminous patchwork of mystery and discovery, of persistent struggle and occasional triumph."

—The Rumpus

"Beautiful and kaleidoscopic . . . Walbert's look at the twentieth century and the Townsend family is perfectly calibrated, intricately structured, and gripping from page one."

—Publishers Weekly (starred review)

"With a sharp eye and deft touch, Walbert explores the ways women's priorities and freedoms have evolved even as their yearnings have stayed remarkably constant."

—Booklist (starred review)

ALSO BY KATE WALBERT

A SHORT HISTORY
of
WOMEN

A Novel

Kate Walbert

Scribner

NEW YORK   LONDON   TORONTO   SYDNEY   NEW DELHI

♨

SCRIBNER
A Division of Simon & Schuster, Inc.
1230 Avenue of the Americas
New York, NY 10020

First Scribner trade paperback edition June 2010

SCRIBNER and design are trademarks of
The Gale Group, Inc., used under license by Simon & Schuster, Inc.,
the publisher of this work.

For information about special discounts for bulk purchases,
please contact Simon & Schuster Special Sales at
1-866-506-1949 or business@simonandschuster.com.

The Simon & Schuster Speakers Bureau can bring authors to your
live event. For more information or to book an event contact the
Simon & Schuster Speakers Bureau at 1-866-248-3049 or
visit our website at www.simonspeakers.com.

Designed by Kyoko Watanabe
Text set in Kuenstler 480

Manufactured in the United States of America

7   9   10   8   6

Library of Congress Control Number: 2008038312

ISBN 978-1-4165-9498-7
ISBN 978-1-4165-9499-4 (pbk)
ISBN 978-1-4391-0054-7 (ebook)

This book is for Delia and Iris

CONTENTS

Contents

LINEAGE

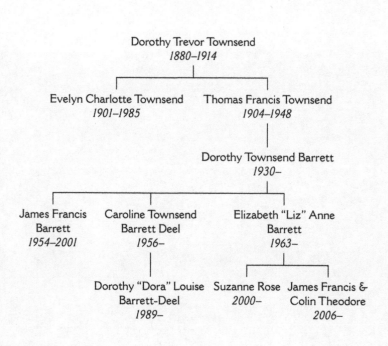

Dorothy Trevor Townsend
1880–1914

Evelyn Charlotte Townsend
1901–1985

Thomas Francis Townsend
1904–1948

Dorothy Townsend Barrett
1930–

James Francis
Barrett
1954–2001

Caroline Townsend
Barrett Deel
1956–

Elizabeth "Liz" Anne
Barrett
1963–

Dorothy "Dora" Louise
Barrett-Deel
1989–

Suzanne Rose
2000–

James Francis &
Colin Theodore
2006–

A SHORT
HISTORY
of
WOMEN

EVELYN CHARLOTTE TOWNSEND

Wardsbury, Grayshead-on-Heath, England, 1914–1918

Mum starved herself for suffrage, Grandmother claiming it was just like Mum to take a cause too far. Mum said she had no choice. Besides, she said, starving made the world brighter, took away the dull edges, the disappointment. She said this in hospital, the place not entirely unpleasant—a private room, windows ammonia-washed looking out to a tree branch on windless days, an ivy-covered wall.

For instance, those, she said. Someone had sent greenhouse lilies, suffrage white, to their favorite cause célèbre, lilies now stuffed in a hospital pot intended for urine or bile. She said she had never known them to have that smell. She'd been blessed by this, she said, the smell of lilies. She said this when she was still speaking, or when she still could be heard, before she twisted into a shape reserved for cracked sticks and hard as that, before they gave her the drip intended for the dying soldiers and here, said the attendant, wasted on a woman by her own hand. Then I was afraid I might break Mum if I breathed, or spoke a word. Before I had tried and tried. Then I gave up like Mum did and went quiet.

Grandmother said to her, "You're too smart." She sat in the chair knitting, like Madame Lafarge waiting for heads to drop. She talked and she talked. She didn't know whom to blame, she said. She had the attendant bring in the blue-veined china soup tureen she'd carried to hospital from her wedding collection, unwrapped from its velvet sack, and a spoon from the silverware she would later promise

3

me, six place settings of a certain filigree. "You're too smart to be so stupid," she said to Mum as the attendant looked on, ladling broth on the ancient blue Chinaman in the matching bowl. "Nobody is paying a damn bit of attention."

But Mum simply turned away.

William wore his barrister's wig to the viewing; the papers reporting he had temporarily lost his mind. I never believed any of it. Besides, this was already December. Everyone had temporarily lost his mind—the war not yet won and miserably proceeding, the trenches entrenched. Wily, Mum had called William. A sparkling prig, she said, as if he were in the room and she were still flirting, arguing in the way they did. That she loved him desperately I understood, though she never fully said it—William still married to an important person's daughter, Mum a widow or worse, an educated woman, and left long ago by my father, lost or dead in Ceylon. What she said was, "William's an old, old friend," or, "Sometimes we misbehave."

Before she died he would come around, or he would not, but at the viewing he stayed a long, long time, wigged and ready. Beside him Mum lay like a dead offering in her simple box, a lavender Votes for Women sash across her small, unquivering bosom, her button-up kid gloves buttoned up to her stiff elbows, her hair à la pompadour.

To my godmother Alexandra's suggestion that I play the piano, I flat out said, No. I was newly thirteen and could do as I pleased. Besides, Thomas would play. Thomas would always play. And so beautifully, who could know whether the mourners were weeping at the sight of Mum dead or the talents of her crippled son? The promise of him drove me mad—the way Mum had always listened, the way Nurse and Penny applauded from the kitchen. Even the bird in its cage, a canary kept to sound the alarm, sat all still and silent when my brother, Thomas, played. So it was around the beautiful Thomas that the mourners gathered, touching him—the top of his head, patting his arm, his shoulder—as if he were holy water. He paid little attention, slouched over the keys performing one of her favorites, his elbows akimbo, slicing the air. Soon, he knows, he will be shipped across the ocean to America. Grandmother said she could afford to keep one of us but two would be a handful. A new family has been found for him, old friends in San Francisco.

Good riddance, I thought, listening with the others—Grandmother and Alexandra and the few neighbors and the ladies Mum called compatriots and William before he bowed and closed the parlor door on his way out. The ladies rustled back to their dance chairs, folding their hands over the printed verse Grandmother said Mum would have preferred. Everyone sat and closed their eyes as if to dream of elsewhere.

I ducked into the kitchen to keep Nurse and Penny company. And what of them? Nurse will marry the milkman, Michael, and settle with him in Wales to live a perfectly miserable life. Children and children. Chores. Michael will drink in the way men do and one thing will lead to the other. Penny will pack her cardboard box and take a train east. She'll disappear like our father did, long before we can even remember him. He fancied himself Lord Byron, Mum said, though he was only a sir and that sir a result of money changing hands. Why she had married him at all she could not say. He vanished in Ceylon, or perhaps the natives devoured him. For my sixth birthday, I received a box containing some of his possessions—cuff links and a blanket woven from hemp; a dictionary of lost words called *The Dictionary of Lost Words* that I, predictably, misplaced, everything and everyone dropping through my hands, even Grandmother, eventually, a few years after Mum died.

She said she thought it best I leave Wardsbury and move to Madame Lane's, an educational establishment out of harm's way. She said she had enjoyed my company, but in light of the endless war and the bloated zeppelins overhead, I should be farther north. There I would learn what I should in the relative peace of distance, peace such as it is, she said. There, she promised, I would find other girls my age and teachers of a kinder disposition and she had last heard that the facilities were still quite respectable: a home that once served as an inn to travelers, near enough to York, in a place called Grayshead-on-Heath. She said all this at the dining table, she and I at opposite ends, where we would meet for meals before returning to our rooms. It had become our custom to live together alone: me in my books and Grandmother engaged with cards or needlepoint or the conversation she called her lifeblood, her friends, the elderly women who lived within visiting distance and arrived in a regular stream to place their small white cards in the silver bowl reserved for guests.

Out the windows I watched a streak of sunset fading.

Besides, she said, you need softening. You are as hard as rock, she said, and for a young woman your age this is not attractive, and, although she did not say it, what she thought was, look what happened to your mother.

"I no longer have the strength to be in loco parentis," she said, slicing the meat off the chicken bone, scraping one of her silver knives across the china. She planned, she said, chewing, to debunk for Newquay, her rheumatism acute. "I'd like a regular week, a Monday or Tuesday on my own," Grandmother said.

So I arrived at Madame Lane's as any ordinary girl would, lugging my suitcase up the wide stone steps—a tackle box my godmother Alexandra bought secondhand on King's Road, saying I was joining the horsey set and it was good thing, too—money there and mine nearly gone.

My skirt bumped my knees as I climbed the steps, period on and that smell you get though you try to ignore it—that smell and oats, or hay, or the saddle soap they use to clean the bridle bits. I climbed the steps smelling like something the horse dragged in, tripping on the last to dump my tackle box on my toe.

Brigid, the one assigned to me, wrapped my toe with gauze and tape. She came from Scotland, though not the Catholic type, which worked just fine, since the idea of Mum scared those other kind mute and I'd had enough of them, anyway. Brigid told me she believed fairies live in plants and at the ends of rainbows. Back in Inverness, she told me, she used to gather dew in a thimble and leave it on a stump and in the afternoon the fairies had already licked that thimble dry. Not the sharpest knife in the drawer, Alexandra said, though she'll do as a friend. This after Brigid told me the colors of my toe—the greens and blues of it—reminded her of Scotland and she took this to mean we would be roommates for the rest of our lives. We'll live abroad, she said, just Sterno and a wooden door somewhere in Florence. Or maybe Paris with a servant attached.

At Madame Lane's we are expected to work. We learn elocution and mathematics. We sew curtains and chisel paint from the stuck, blackened windows. We sweep the corners of webs and the dust that settles from the quarry. We are too young to do much more, but still—we wrap bandages, we gather rags. We are girls who have come to stay for the duration: Brigid, and Josephine, whose parents are divorced and whose father will, before the end of the year, blow his brains through the roof, and Abigail, who arrived in April with seeds to plant, tiny specks in an envelope she carried to the girls' garden and sat to watch grow, and Rebecca, a Jewess, someone said, though we had never met one, and Filomena, who refuses to speak and rarely bathes, and Harriet, God, Harriet. We are a few more than this, a dozen or so enrolled from the far corners, here to join the effort out of harm's way—harm meaning the Kaiser himself. There are posters of his soldiers looming over girls like us, fallen and helpless beneath their big, black boots. We see the posters at every rail station and in the windows and doors of the shops in Grayshead. We are whom the men are fighting for, they suggest. It is one long duel.

The posters give some the chills and others nightmares, though we are in God's hands, Madame Lane says, and must trust faith. Faith here is a silence near to unbearable. Everyone has gone away. Horses were once harnessed and ridden in the neighboring saffron field, but the horses have been sold, Madame Lane says, the saffron fields plowed under for corn and root bearers. There is little food and we are often hungry.

Still, we keep neat rows, military rows, and listen to the men who instruct us, men on leave or those who have never been; everyone nervous. They speak too quickly and startle from a raised hand. The women who look after us aren't nervous, just mad. They have worked their fingers to the bone, they will tell us, a thousand and one jobs—have we seen the pictures?—men's work. One even read the manual and repaired the tractor crankshaft. Fancy that, they say. Fancy that and now here, and now this.

What? we say.

This, this, they say, gesturing out to the cold blue hills beyond or the pile of rubble, a former castle, on the crest, or the rotten silver oak they have hacked to a stump, the weather already turned and Madame Lane's in need of heat. There is never enough heat, and the women who look after us rise earliest in the morning to scour the dead limbs of the silver oak for kindling, the heels of their palms riddled with splinters, hard blisters. They were once dainty, though it is hard to imagine.

In late October, my godmother Alexandra visits. She wears her fox stole and a ruby signet ring and she writes a permission slip for Brigid and me to accompany her to Grayshead for scones with clotted cream. She knows someone and she can order what she likes. Afterward, we walk the maze of cobbled streets looking for the milliner's tiny yellow flag. Alexandra believes I am in need of a hat.

The town is in a dale far north of London, closer to York, as Grandmother said, and ringed in medieval walls Brigid and I climb and balance on with our arms out, as if we would fly if we fell. Thunderheads bunch in the distance though it is only weather, says Alexandra, looking toward the ruins of the castle. She suggests we climb the path and explore, which we do, though the castle looks like nothing more than a pile of stones, *is* nothing more than a pile of stones, tossed onto what would have been a good cricket field, Alexandra says. She says this and other things, and then she says what she has been waiting to say: that she has decided to leave, that she has wrangled passage on a freighter to Buenos Aires later in the week, that try as she might she can no longer abide this proximity to slaughter, a million dead at the Somme, alone, including four brothers next door and her cousin, a shy boy newly sixteen who had lied his way in. And for what? she says, as if I might know. "His honor? Ours?"

I cock my new hat on my knee, bruised as my toe from some other tumble. The hat's been fashioned from red felt, formed and set on a wooden head, a partridge feather within its band—for luck, apparently, like a coin at the bottom of a wishing well.

"*Adios*," I say, my only Spanish.

"*Adios*," Alexandra says, and we laugh and then she too is gone, walking the piers of that city, squashing the squashed fruit with her high heels and waving to the men on the infirmary boat. She wears her fox stole and her thick hair twists over one eye. She is not yet too old, nor is she too young. She is neat, smart, a typist or a teacher. She is an educated woman, who knows? She has to make do, she later writes. And she will do what she must.

Father Fairfield comes from a distant parish, near Birmingham, and though he is still a father, he no longer believes. Once, he tells us, he led quite a flock.

He arranges our desks in a circle so we might look at one another rather than pepper his back with glares. "I stand at the ready," he says. "What do you need to know?" He wears a black robe of sorts, tied with twine, and his hands are the hands of a laborer, though his face is different than his hands suggest, delicate and soft.

Father Fairfield is God, I write across the book reserved for notes, blue-lined and empty and entirely full of promise. We've been issued five, one for each subject, and a pencil that can be repeatedly sharpened. I shove my pullover to my elbow and write the words again, this time in script: *Father Fairfield*, I write, *is GOD*.

They will draft him by March, Archbishop of Canterbury be damned for sanctifying conscription of the clergy.

"I'm no Bertrand Russell," Father Fairfield will say, and go, killed within his second week, but for now he stands before us beautiful and ruined and not yet dead.

We wear leather lace-up boots for sustenance and seamed, five-pence stockings and our hair should be brushed fifty times and from our eyes as well, even the curly kind. Madame Lane doles out rules as if we are still children, but we are no longer children. We are fifteen, sixteen, seventeen.

Our blue pullovers are required, even in summer, but now, in January, we are freezing, the winter draft whistling through the walls, swirling around us as churned waves would if we were mermaids. We are trapped undersea. In the mornings the ice is so thick on the windows we must crack it with the silver letter opener Josephine has brought from home, the tarnished one with the sharp point. The ice cracks as the world once did, Josephine says, to form the continents. "Look," she says, holding up a shard. "Australia."

We don't know about that. We are simply mermaids, sirens ringing the locals in—the boys too young yet to go kicking past on their way to Top Hill—snakey boys, Brigid's word, from the quarry families, boys with shorn hair and looks on their faces and black pants pinched at the knees. If they could, they would have dangled cigarettes, the rolled kind, from their lips, too dry for our likes. We'll take the wet kind, the ones frequently licked, the full ones of Father Fairfield's. He'd seen so much! Tell us, Father Fairfield. Fill us in. We are bleating over the moon.

He sits at the windowsill, smoking. He says his preference has always been silence. He tells us how there are many Quakers in Birmingham. He tells us how they conduct their Quaker meetings in their meeting houses, simple constructions of wood painted white and benches that line each wall where the congregants sit and wait and think until compelled to stand and speak. He believes this is a good idea, he tells us. Something we might try. He smokes for a while and watches us from his place on the windowsill, the smell of the smoke intoxicatingly warm. I sit on my fingers. I scratch an itch. No one, it appears, has anything to say, nothing rising to the surface out of the rumble of our own minds, although Father Fairfield doesn't seem to notice. He doesn't seem to remember we are here at all. He pinches the end of his cigarette and sets it beside him on the sill, then he stares out the long windows at the cold blue hills, or maybe at the remains of the castle on the crest, and it is not until we hear Miss Peach ring the bell for Domestic Duties that we are brave enough to stand, to remind him we are here.

"Miss Townsend," Father Fairfield says as we file out of our classroom, a former library of sorts though our bookshelves have been emptied, donated to the Red Cross down the road, and the ladder that reached the higher shelves donated, as Madame Lane likes to say, to the stove.

Brigid has offered to wash the blackboard and Harriet has presented him with the scarf she was knitting, loopy and intended for a soldier, though here twisted in Harriet's hands as she says, "Welcome, Father," and curtseys. Father Fairfield ducks and hangs the scarf around his neck, the standard green yarn of it greased from Harriet's dirty hands. She knitted everywhere, Harriet—at meals, at vespers, even after lights-out, when the rest of us lay like so many corpses in a trench, waiting for sleep, the blankets brought from home piled high and never enough, our toes freezing. "Thank you," Father Fairfield says, turning away from her to me. "A word?" he says.

"Yes, sir," I say, the other girls looking wide then moving on, leaving and sorry to go.

Dreamy Father Fairfield, with too-white skin and black hair and lips that curve just so and wet. He looks like the pictures of actors Penny showed Thomas and me in the kitchen some afternoons when the rain kept us in and we were waiting for Mum to come home or Nurse in the parlor, loitering with Michael. Penny had been the kind one, crying for hours when Mum passed on before packing her cardboard suitcase. We were on Mum's order to be good to her and never cross and never rude and never to raise our voices. She was simple-minded, Mum said, and though there were times I wanted to say to her, bugger off, I did not. I never did. Alexandra said that I had inherited Mum's will, not to mention her temper, and that this could either float me in good stead or kill me. I think I'll float. Why Mum chose to go down I'll understand when I am much older, everyone agrees. I'm dying for you, is what she said, but Alexandra said, no, she would never have said such a thing and besides, she was delirious and spoke stuff and nonsense. Her mind overwhelmed her, Alexandra said.

It takes me a moment to hear Father Fairfield talking. I am always drifting, my own mind loud.

"I admired her," he is saying. "I just wanted you to know, I admired your mother."

I stand stock-still in my uniform, though when he offers me a chair, I sit.

"Smoke?" he says, and I say yes. He walks to the window, left open a crack though the wind blows, and picks up the cigarette pinched on its sill, lighting it with a match from the pocket of his robe. He draws the smoke in, unwrapping the scarf from around his neck, breathing out. "Don't want to catch fire," he says, passing the fag to me. I hold it in the way I'd seen Mum occasionally, and Nurse in the kitchen with Michael. I let it burn between my cold fingers and then take a puff, suddenly giddy from the cigarette and from Father Fairfield talking. He is saying he had read all about her in the papers—between the lines, he says, where the news is: a real hero she was. She would not compromise, he says. She did something, he says, though it must have been a sorry lot to live through. And wasn't it cruel the way the press eviscerated her, the word itself like taking Mum from his other pocket and slicing her down the middle.

You can learn a lot that way, he says. Reading the papers. Do I read the papers? Just this morning he has learned how our new allies, the Americans, have tortured four Hutterites, he says. Do I know of them?

"No, sir," I say.

"Farmers, mostly, descended from mountain men. Bohemians."

"Oh."

"They wanted to farm in America. Someplace west."

"Yes, sir."

"The Americans killed two of them. Beat them to a pulp for refusing to fight in the war," he says. "The other two, God knows."

This I do believe, given the way the wind is blowing, he says. The dead ones were chained to a wall and so badly beaten, according to the papers, that the wife, the sister-in-law, had to come in to identify them—brother, husband. "These Americans, our new allies," he says, "our brothers in arms."

Father Fairfield stops then and waits. I cannot imagine what he expects me to add. I have learned that adding, embellishing, decorating with words is part of my finishing, or at least this is what Miss Peach of Domestic Duties expects of us. We are to elevate the conversation, to egg it on. Think of the sweet flourish of a frosted buttercream rose on a many-layered cake, she says, and our mouths water hearing it, since it had been some time since we ate cake.

The ash sifts down, burning. I should put the cigarette somewhere, what remains of it, but where? Father Fairfield occupies the desk and shadows the ashtray and I would have to stand, straightening my legs. It all seems too complicated and awkward and lacking in female *grace*, a word we discuss in the evenings after vespers, when Miss Cordine and Miss Long speak to us on the many graces.

"And who looks after you?" he says.

I cough, passing the fag, nothing but ash and paper, back to him.

"My godmother Alexandra," I say.

Father Fairfield smiles, then leans over to wrap Harriet's scarf around my own neck. "You're shaking," he says.

"Yes, sir," I say.

"I just wanted you to know that I admired her," he says.

"Yes, sir," I say.

His eyes are a bit green instead of all brown. They are algae green and perhaps that's what comes to mind because they are tearing, not tearing as if he will cry right then and there, but tearing as if he is suddenly caught in a wind tunnel, or has found himself reading too long, the way tears come on from too much concentration, or thinking.

"How old are you?" he says.

"Pardon?"

"How old are you?"

"Sixteen," I say. "Almost."

"That's right," he says, as if this were an examination.

"And when she died?" he says.

"Thirteen," I say, too quiet, but he hears.

I am a fighter, Grandmother says. I am just like her, and stubborn as a goat, and willful and determined and entirely lacking, she says, in female wiles, so that I will not cry. I should not cry.

Besides, I could tell Father Fairfield, I would rather hear something else. I would rather hear about the woman who had to identify her brother and her husband, beaten to a pulp for refusing to fight. I would rather hear whether the woman found the two dead ones who had wanted to farm west sitting in chairs, their hands tied behind their backs, their faces sprouting like purple cauliflowers and blood from their noses, or if the woman found them as if they were asleep, the sheets pulled over their bodies so that she had to turn the sheets down to see, so that she might have, for just a moment, imagined she would find no one there she knew, though of course she could tell from the outlines, from the shift in the air. She knew from the wind and the sudden sun, just as I did. I knew from the way my eyes teared so that no one ever had to tell me. No one needed to say the word *dead* because—I could tell Father Fairfield now and I could have told him then—I already knew.

And knowing, I took the birdcage outdoors and opened the little latch that so many times I had been tempted to open before, the little latch that fit through the tiny loop, the coil of brass there. I let the door swing open, the canary with its seed eyes and thorn beak stunned by fresh air though mostly—I will think about this later— by the absence of that horrible room: its four walls papered and browned at the seams as if all the tea in all the teacups from all the sitting and waiting had stained its joints. Nowhere is the oiled piano with its spinet legs and raised, ridged spine waiting for the swing of the metronome and Thomas's long fingers, and the green velvet draperies thick as blankets for the draft and the chairs, two, and little writing table with its smaller stool and inkwell and pens and blotter to answer the letters propped between the bookend Bibles Mum had said were put to best use there.

Who can blame the canary? What does the canary know of sky and trees and air? The little door swings open on its tiny brass hinges but the bird does not move nor sing nor ungrip its maddeningly rigid claws from its swing, its hanging perch, nor blink its seed eyes nor do anything as I shake the cage. I shake the cage hard. The door is *open*, the tiny door no longer latched with the tiny brass spike through the tiny brass loop. It could have done it itself, idiot, no trick to this. It could have used its thorn beak to lift the latch, but it is an idiot bird, an idiot canary, a birdbrain, an imbecile, and I must turn the cage upside down and shake the cage again and again to watch it swing upside down until with a jerk it wings for balance but too late, birdbrain, I pull it out, yank it out and it bites the skin of my thumb, the tight skin there, and that hurts so much I fling it off toward the tree so that it falls a bit into it, then up, flying! And then it's gone.

And when the bird flies away I am not as happy as I imagined I would be. I would do anything to bring it back.

I could tell Father Fairfield about the canary, about letting the

Kate Walbert

canary go, but I do not. Instead, I wait for Father Fairfield to explain something more, to perhaps explain the point of it. But Father Fairfield never explains the point of it. He simply flicks the nub of ash toward the empty bookshelves, his feet beneath his robe planted in lace-up leather boots not so different, I might have shown him, from my own.

DOROTHY TREVOR TOWNSEND

London, England, 1914

Bloody hot that day and earlier a trip to London for an insuffer-able luncheon at the Victoria Club, the speaker someone's bril-liant son, a certain Richard Thorke, la la la, here to address them on The Woman Question or rather to enlighten them on A Short History of Women. So it said in the program in the shaky hand of the poor scribe assigned to such tasks—wedding invitations, funeral announcements, lectures delivered to the willing. A Short History of Women, again and again, Some Observations on The Woman Question, again and again, dedicated to Mrs. Joseph Allen Thorke, again and again, tireless in her cause, peerless in her principles.

The gathered are propped in mandrake chairs around ordinary curtained tables; hot and they can barely move, draped wrist to ankle, corseted, as Richard Thorke stands in cool white jacket and trousers, his hair combed bristle. Don of philosophy, he is, though with a greater interest in eugenics. They all have a greater interest in eugenics now, don't they? A result of the recent Galton conference and what William calls the clear regression toward the mean on dis-play at every bus queue. No doubt Richard Thorke might have just as easily stood at the lectern to speak of the delicacy of a woman's skull, how he could read the cranium with his hands though, one would guess, he might prefer to crush it.

She's too hard on him, of course. She's too hard on all of them.

And why Richard Thorke stands before them at the Victoria Club at all, neither in France nor going, is a question, though he must be missing a kidney or blind in one eye.

He taps his water glass and waits for the women to find their seats.

They like to talk, women; this Dorothy imagines Richard Thorke thinking along with, what else? What men think. She has no idea, truly. William will, on occasion, *enlighten* her—"women think in circles," he said recently, "men in lines"—as did Dr. Vaughn, the sole professor at Cambridge who had agreed to let her and the other girls from Girton attend his university lectures, Dorothy and the rest bored with the mistresses who had been hired to instruct them at their own college, brilliant women, but no more known than shopgirls. She wanted to hear the famous men, the authors of the books she had read.

"And you're, what? Fifteen? Sixteen?" Professor Vaughn said, staring up at her, his bowl of soup before him cooling. She had knocked on the door to his rooms, directed by a few sulky students. ("Permitted," one said, "but never tolerated.") She stood very straight in front of Vaughn though her hair, piled high on her head, felt too heavy and she would have liked a warm bath—Girton far from here on its windswept hill. She rode her bicycle, her mum's one concession.

"Eighteen," she said, regretting it, her age, the question, him with his stained robes and hair sprouting from his ears.

"And you'll be quiet as mice?" he said.

She nodded though Vaughn had already returned to his meal, the spoon disappeared in his huge hand, gnarled from psoriasis. He'd scratch himself away, eventually, until he remained merely flakes and a robed hat.

"So be it," he said, slurping.

"Ladies," Richard Thorke calls, his voice loud, commanding.

Her table fills with several women she has never met. They wear the requisite lavender, or cream in support of woman's suffrage, though their attentions have been diverted to war, to The Voluntary Aid Detachments, to wrapping surgical dressings and packing Red Cross boxes, their labor evidence of their patriotic intent and good, bloody conscience. Now their silks shuffle as they settle in, their hands folded, yes, *folded*, she would say to Dr. Vaughn, this not, she would argue, female, Latinate prose as he would have corrected, his belief that a woman's ability to think clearly at all was hindered by anecdote, emotion, unnecessary drama, butterflies that fluttered about and tickled his nose, he said.

But the gathered have now settled and are waiting for Thorke to begin, as he promises, with Darwin himself, whom he will argue constructed a new life for all of them.

"Leading then to the work of Havelock Ellis," Thorke says. "And so forth."

Dorothy listens and then she does not. She hears instead the sound of Thomas. He sits at the piano practicing his scales, jaw clenched as his clubfoot, his good foot pumping the pedal, the other tight as a fist from what the doctor would not tell her though she has read what literature is available: *A mother in distress may cause the fetus to recoil from the natural course of growth, the cells understanding defeat and the mother's Attitude revolt to abnormality of the limbs and possibly of the brain. There have been numerous—*

Concentration, Dorothy thinks. Here and now.

She looks around the table to see that many of the other women have shut their eyes.

"—Ellis for whom I am entirely grateful, given his scholarship on Individualism and After. How this pertains to you, to all of you, I will attempt to make clear, though I would like to begin by acknowledging the great debt I owe to Mr. Herbert Spencer, for his work on natural and parasitic evolution, and for his understanding that only the fittest among us, as he wrote, will survive.

"But first—"

Again?

"My mother, to whom I have dedicated this talk."

Dorothy imagines Richard Thorke's mother: short and hearty, as these brilliant men's mothers mostly are, red wrists and boiled hands, feet blackened by the fire.

"To deny her the scholarship she craved, to relegate her to a position next to the fire—"

Ah-hah!

"To insist that Woman did not matter in the functioning of society, nay civilization, from the time I was a young boy, struck me as terribly wrong—"

How astute!

"And I would hasten to add that she, far more than my father, might have made a lasting contribution—"

Shocking!

"—to what is good and right, to what is fair, about our system of governance. We know from the work of the adventurers in the Explorers Club that there are certain societies that celebrate women's work, that rely on women to sustain their very existence. I'm thinking of South American cultures, many of the tribes from the Amazon Basin—"

The names of the tribes from the Amazon Basin roll off Richard Thorke's tongue to land in a series of thuds on the lectern. He pauses, then, lifting his glass to sip and looking up. He *is* blind in one eye, Dorothy thinks, and not for the first time imagines she must be a witch. From here she can see the sharp flecks of white that explode the iris, or is she only dreaming? How can she see from this distance so clearly and yet she can, there! The eye remains rigid, fixed, trained on the aisle that separates the two rows of curtained tables, the towering centerpieces—no doubt lunch favors—like so many preening peacocks. It is too much, the adornment, and so perhaps the dead eye, his dead eye, seeks emptiness, as she will the sky over the horizon, or the sea. Emptiness, quiet, a certain release from expectation—from *seeing*, in this case, from the burden of *the thing itself keenly observed*. But then this may be singularly her burden and not his.

"Take the Onimapoe tribal women," says Richard Thorke, setting down the glass and straightening his notes, "who make their home in the Amazon Basin where they have collected medicinal components of certain unique vegetation for decades and thus composed an aural language expressly for the purposes of health. The names and properties of the remedies are apparently communicated great distances, by that I mean jungle to jungle; as evidenced by the witch doctors of the central countries these remedies have traveled as far as southern Mexico and have had a profound effect on the populations of the entire continent. The work of the American anthropologist Franz Heiniker, whose studies of the Onimapoe women have been widely published and may be known to many of you, confirm the extraordinary reach of this knowledge."

Thorke clears his throat over the faintly interrupting sounds of London, busier near the end of the lunch hour. Thankfully someone has pried open a window. It is a relief, the air, and the clang of the street as well.

"And I use the word *knowledge* here with great care in your midst because it is my desire to emphasize to those of you who have chosen my company this afternoon the work of my colleagues in the Darwinists, whose understanding of the fundamental principle of the *ideal*, or rather, of women who labor toward that ideal, informs my own knowledge and subsequent scholarship. In the Onimapoe that ideal is the health—dental and otherwise—of husbands who preserve the order and hunt for the tribe, and sons who will inherit the governing traditions aforementioned. In our civilized society," Richard Thorke continues, "that ideal has evolved and shifted from survival per se—men have assumed these responsibilities—to what I propose might best be called 'comfort.' Simply put, women have traditionally maintained comfort; and, consequently, they have exhibited a physical drive—as manifested in their propensity toward impulse rather than intellect—to *advance* comfort."

There is a shift in the interrupted silence. A few women take notes, one coughs. This seems to be a stopping point, or at least a pause. Richard Thorke wipes his brow and removes his jacket. Dorothy sees sweat stains under his arms and that he wears braces, which she's always liked, wide blue braces, and that in his pocket is a small notebook that contains, she imagines, important thoughts that occur to him at irregular hours, or at those hours of the day when he finds himself not at his library desk or in the solarium, but riding on the bus or walking. A luxury, pockets. But then in truth her thoughts, these random ones, only occur to her when she should be listening, or rather, when she is listening. It is as if she lives in a heavy fog; even when reading the children their stories, she is elsewhere.

"To return to the Onimapoe," says Thorke. "Vis-à-vis health, the Onimapoe tribal women have similarly worked toward their ideal of comfort and by dint of purpose suggest a woman's *capability to advance toward* a certain intellect—and here is where we, the Darwinists, become interested in Heidegger's research—suggest a woman's *capability to solve* complex problems by using empirical evidence to the sole purpose of reaching this com—"

Apparently a hand has been raised somewhere within the sea of tables. Dorothy turns with the rest of them to see it frantically waving, as if desperate to summon a passing ship. "May I interrupt?" the woman is asking. She bobs somewhere in the back; a voice.

Richard Thorke stares, the dead eye fixed. "Briefly," he says.

The woman stands. She looks like all of them from this distance, stout, a shroud of cloth, a hat, a handbag or something similar, one would guess, wedged beneath her chair—and what would that contain? All the tools of the trade—a hairbrush, a small mirror, some missives from the Bible to keep her spirits up. The woman clears her throat. "Are the Onimapoe of which you speak the ones who elongate their lips with clay palates?" she says. She has clearly rehearsed the question. Perhaps she has even written it out beforehand, having routed out the work of Richard Thorke, read a pamphlet or two in which the Onimapoe were mentioned, his interest in, his specialty regarding, his expertise. She says the question bravely, her voice strong.

Richard Thorke pauses. "What?" he says.

The woman shifts as a horse would, kept too long standing. "I asked," she says, "whether the Onimapoe of which you speak were the ones who—

"Right," says Richard Thorke. "Right." He sighs and sips his water. "They engage in much ornamentation that has a scholarly significance I wouldn't dare to address," he says.

"So it means something?" she says.

"Of course," he says.

The "thank you," can barely be heard within the rustling of the women turning back to face the lectern, the stout woman forgotten, humiliated for asking; the others are on Thorke's team and would cut the stout woman down in an instant.

"I've lost my place," he mutters, and she is close enough to be one of the few to hear, though she knows she is not meant to answer. If she were, she might say, *comfort*; she might say, *by dint of purpose*.

"Think of her as simple: Woman. Yet think of her also as a soft flower, a bud newly opened, delicate yet sturdy in her determination to bloom: she shall not wilt on the vine. She shall grow toward comforts yet to come regardless the age, the year, the moment in history.

" 'What can be done?' asks Man. 'What cannot be done?' answers Woman."

There is an inexplicable burst of applause at this, a rallying burst. The woman to Dorothy's left leans in and whispers, "What did he say?"

"What cannot be done," she whispers back, noticing, as she does, the smell of the powder thick on the woman's face and how, with a fingernail, perhaps in answer to an itch, the woman has streaked a rut from eye to chin.

Richard Thorke has paused to wipe his hands on the linen napkin provided for him. He returns to his notes.

"Consider what is known as social evolution, or rather, Woman's innate or natural abilities and how, given the work of Havelock Ellis and Herbert Spencer, whom I have mentioned and whom many of you must know, and, most recently, Alfred Wallace's 'On the Tendency of Varieties to Depart Indefinitely from the Original Type,' we see now that type can transmute, transform, transcend type," he continues.

"What is a woman's type? She fluctuates with the tides, her watery blood leading to a constant irritability, and she dislikes analysis and rigid rules and grows, in Ellis's words, 'restive under the order which a man is inclined to obey.' She has, in the face of this, compensated well: Think of Dr. Gregory's classic "Legacy to His Daughters," a primer in which she is advised to cultivate a 'courteous mode of expression,' by avoiding conversation altogether—'if you happen to have any learning, keep it a profound secret, especially from men.'

"So the type still holds. And best not to quibble mathematics. We could call it Differential Availability of Aptitude at the High End— we observe the phenomenon everywhere—little girls turning trucks into baby dolls, little boys turning trucks into tanks.

"So let's turn from what we cannot amend and begin again, to Darwin. Evolution! Here is the hope: Havelock Ellis believed that the natural existence of Woman is quantified, validated, so to speak, as the *natural*—emphasis mine—counterbalance to the existence of Man. The harmony *possible* between Man and Woman is the one that occurs between two warring forces, and by that I mean the very construct of the universe, the pull that keeps the earth spinning on its axis. And he addresses the defects of Woman, the stupendous natural obstacles Woman faces (though he did refute the frontal lobe argument and there it is) with a brilliant analysis: Every inaptitude of Woman will be in its time accompanied by some compensatory aptitude 'even if it *has not itself yet developed* into an advantageous character.'

"So. Full stop. And a question.

"Where have you been; whence are you to go?

"Now, in this hour, we are finally put to the test. Are women made of that mettle? Can women rise to the challenge of the times?

When you are asked to vote, and I believe, if you are patient, given the way the wind blows, you will be asked to vote in this century, nay, in this decade—"

To this a scattering of applause.

"Will Woman, and by that I mean You, step in line, show the naysayers and the soothsayers—"

Laughter.

"And your husbands and fathers and sons that you have had it all along—courage—that you have understood all along certain incontrovertible necessities and by that I mean war, the necessity of war. This is not dollies in nappies, ladies. Do you understand the elemental nature of the question?"

To the scattering of applause Richard Thorke slightly nods. Then a cloud passes over the sun and a storm of violent shadows sketches the walls of the Victoria Club—troubled oceans and sliding continents.

"We owned the second pew," says Richard Thorke. "Mum's knees were bruised from it. And still, we cleaned the church on Thursdays. Sang choir Tuesdays. Mum's hands did the braiding of the church bread, and my father, the man for whom I was named, refused to attend on the matter of principle, his principle, though that would be the principle of the belt."

Thorke has turned a strange corner, Dorothy thinks. They all stare down the alley with him. The shadows now are buildings cast on brick walls, the dark of it grime and soot. He clears his throat and mutters something inaudible. What should they do? They could sit him in their laps and tell him it's all right. They could stroke him with their watery hands, tend to him, she thinks, provide, what had he said? Comfort? They could explain to him that his father is long since dead, that all those men eventually die and that his was not, after all, so unlike most of theirs. She could have stood up and turned and cleared her own throat and said something. Anything. What is this gibberish? she might have said. Is anyone really listening?

But she does not. Instead, she applauds as Thorke abruptly concludes, thanking them for their attendance, complimenting the cooks on the fine luncheon they are about to enjoy, suggesting that afterward they might take a moment and pick up one of his pamphlets in the solarium for a small donation. Thorke is shaking, she can see, as he tucks his notes back into his pocket and bows, appearing, from this close, as if at any moment he might faint.

Richard Thorke's invitation for coffee doesn't surprise Dorothy in the least. He has recognized her all along, he says, the Girton girl who interrupted the Anarchists.

They were at Cambridge together a dozen years ago, he will remind her, and then she remembers him—Richard Thorke, one of those earnest men in flying black robes hurrying to Evensong, hymnal tucked underwing.

And did she know, he said, that Terrance Gibson had recently been made Chancellor of the Exchequer?

And did she know, he said, that Richard Paul would soon be appointed to bishop?

"And what of our esteemed leader, William Crawford?" he asks. No doubt Richard Thorke has read of their resumed affair, of what the press has called William's shady shenanigans: his lack of moral fortitude, his rumored pact with the Hun devils and the wheeler-dealers and the men of industry who fuel this war. William has told her practically nothing and yet she understands enough to know that he will be made rich or rather, richer, and that he will live down the scandal.

They leave the Victoria Club, strolling past cabbage on the walk and potato peels and cigarette stubs, the rubbish collectors unemployed or enlisted. He pauses to light his cigarette and hers.

"You liked it?" Richard Thorke asks. "What did you think?"

She exhales as Richard Thorke waits, his dead eye wandering off to gaze at the moon, just visible now in the beastly sky. Richard

Thorke. Fellow of Trinity College, Cambridge University, and recent inductee to the newly established Men for Women's Suffrage, or MWS, professor of eugenics, Cobbett Chair in evolution, waits to hear what she has to say. They stand momentarily on the walk, or perhaps in a doorway, at the entrance of a pub or eating establishment into which she is not yet allowed. He has pulled her aside. Is his plan then to kiss her? What exactly does he want of her? To advance comfort, is her job. She could do that, couldn't she? Be useful that way. Women want to be useful, after all, and young boys are dying. They're bred to be useful, or maybe, they're bred to breed? She can't remember which and there's no time, truly, to think. Richard Thorke needs something. He wants something terribly.

Again she must apologize. She truthfully wasn't listening.

He smiles, then. "I asked," Richard Thorke says, "whether you found my talk interesting."

Dorothy reaches out to take Richard Thorke's arm, her laugh distracted, automatic, complete.

"Full marks," she answers. "Bloody brilliant," she says.

Dorothy makes the hourlong journey back to Wardsbury by train. It is the time of early evening when the heat should magically drift but does not; it settles, solidifying, like too ripe fruit, gelatinous and capable of rot. Bees are out, hideous swarms around the trash bins, and the battered soldier who tears the tickets sits on the shade bench reading, his leg unbuckled and propped against the arm of the bench. The look of that! The saturation of color and the smell—the stench of garbage, the swarming bees, the soldier, leg off, the amplified sun at a slant descending (it occurring to her for the first time how tremendously hot that machinery must be to cart around, buckles and straps and a solid piece of wood, or is it hollow?)—and the memory of Richard Thorke's lecture, Thorke fresh from Trinity College, Cambridge, fresh from the American Museum of Natural History, New York, fresh from Munich or Bonn: A Short History of Women, the program read: Some Observations on The Woman Question, with apologies to Havelock Ellis, Charles Darwin, and, God knows, she thinks, Jesus Christ. Thorke had smiled when introduced, the sound of the applause in greeting loud before the unbearable quiet as they sat with their small hands in their laps and waited. They were always waiting. Waiting to hear, respectfully listening. Who are we? they wanted to know. Tell us, who? And what should we do next?

Returning to Wardsbury in the early evening heat, everything feels under siege. Dorothy looks at the unbuckled soldier and wonders what he reads though she knows it will disappoint her: elementary verses or the masters Fledge and Doyle on their walking tour of Norway. "Water?" she offers. She has brought a thermos refilled from the luncheon and a pocketbook full of sweets, intended for the children, Nurse, and Penny. "Biscuit?" she says.

"Thank you," he says.

Crumbs on his lips, he asks her to sit and she does, no other passengers departing or arriving, and she in no hurry to begin the walk home. The station she has known since childhood, the red bricks of it, the rusting Wardsbury sign, enamel blue with white lettering, the papers stacked beneath the conductor's window where a young man in a greasy shirt once sold tickets to everywhere. She had wanted to go everywhere, had tugged her mum's hand to take her: the view from the train, first the smokestacks and then the city, and all the places her mum promised she would visit as a bigger girl—St. Paul's Cathedral, Big Ben, the Tower of London—so much grander, she came to know, from a distance.

She turns, understanding that the soldier has been talking.

She hasn't heard a word.

Even here she seems no longer capable of listening.

"I'm sorry?" she says, but the soldier moves on, leaning into himself to stand. He has buckled his leg and pulled the pant over the stump to hide the block and leather straps of it, the chiseled wood. He wears a woman's ring—engagement, or similarly ornate—around his pinkie finger; this she will always remember.

* * *

The battered soldier kicks the rubbish can with his good foot, the buzz of flies loud in the thick heat. There must be blood in the trash bin, something that has frenzied them. Dorothy nods good-bye though he is no longer looking; he is on his way back to the little cage in which he waits for customers on his three-legged stool.

At home the children will be in the kitchen finishing their dinner and Penny will have scrubbed the wood with the steel bristle she packs in the toes of her boots to keep the wet out. Nurse might be sitting, too, urging Thomas to eat more. "Eat, Thomas," Nurse will say, babying him, as if his fisted, crippled foot were jammed down his throat.

She feels sick at the thought of poor Thomas chewing, pushing away his plate. Is this the moment she decides? Or is it later when she arrives, when she steps through the front door, discarding boots and shawl, yelling out for anyone, her breath flat, airless, as if caught in the wooden press Evie received last Christmas, where now bleed too many nosegays from too many of her benefits, meetings, rallies, everything eclipsed by war. And again the thought occurs to her, the magical intuition: her idea, her better idea—and isn't this the way of intuition? The hunch more formed than one fully understands? The outcome set? Something will happen, she thinks. She will make something happen.

"Tea and toast?" Penny appears and wants to know.

"Tea," Dorothy says; her first refusal.

Thomas hobbles toward her, her beautiful boy. She sits down on the boot bench and he flings himself across her lap for the cracked egg.

"Make them scrambled," he says. "A dozen."

"I don't have a dozen," she says.

"Yes you do, Mum. You do," he says.

"Let me look," she says, and out of her bag (and even this, the bags they must carry, carpet bags, needlepoint bags, cloth bags,

31

seems tedious, ridiculous) she pulls the wrapped sweets they served for dessert.

"I found this," she says, offering Thomas the handful, which he takes without moving, his body, heavier than he knows, slouched across her lap, his back to her, waiting for their game.

"Oh and my," she says. "A dozen eggs!"

"I knew it," he giggles.

"Let's see about this pan." She smoothes his shirt with her flattened palm, smoothes him out like kneading dough and from somewhere beside her reaches for the egg, pretending, changing her palm to a fist which she brings down hard on his back and then the tickle of a cracked egg, the white and yolk of it slipping out.

"There's one," she says. She pounds, again. Cracks the imaginary egg. "Two," she says. "Three," she says. The eggs are cracked, the entire dozen, Thomas squirming on her lap, sugary drool on his lips.

Evie must be in the kitchen with Penny, or perhaps she's already retired to her blue room. She's lost in books, pulling them one by one from the bookshelf Dorothy has painted with bluebirds and robins. What had they said at Girton? Blue for fortitude, for strength, some wealthy patron long ago donating the blue draperies and blue carpets.

Now the lamp beside Evie's bed is blue and the rocking chair that had belonged to Dorothy, blue. A blue girl? Ted had said, returned from Ceylon near the time of Evie's birth to check on his women, whom he pronounced well before he set off, again. Alexandra had been right; he had adored her, though there was work to be done, he said, in the field, and she was busy besides. He brought something remarkable then—the peacock? It strutted here and there before killed by the fox. She found the dead bird while out for a walk with Evie in the woods up the hill, near the edge of the long lane bordered by lilac and stone that leads to the orchard. There she had planted the apple trees and commissioned the mason to build a wishing bench. She told her husband she'd be fine.

She painted the girl's room blue and would, three years later, paint the boy's room yellow, though Ted did not return for the boy. She sent him the news by post—*The atrophied limb retracts, the cells, contrary to current thinking, not diseased rather multiplying at an alarming rate. The resultant thickening of bone inhibits natural development. Speculation suggests given the state of the Mother during pregnancy and possibly due to unhappy Thoughts, she has encouraged the Condition by willing, ironically, too much health for the child.*

Dorothy slides Thomas from her lap.

"Off you go, soldier," she says. "I've had a day."

DOROTHY TOWNSEND BARRETT

Dover, Delaware, 2003

The soldiers keep Dorothy in view. She carries the tripod, unsteadily, and an extra poncho for a bib. That they have let her come this far might be due to weather, or possibly the kinds of amusements of which she remains unaware. Still, she assumes that they watch, tracking her as she stomps along the fence and positions herself by the sign that clearly states: No Trespassing, Government Property, Photography Forbidden.

It has turned a wet September, everywhere raining so the leaves, black and slick, paste to the soles of her boots. Really, they are Caroline's, Wellingtons borrowed from the back of the hallway closet where earlier Dorothy rummaged as Charles watched, wondering where she could possibly be going in such weather.

She turned, boot in hand.

"It's raining," he repeated.

Deaf at most decibels, Charles refused to wear aids (vanity? fear?), preferring to cast his voice into silence, hoping for an echo or a nod.

"Nowhere," she had said, because this is nowhere, or anywhere, or somewhere not particularly known: an hour's drive north if you took the busy roads, and then country, mostly, the drizzle graying the already gray landscape. Ye olde etcetera—cornfields, silos, a ravaged billboard for Daniel's peas, fresh from California, though this is technically Delaware and the land of soybeans. Ducks, too, the fall season in full swing; the drizzle split by the crack crack crack of the hunters' guns.

She parks near the drainage ditch that edges the fence, chain link, as if for dogs, though there are no dogs here, only a guard tower, a landing field, and the soldiers who wait for the planes. But that isn't right, exactly. The place is vast, a city of a place, with barracks—are those called barracks?—and trucks and cul-de-sacs and no doubt children sleeping, army brats—or is this marines?—in the two-story housing labyrinth not so distant from where she gets out, near the drainage ditch, near the landing field, near the place where the plane will descend. This she knows. The rest—the presence of children, the numbers involved, the ranking, the hierarchy—she truthfully has no idea.

Dorothy skewers the tripod in the mud and adjusts the poncho to cover her. Today, she plans to fight back. She can almost taste it; see herself in her resistance: Dorothy Barrett, granddaughter to the suffragette, mother to three: Caroline, Liz, and the dead one, James; wife to Charles. She mounts the camera on the track and angles the lens toward where the plane will descend—they come from the East, she has learned, out of Mecca, the bodies mostly coffined, then wrapped in flags, but sometimes carried in a tiny box.

"Christ, Mother," Caroline said after the first arrest, the fine. "Get a life."

"Your great-grandmother starved to death on principle; she literally ate nothing."

"I know, I know. I've seen the postage stamp," Caroline said.

"I think it changed things then," Dorothy said. "To do something. She made up her mind; she took a stand—"

"And look what happened to your dad? Anyway, you said she might have been unbalanced. A bit insane, wasn't she? You've said that before. She might have been suffering from—"

"Hysteria?" Dorothy said, hearing her own tone of voice—hysterical. "The point is, she did something."

"It's illegal to take pictures there."

"This is a free country."

"Please," Caroline said.

The two sat at Caroline's kitchen table, Caroline in one of her suits meant for business, her cigarette burning in the ashtray a ten-year-old James had spun out of clay. Caroline's daughter, little Dorothy, is elsewhere, having reached the age of the disappeared—her voice shouting orders from behind the locked door of her bedroom or even standing present, her body a studded cast of her former self; if she is somewhere within it she is very, very deep.

"I should never have told you I voted for him," Caroline said.

"I would have guessed."

"Consider my client base," Caroline said.

"Please," Dorothy said.

"Anyway, the law has to do with respect," Caroline said. "Or something. They make the rules for a reason, I'm sure. It's none of our business. None of your business."

"Says who?" Dorothy said, to which Caroline had some sort of reply.

Dorothy listened for a while, and then she did not; she thought of other things, how she would like to have believed that not so long ago Caroline would have stood beside her at the fence, that she, former president of the student council and Future Leaders for Justice, might have carried a sign or at least shouted an obscenity. But this was before Caroline divorced and took that new job in the Financial District. The Dead Zone, she called it, but the money's good, she said. It's serious money.

"Mother?"

"I was listening," Dorothy said.

"Forget it," Caroline said. She tapped her nails, those nails, on the table, then the doorbell rang—pizza delivery—and the conversation ended.

"Dinnertime," she yelled in the direction of the door.

* * *

Crack. Crack. Crack.

The soldiers have had enough. They climb down from their tower to slog through duck country, technically Delaware, the first state, though most have trouble with the history; one can hear their boots, or is that frogs? The sucking. Soon enough they'll reach her. Dorothy records their magnified approach; records them unlocking the gate and stepping to the other side, records their blank expressions. The trouble is she can only pretend to hate them.

"Good morning, Mrs. Barrett." This from the one Dorothy calls Tweedledee.

She straightens up, adjusts the poncho.

"We'll remind you that you're trespassing. That taking photographs is forbidden."

"Today," she says, hand on tripod. "I plan to resist."

Their arms remain folded. Four pair, as usual; a pack; a team; a unit, perhaps, or would they be a regiment? No, a regiment is bigger, a regiment is many. She tries to remember from mornings James explained the exact order of things—sergeant to lieutenant to captain to king—his miniature warriors arranged throughout the house in oddly purposeful groupings. She would find them everywhere, assaulting a sock, scaling the Ping-Pong table, plastic, molded men with clearly defined weaponry and indistinct faces. When she banished them to his room, fearing someone would trip and break a bone, James had cried and cried.

"That would be more than your usual fine, Mrs. Barrett."

He is a horse's ass, but then again, a boy once James's age, who should be pitied.

"I plan to resist," she repeats. One of the Mute Ones has his hand out as if to help her across the muddy plain. They are waiting, she knows, for Dorothy to do something. Collapse, she thinks, then does, more a buckle than a collapse, knowing full well the ridiculousness of it, how small she'll become. The big one bends down to help her. *Now*, she thinks, though it is not until it is done that she understands she has found the courage to do it, biting the soft part of that hand, the hammock of skin between thumb and forefinger.

Caroline sits next to Charles in the detention waiting room, no question who's the boss. That girl could split atoms, Charles had once said. We ought to lease her to GE.

Sorry, darling, Dorothy mouths to him. He looks at her with his doggy yellow eyes not hearing a thing; then Caroline leads them both out.

In the fresh sunshine they blink; "Look how the weather's changed!" Dorothy says, reflexively. "What a treat!"

Caroline has opened the car door.

"Get in," she says.

They sit in silence all the way home, the radio punched to static and static and static then punched off, again, then the familiar drive, the front door, the hallway, the kitchen. Caroline makes tea and calls a what-there-is-of-the-Family Meeting, Liz trapped in the city, attempting another pregnancy (busy, busy, busy!), and the hole in the place where James would have been. Dorothy steps into it and wanders around while Caroline speaks of Responsibility and Reputation and Appropriate Behavior, and yes, Patriotism, but mostly, mostly, mostly, Mother, Embarrassment.

"And what of history?" Dorothy says. "Lineage?"

"Mother," Caroline says. "I'm at wit's end."

Dorothy would like to cradle Caroline in her arms, Caroline sleepy and hatted and a bit jaundice yellow, but she cannot. Caroline has grown; she's taller than Dorothy and now divorced and a multimillionaire, she has confessed. Mill-ions, she said.

"Where are your friends, Mother?" Caroline asks.

Dorothy shrugs. She hasn't thought of friends recently, nor her standing Wednesday at Sheer Perfection; her hair's gone shaggy and her cuticles have grown over their moons.

"I'm sorry, darling," she says. "I'll stop."

*   *   *

How has it come to this? There was what there is of Youth, Dorothy thinks. Then a calculated abandonment to marriage—clubfooted father to emotionally crippled husband, she came to understand in the seventies, amidst all that explosive talk talk talk of feelings that women suddenly did and the gin they drank and those dresses they wore—what were they called?—babydolls or cupie pies or swing sets. Something infantile and slightly obscene. They wore those dresses and talked, but they drank, mostly. There were affairs but she never had one. She wore boots. She wore a beehive. She wore babydolls. Maybe she just wore out. The point is, she was nineteen once and she wouldn't be again. She had hoped for, had imagined, a proper evolution to Love, she had soldiered on under the principle and found her greatest devotion her children, and books, and, truthfully, certain friends, Charles, too, as a friend at times, an unshakeable companion, a sturdy walking stick. Throughout it all, she had summoned an indefatigable, copper-colored Spirit, a shimmery bright thing. She had kept it bright, hadn't she? Wasn't she the one who had convinced Charles to do a U-turn on the GW Bridge? And what of golf and bridge, the Tenni-Tour and various hospital fund-raisers? She'd worn a blond wig and pharmaceutical pearls at Charles's retirement, hula-hooped her toast, gyrating the thing to her knees. She used to leave it all to chance, or Certain Men, actually.

Now she is blindsided by fury; she feels the tide of anger rise at certain unpredictable moments (yes, the *tide*), as if drawn by an internal moon, waxing and waning, though mostly waning.

A disclaimer, first: she lost no one in The Tragedy, no Hero her James, just an ordinary mortal, his (by inference) an unheroic death: cancer of the blood—blah blah blah—one cell fried—blah—and then another—blah blah until nothing remained but bone and sinew, James's lungs mechanically pumping, a ring of them singing before the doctor switched off the machine. Godspeed. And the machine stopped. Godspeed. Which is not to say she didn't know someone who knew someone; which is not to say she forgets we are living under the Cloud of It, as her daughter Liz would say, and that there are Reliable Threats, that Evil Lurks, that there are those who seek to undermine our Way of Life.

Crack. Crack. Crack.

The next time Tweedledee steps away from the others, approaching alone, the Big One with the bandaged hand hanging back as if on lookout, cradling the thing like a club.

"Did it hurt?" she calls to him. "Am I toxic? Infectious?"

"Another assault and there'll be no bail," says Tweedledee.

"It's a free country," Dorothy says.

"Not exactly," he says. Clearly there's a manual on How to Speak to the Protesters and/or the Criminally Insane.

"I'm not interested in the bodies," she says. "It's the wildlife I'm after. Mallards."

"Camera's forbidden," he says.

He stands, square and sharp, against the autumnal reds, his camouflage humorless, stuck in the sole season of winter. If she could see his eyes she predicts she would see embarrassment there, but they remain mirrored lenses, and anyway she is wrong: he is doing his job.

"Glorious day," she says, but he doesn't bite.

"So you can shoot them but you can't photograph them? I find that ridiculous. Ridiculous," she calls out to the Big One. "Does it still hurt?"

She grips the camera with her dirty fingers, though it is looped around her neck and going nowhere.

"You're trespassing, Mrs. Barrett. This is Government Property."

She plunks down in Tweedledee's shadow, her arms crossed.

"In Sweden there's no such thing," she says, squinting up. "You can camp anywhere. It's allowed. You could take a walk across the entire country if you wanted and no one could say, private property. I'd call that democracy, wouldn't you?"

He looms over her like a man mountain—trees and shrubs the pattern—his mirrored glasses the stone at the top, the place of the vista that from a distance could be snow, or water; bright, regardless, and glaring sun. She waits as he gestures to the Mute Ones, to the Big One with the bandaged hand. They are tired of her frequent visits, and bored in general. They step forward, unlocking their handcuffs, clicking and unclicking as if they'd rather be elsewhere. Even Tweedledee wipes his forehead in an exhausted, parched gesture. She thinks of how he sees himself now, how he *pictures* himself—soldier or statesman—protecting the all of us from God knows what: nothing; everything; an old woman with a camera. He protects is all, he's like a postage stamp or a flag, a symbol bought and sold, something with an adhesive strip to stick on an automobile bumper or football helmet—thirty-seven cents or a dollar ten in the big bin at Rite Aid.

The handcuffs are tighter than she would have imagined, and she finds herself humming the only song she can think to hum: "Amazing Grace," knowing, even while humming, how ridiculous she sounds, how outdated it's become, even quaint: Peace and Protest, a unit in the textbook on Sixties Rhetoric Caroline brought home from college, a chapter to be highlighted in fluorescent pink, an essay question. She thinks to mention this to Caroline, to somehow explain: What I am trying to do is to aim for something real, she'll tell her, something that is not just an approximation of real.

Here the two of us, she'll say, the all of us: the soldiers, the protestor, were all from a scene already enacted; so that even my own inclination to *be*—

Caroline interrupts. "To what?"

The bail has been paid, though this time they fingerprinted and there's a court date deferred—"Ma'am," Tweedledee had said to Caroline. "Tell your mother to keep her mouth shut."

"*Be*," Dorothy says now. "To *be*."

"Or not," says the Millionaire.

"When did everything stop being real?" Dorothy says.

"Don't bring James into it."

"He would have—"

Caroline plugs her ears; she might be eight, again: a girl in braids and kneesocks, six missing teeth so that she could no more blow a bubble than recite Pope, though James, a teacher at heart, had tried for weeks.

"I don't care, Mother. I mean, I do, but at some point you have to put yourself first."

"Like hell."

"What?" Caroline unplugs her ears.

"I said, I know."

"You know what?"

"I know you don't care."

The bubble burst, the lopsided attempt. James picked it himself out of Caroline's braids, though Dorothy had still given him a scolding and threatened the back side of the hairbrush. James put it all in his Feelings Jar, a jar that, in its earlier life, contained dill pickles.

I was just trying to DO SOMETHING. I was just trying to teach her how to blow bubbles and you got so mad you could spit. You always get so mad.

"I am just trying to Do Something," Dorothy says, though Caroline is busy looking for dinner inspiration, for anything other than pasta. "You don't care to understand. It's like everything. Conversation, for example, is now just approximations of opinions adopted from other opinions that were approximations of opinions, *etcetera*, *etcetera*. I'm just trying to be real when everything is an approximation."

But this is not true, exactly. Death is not an approximation. It is completely real; it is unchangeable, forever—an approximation of nothing. Hadn't she seen it that first time she'd found the base, the barracks, the military galaxy? Where had she been going? She can't remember anymore. She was lost, she knew, had taken to driving, punching the radio to listen to men and women discussing God knows what, anything to drown out her own inside voice. Use your inside voice, she used to tell the children, meaning quiet. Softly. Hers shouted now; tore its hair out. She had followed the convoy of jeeps, had stopped across the highway, curious at the rows and rows of them idling like so many school buses by the chain-link fence that surrounded the complex of guard towers and apartments and houses and a post office there in the middle of nowhere, or everywhere: soybean fields, corn crops, a *V* of geese heading south, and somewhere else, just beyond, an abandoned barn where starlings roost in rotted eaves and a boy necks or smokes or pings his pocketful of stones one by one against the glass, wanting breakage: all boys do. At the center sat the plane, exceedingly complicated, wings folded and a scissored tail—more like a jackknife than anything that could fly—and from it soldiers transporting bodies, their families there to receive them, to take them back as real, as dead.

"This is no approximation," Dorothy says. "This is what that idiot has the audacity to hide: the one thing true in the mess of it—death, destruction," she says, attempting to name it all for Caroline, who some time ago surrendered, running the sauce jar under hot water, her back to Dorothy though presumably listening.

Now she turns, her hand dripping.

"I hear you, Mother," she says, popping the lid. "And I am trying to be sympathetic. I mean, I get it, sort of. I sort of get it, or get it as best I can. It's just, God, do you have any idea what I'm up against? And now I have to bail my mother out of jail? I mean, can't you find some other project?" The question, Dorothy understands, is rhetorical, so she says nothing as Caroline forks a noodle from the boiling pot and holds it out to her. "Finito?" Caroline asks.

Weeks later Dorothy dreams of James. In this one he steps out of the Cape Cod surf (those were the years!) wet and gleaming; he is as he was, a young man, a boy who loved books, who copied passages in letters to his mother, certain things he believed she might like, under-standing her taste, he once wrote from college, in these matters.

Dear Mother,

His name is Professor Burns, which is ironic, because he smokes like a chimney and even when not keeps the cigarette, somehow lit, behind his ear. There's a rumor his hair once caught on fire and he lost his place in his notes and for the rest of the semester kept one step ahead of the syllabus oblivious. He is a little odd, but I like him and this is my favorite class. I don't know if I love romantic poetry or just love the way he talks about romantic poetry. I don't know if I just love that anyone can talk about romantic poetry at all how many years later and still weep. Yes, he weeps. Or did the other day after his lecture on Wordsworth, after reading the one about wandering with his Dorothy, or maybe the one about the daffodils I can't remember. A few of the girls went up to console him; maybe it was just a ploy (ha ha).

Here he is! Dorothy thinks in her dream. Look, here he is! He's been swimming—that scamp—all along!

She hears the waves roll out behind him, the crash of it so clearly. She is fearful he might decide to return to that riptide; how often has she warned him it could carry you for miles! But, no. He walks toward her, the sun behind him dazzling. He is a dazzling boy, a young man of promise without a single broken bone, nothing to be mended, stitched; strong-hearted. He takes no medications, she could tell you, and on that repeatedly filled-out form that has so many boxes in which to check yes he checks no, no, no, no! every time. He is no more an approximation than a red tulip in May and here is the great joke of it: He is Real!

A delicious pain, almost sexual, wakes her. It is the great cruel trick of the night: to wake alone, regardless. She can scream or cry if she wants—Caroline's gone home and Charles is deaf asleep, long in the habit of covering his eyes with a towel to block the light. She elbow-props herself to watch him breathe, he the father of her children, but he floats away from her, somehow, into outer space in his bubble. It will burst, eventually, and he, like the rest of them, will be gone.

To where?

An approximation of this, perhaps, or the curl of a shell, the color of leaves, a gesture; here but somewhere deep within.

When James was very sick, he had asked her what she believed; this was toward the end, she remembers, very close. And she might have lied; she might have given him something more, this man her boy had grown into, his body wrecked now into old age though he was still young.

"Nothing," she had said, already furious. "Absolutely nothing."

He sat in the hospital chair by the window. She had brought a blue shawl and oatmeal cookies she would set by the door for visitors—his friends from college, his young law colleagues. They had a train to catch and could only stay an hour, though they were often out the door sooner, worried they might miss something, that there would be a crowd.

"You're an original, Mom. I've meant to tell you," he said.

"From a long line, darling," she said, wanting to hear more and wanting him to stop. She still had to tell him so many things, things she could remember: her father, Thomas Francis Townsend, the Francis James's own middle name, playing the old upright in the living room, the little ceramic bust of Beethoven balanced on top and frowning out at all of them, the bust a gift from a nurse or a housekeeper or some stand-in for his mother, the original Dorothy, when he was still a boy, still in, as he would say, the bosom of the devil, during a particularly rainy day or maybe it had been a sunny one. He spoke of a music room. He spoke of thick, green draperies pulled and a view out the French doors to hills and a peacock (they had owned several, each a sacrifice to the fox) drawn to the sound of his playing, when the door on this rainy or sunny day stood open and the draperies were pulled and the metronome tick-tocked and he sat on the ebony bench, his bad foot lifted with his good hands to rest on the pedal, and played and the screech of the peacock or possibly the canary she insisted on keeping in a cage interrupted him so he stopped. He spoke little of it. It had been a terrible interruption, he remembered, though why—a bird?—seemed ridiculous and wrong. The nurse had given him the bust, had presented it to him. She said it was magic somehow; that if no one else listened it did.

She had tried to play, she might have told James, and never got it: music. There were so many things she never got, she could have told him, yet even here, even here with him, she wanted to paint herself in a different way, to flaunt the new lineage, to be the lineage he had helped her discover so that she could stand for something other than mother. And what was so wrong with that? Why couldn't she just be that? It is all he needs now. It is apparently all that they ever need.

She stood by the edge of his bed; she liked to stand there. She even liked this hospital room, or well enough. They had moved him to the quiet floor, the dying floor, he called it, with its view over the low rooftops to the sliver of river when the light went right, which happened more often now, in this season. It had miraculously become autumn.

"So I forgive you your trespasses," he said.

"Hallelujah," she said.

"And besides, I'm hoping you're wrong," he said.

"It wouldn't be the first time."

"If you are, I'll come back and rattle the windows," he said. "Think of it as my 'so there.'"

The windows more than rattle; so there. The wind more than blows. And somewhere else the terrified children must listen for what else—the cavalry, the infantry, the artillery—what had James taught her? Nothing. Everything. The names run together to a pooled point, the way blood will when the heart stops beating, when the machine stops. The machine stopped.

That she gets out of bed after her dream of James is almost beside the point. She no longer needs to write a note for anyone. She can do what she likes. She throws on loose clothing and goes, forgetting her empty camera—It was just like in the movies! she told Caroline; the soldiers rolled out the film and flung it in the garbage! They called her bite his wound!—forgetting her purse, backing the station wagon out the long drive to swerve down the road toward the highway. At this hour there's little traffic and she can speed as much as she likes, the cornfields and rows of soybeans saluting as she passes; in the end her only ally, the landscape, the actual black dirt of the country. Government property my ass, she thinks.

Her headlights flood the woods she turns into: wild, brush grown, skunk cabbage in the hollows and arrowheads to be found; the all of it rattling in this strange, Halloween wind. There might be children behind the trees, trick-or-treaters, Frankensteins and ghosts and ghouls with bloody wounds shaking the skinny limbs of the aspen saying, I'm here! No, here! But they'd be flushed out, of course, by her, by the klieg lights on the landing field: in case of emergencies, no doubt: the jackknife slicing the air into ribbons, the families the only witnesses to the dead.

And what had she planned, anyway? To whom would she have shown her pictures? Charles? Liz and Caroline? Absent friends?

She parks near the guard tower and slams the door. The steel latticework seems to glow in the moonlight, rising to the little booth of their treehouse watch. She might see breath on that glass, it is that cold and not so far up, or frost; she knows he is in there and she could find him if she climbed.

When did it become the boy she is after?

Does a radio play in their guard tower? Does Tweedledee sit by himself writing a letter home?

She wants to know where he's from, what he studied in school. She's interested in his early artwork, she could tell him. Elementary. Preschool even. Did he begin with circles? Those circles! And then slowly, no; she had seen it in her children and her children's friends and her grandchildren, even. The loss of circles, eventually. Don't despair, she could tell him. It happens to everyone.

She would like to know where he sat in the cafeteria—with the popular children or off a little by himself, like her James, his sandwich crushed from his bookbag, a tuna fish on white bread or maybe peanut butter. Did his mother include notes? An *I love you*, or *Hi, Handsome!* Perhaps he was not a son who required encouragement; perhaps he did fine on his own. His were not elaborate tastes—she can guess this—nor particularly demanding. He seemed fine with what he got until he wasn't; and when he wasn't he didn't complain. He made plans—how to leave, how to get out, how to make do, survive.

Was he interested in trains? Did he play a musical instrument?

Dorothy stands at the fence looking in. The worst thing, she would tell him, is that she can no longer distinguish stars: When I think I have found one it moves out of view, just metal in orbit or a transportation vehicle. There are no longer fixed points by which to determine my direction, she would tell him. How can I ever make a wish?

You are not responsible, she would add. It is shameful what we've done to you. We should all of us be ashamed.

"You are just like the rest of us," she says. "You are only trying to Do Something. "

Does Dorothy shout this or whisper? It no longer matters. She is suddenly tired and aware that she should go. She'll return home the way she came, driving back through ye olde etcetera to her rightful place beside Charles: Dorothy Barrett, Mother to Caroline and Liz and the dead one, James.

Hormones, she'll tell Caroline, by way of explanation.

I miss him too, Caroline will say, by way of apology.

"Good-bye," Dorothy calls to them, though none can hear for the crack crack crack; the hunters particularly ravenous at dawn.

DOROTHY TREVOR

Lost, Dorothy interrupts the Anarchists—a crowlike flock of young men sitting circled around a tall leader. She had been looking for the door with the round brass handle, the Tillinghurst Room, Rabia had said, in the northwest entry of Trinity College, something easily missed but she'd see other Girton girls. She had been looking for the Spiritualists and entered the wrong room, she said to the men.

Come in, come in, the leader says, raising a book in hand. He stands against a narrow, stained-glass window—Christ-shepherd minding his sheep, it looks from here, beneath two doves spearing a Latin inscription. Too dark to see much else, though warmer in this room, the candles shifting as she enters and shuts the door. She had intended the Spiritualists, she might have repeated, but she did not. It seemed silly to explain and besides, she had sought the Spiritualists on a lark, Rabia claiming Dorothy might, if she dared, contact anyone she pleased—Lady Godiva or Anne Boleyn. Just last week, Agnes Amy spoke directly to Catherine the Great, who advised the gathered to pay closer attention to Mistress Francis's new lectures on hygiene.

Dorothy finds a chair outside the circle and sits—might as well—releasing, as she does, the vague idea of levitating the dead, or at least listening to their bangs and whispers and—what is it Rabia had said?—something about a freezing wind. They came with a freezing wind, Rabia had said, her yellow eyes wide. She said the spirits rode the wind right into the Tillinghurst Room and gathered beneath the music table, though sometimes they hovered in the draperies or thumped the piano or rattled the windowpanes. They seemed prepped, the ghosts, to be as ghostly as the Spiritualists imagined them. And why wouldn't the Spiritualists be ghostists, what turned a ghost into a spirit or vice versa? Did it have to do with souls? The age of the dead and/or dying?

Plenty of questions and here the wrong room.

Still, she sits, and why not? No one seems to be paying much attention to her, or perhaps they are simply pretending not to notice, she the one woman in a dozen or so men. Best to go along rather than make a fuss leaving. She will listen to what she can. She has become a good listener.

She concentrates on the leader in front of her, interesting with his book, leather-bound, it looked from here; he was still talking, defining something, the epoch of the proletariat, the injustices of distribution and wealth, and now he held up the book again. A Bible? Marx? Literature entirely predictable, she guessed. Wordsworth's poetry? Dorothy raises her hand. Why shouldn't she? This is merely a group, a club, not a university hemmed in by undefeated laws nor Dr. Vaughn's Greek Civilization with its seven Girton girls, the brainy lot, lined like stuffed monkeys in the back row. She guesses Wordsworth. She guesses this a meeting of romantic minds.

"Wrong on all counts," the leader says. "We're Anarchists," he says. "And this?" He shakes the book. "Engels on military history and theory."

The men shift to look at her, uncomfortable. "An Anarchist Communist?" she says.

He is against idealism, he explains. Last week they read the *Communist Manifesto*. "Bravo!" she says, clapping.

A few of them laugh, though most do not. They take their lead from him, whose name is William, he says. William Crawford.

William the Anarchists' leader, she thinks, or is that yet another oxymoron? She cannot wrap her arms around it. She should walk out, she thinks. Go find the ghosts.

"I've got to find the Spiritualists," she says, standing. The noise she makes! Coming and going there is no way to sneak, no stealth possible: every skirt with its rustle. The beauty of them all to be accentuated, Queen Victoria has said. Now those not wearing bloomers balance birds' nests on their heads. Why must they always look like fools?

"Pardon?" William says.

"The Spiritualists," she says.

"We are speaking of Positivism," William says. "It will be a debate, of sorts. There's a proposition and then a response. You may stay if you choose."

"Delighted," she says, sitting back down.

"And you are?" he says, waiting.

"Dorothy Trevor," she says.

"Dorothy Trevor," he says.

"Yes."

"Positivism, Miss Trevor. That which is understood must be observed and verifiable as such. Do you understand the term?"

He levels her in a gaze, the candles lit around the darkening room shifting, again, as if the ghosts are shoving in. She stares back, why shouldn't she? He looks all of eight years old, hair over his eyes, as he leans, book in hand, against the narrow stained-glass window.

"Enlighten me," she says.

Dorothy listens to the men argue the death of the bourgeoisie, the decay and disappearance of the classes, the certainty of their voices, their declarative sentences, oddly comforting, or perhaps it is merely the warmth of this room, far warmer than anywhere to be found at Girton, the Old Wing drafty, its halls trapping the cold, its blocks of red bricks already in need of repair. More than once she has tripped on a carpenter's tool. Our college is listing rubble, she wrote to her mother, a red elephant lumbering among the swift gazelles, the swiftest among them Trinity, its men future prime ministers, kings.

She has come once before, wandering the famous Wren Library, seventeenth century, she is forbidden to use, where needlepoint tapestries hang over the thick stonewalls keeping the damp out and preserving the ancient books, the unicorn tapestry guarded by various fellows—legend holding that after the monks buried it in ash, the unicorn's horn turned gold. She had looked through the long rows of drawers in the wooden catalogues that held the typed names of the books and inked impressions of long-dead librarians, cards slowly eaten to dust by silver wings—"a bit dense"; "better would be, *Life and Letters of Benjamin Jewel*, by E. Abbott and L. Campbell"; "a fascinating study of the identification of Gibeon." The ghosts are there, too, she might tell the Spiritualists, not only in the Tillinghurst Room, but there, in the books. They rise from those narrow drawers like steam.

Tonight, she had followed Rabia's instructions, counting the chain of gates to the far staircase, then continuing down the walk that led to the northwest entry, Trinity a maze, a puzzle to construct, interior to interior, the room she found herself in now one of many behind arched wooden doors donated by a viceroy or prince, its stained-glass windows no doubt stolen from a chapel in the Basque region of Spain. The all of it built above dungeons crammed with relics—a strand of Mohammed's hair, Christ's tooth—and armor: scepters, granite bowls and pestles, minerals once ground and shaped to bullets, diamonds used to pierce the skin.

"Onward, gentlemen," William says, concluding. "We reconvene next Wednesday." His hair hangs in a crop, swept up with a cowlick then dropped, again, black hair, eyes difficult to see in this dark, maybe grayish. His shoulders stoop as if anticipating a low door.

"I'm going to tell you something that will break your heart," he said later, still explaining, though this after he insisted upon riding her back to Girton, insisted on standing and pedaling as Dorothy sat on the seat. I have been practicing, he had said. I am a very good pedaler, he said. The best pedaler. Watch, and though she watched it was dark and a long way and they only found Huntingdon Road by the light of the moon.

"The average, by that I mean, calculated average woman in this country is an instrument of labor. She lives in poverty and servitude simply to put food into the mouths of her children, many of whom are born completely against her will. They call her a breeder and are done with her; round and round," he said.

"Tragic," Dorothy said, though she didn't mean tragic, she meant something else. It felt as if she might say anything. It felt as if she'd been suddenly untied, let loose, forbidden to speak in Dr. Vaughn's lectures, where she had so much to say! and then so lonely in her rooms with their double door and blue carpet and draperies and latched windows. The Building Committee had originally considered iron bars for the girls, she told William as they slipped in, but these were sixty pounds and so they counted on watchdogs. This one she had already ("wisely," William said, smiling) tamed with scraps.

Mistress Francis supervised, the rules spelled out in a notebook coupled with the Bible at every bedside. She must always consult the parlor ("please consult the parlor on your return") before retiring to these rooms, her rooms, with their rickety bookshelf and hand-me-down volumes from Girton's own library, donated by the wealthy friends of its founders. (Look at this one! Dorothy says, showing William the inscription: "To Charles Robert Darwin, with affection.")

Her sole luxury is her piano, brought into her rooms by six men struggling. It had cost most of the allowance her father had provided for the year, and she had been required, in Latin, to write a defense of her decision for him, a defense of music. He was not an unkind man, she said. Just stern.

She didn't mean tragic, she told William. There were worse things she could tell him and no, it didn't, quite honestly, break her heart.

"I was looking for the Spiritualists," she said. "Don't think me unsympathetic."

"You'd rather talk to ghosts than Anarchists," William said.

"I wanted to watch the table shake. There's much rattling and then, if you're fortunate, the wind blows and you lose a pane or two." She smiled, flirting or doing her best. She felt too old for this, unpracticed. If she looked straight at him she had to look away. She was breaking every Girton rule by inviting in a man, by smoking, but then again, all rules were made to be broken, her friend Alexandra said.

Dorothy sat across from William in her sitting room and her hands suddenly shook and her voice went off and even though they were whispering she felt as if she shouted, saying as much as she said, talking and talking. And who was he? Perhaps one of the men who had hanged their effigies last spring, declaring war on them, she and Alexandra and the other Girton girls who listened to Dr. Vaughn and wanted more, wanted to come and go and be given proper degrees so that they might do something—Charlotte and Constance, the brilliant twins, and the Indian, Rabia. Perhaps it was William and the Anarchists who had hung the banners: Here's no Place for You Maids! Much Ado About Nothing! And now here he sits in the very place he swore he would never be.

She was against convention, she was telling him. She was a contributor to the National Society for Women's Suffrage. She was interested in the supernatural. She had attended one of the laboratory schools and then sat for the entrance exams. Latin and Greek she knew from her father, though her mother had insisted that French would be more useful for a woman. She had a great interest in history and felt perfectly comfortable attending Dr. Vaughn's lectures. She had been the one to ask! Yes, she was an agitator, and why not? Women should be given full right to an education and rewarded for it. They should have more than this deplorable position of parasitism. They should be permitted the vote, even unmarried women and debtors and those with nothing particularly interesting to add.

She took a puff of his cigarette, blowing the smoke out the unlatched window then handing the cigarette back to him. She stroked the little watchdog on her lap, a pug. She felt a slight nausea from his cigarette. She would like to hold his hand but she didn't dare. He had pale skin and a sharp, patrician nose, and his black hair cut across his face like a shadow. They sat opposite one another at the small table where she at times wrote papers no university lecturer wanted to read. She read them to Alexandra, who declared them brilliant. They would do just fine, they knew, if they changed their names and sliced off their breasts: she would be Diderot, or Delacroix; Alexandra, Alexander.

"Not as glamorous as it looks, rebellion," he said, reaching for her hand.

She looked at how his long fingers tapered down to fingernails she thought too ragged. He must bite them.

"Terrible habit," she said.

"I can think of worse," he said.

She had been able to look at him then, for an instant.

"Enlighten me," she said.

Sometimes she played the piano and he listened with his eyes closed. She liked that and she would have liked, at the time, to correct him, to say that what he had said when they first met didn't exactly break her heart, but that it broke her heart that it broke his heart, and that he had appeared, that night, to be a man who might think differently, or rather, speak his mind more honestly. But the truth was she didn't entirely believe him. And now it no longer mattered.

They saw each other every day. Sometimes he would climb through the unlatched window or they would pick an hour, late, and she would pedal her bicycle to town, to Trinity and the Anarchists Club to meet William again in that first room, named, she now knew, after someone's comely wife, the Mrs. Theodore Jacobs Room, 1723–1794, God Rest Her Soul: a life for a room, a fair exchange; table and chairs nicked from too many bored students.

The stained-glass windows were indeed stolen from a chapel in the Basque region of Spain. William told her this. He knew the college well, him from a long line of Trinity men, father and grandfather and great-grandfather and so forth. He'd been spoon-fed the history from the beginning of time, he said. But the world would soon erupt, he said, given the decay and disappearance of class. Then history will not stand a chance.

The night William was beaten, the assailant after his pockets, some pounds and nothing more, he said, finding him on his return from her, midnight or near enough, he changed his tune. So much for the plight of the breeders, she said. They were lovers by then; she exactly what her mother had feared she would become. She didn't give a damn. Freedom! she said to Queen Victoria. Liberation! she said.

She felt drunk from it, from the feel of him. She listened to Dr. Vaughn's lectures with a look on her face, Alexandra pinching her leg. She read books. She played notes. She breathed in and out. On several warmer days, she and William went on a hike and brought lunch, his funds limitless—bread, fruit, bottles of ale. She sat up from the blanket and ate and afterward lay back on the blanket again, waiting for him. When he turned to her, she felt she disappeared, slipped into him like a coin cupped by a hand.

Sometimes he would read to her; sometimes she to him.

"You're in love with him," Alexandra said.

"Brilliant," Dorothy said.

"Him?"

"You."

"Pleasure," Alexandra said.

"That would be the first thing," she said.

They sat in the larger parlor, the room Mistress Francis expected them to consult every evening. Here the other Girton girls played Speculation or read after vespers, Mistress Francis in their company stitching something god-awful—a verse from the New Testament to be framed in wood—or at her table in the far corner preparing another talk on hygiene. But today the larger parlor was empty, Mistress Francis and the girls on the banks of the river. There were daffodils there, hundreds of them, and grass so green it looked painted by a hand, and even here the trees and shrubs had finally blossomed, the grounds of the redbrick building not so stark as at Michaelmas, when they had arrived.

It is that kind of spring day. If Dorothy and Alexandra were to draw the draperies they would see a cloudless sky but they drink their tea in lamplight, the parlor dead-still except for the occasional rustle of the draperies, the Spirits insisting.

"Mind, looks, money," Alexandra said.

"Two, three, four."

"He's a bit of a twit," Alexandra said.

"Who isn't?"

"Ted Townsend," Alexandra said. "He seems keen for you."

"The Explorers Club?" Dorothy said. "God, I thought I heard he'd contracted something. Didn't he contract something? I read it, didn't I?"

"There are rumors," Alexandra said. "He knows Darwin. Assisted him in the field several times and is working on some paper. He'd make William green."

"I might jump out of my own skin first," Dorothy said.

"He'd love to examine it."

"Relic of the beast formerly known as Woman."

"Gone the way of the dodo," Alexandra said. She picked something from between her teeth.

"Frankly, I'm bored with that," Dorothy said. "Science. The whole business of it. Can't the men find another subject?"

Alexandra raised her cup and sipped. They had a plate of sweets before them and a copy of Florence Nightingale's "Cassandra"; these days they might read it aloud just to hear her words in their voices. "What we want is something to do, something to live for," they would recite together.

"Three new girls coming in," Alexandra said. "They're from Miss Ina's School in Worcester. Brainy brainy. Reception's planned."

"Sherry?"

"Believe so."

"Excellent."

The sugar cubes are from Bengal, sent last week to Rabia and shared with all of them, each cube painted with a tiny purple violet and a sprig of green. The wallpaper velvet, a faded red. Round and round are hung the mementos, the framed invitations, the missives, the verses of the Bluestockings.

Two cubes dissolve in the saucer of Dorothy's china cup. She watches as the violet bleeds into water.

"You know who William's father is," Alexandra is saying. "He will have his degree by May, be married in June. There's a government post, apparently."

After William left Cambridge, Dorothy and Alexandra rarely spoke of him. He'd come and gone, Dorothy said, as if she had indeed found the Spiritualists: William a ghost risen up next door, summoned from the Netherworld, the Underworld, the Other-World, summoned from across the Thames. He'd returned to the place where the ladies lived, the ones sent to the schools intended to teach them the ways in which to serve the men who would inherit all this, who owned all this: the piles of stones and the chairs within, their leather seats and backs worn as old gloves, their arms and legs elaborately tattooed with the carvings of naughty boys. They were all of them naughty boys.

Still, Dorothy would, at times, allow herself to remember that first evening, and the way in which William rose up to her out of the circle of Anarchists—Positivism, gentlemen. Do you understand the term? he had said to her. Do you get the mathematics?

She should have done it differently. She should have spoken up, said something. She should have claimed her place. She might have told them the story of her old friend Hilde, dead in childbirth a few years back. She hasn't thought of her since; willed herself not to think of her. She and Hilde were taking their time, she might have told the men. They were strolling back from practice. Hilde dragged the hockey stick and made a snake of it in the dust of the road.

Dorothy, look! she called. A cobra! And then from nowhere came the boys. A team, apparently—a group of them on their way back from school, or maybe a game, she didn't know. She could see them still, ringing her, ringing her friend Hilde, locking their hands and closing in. They came from nowhere, she and Hilde alone on the road, a dirt road, empty but for the milkweed and the Queen Anne's lace in the dried-out ditches—there's been no rain—the goldenrod and the dragonflies and the other insects she can no longer name though at the time she had been quite a naturalist. The boys were watching; they had a plan. She and Hilde walked down the dirt road, Hilde dragging the hockey stick, hot for June and dusty, the stick making snake skids in the dust, Hilde telling some story, something about a snake following her once all the way home, the snake chasing her, even, the snake being the kind that could chase, could smell fear. She was afraid then, she said, but she is not now. She's going to walk as if the snake isn't there.

The snake isn't there, Dorothy said. It's your stick, Hilde.

Blow off. I'm pretending.

You played well.

The best.

Too bad your mum wasn't there to see.

She can kiss my arse, Hilde said.

Dorothy felt the thrill of the word, felt the swell of power in Hilde speaking this way of her mum, too strict, they both agreed, and capable of evil—but Hilde was already twelve, two years older than Dorothy, so she said what she liked.

She can kiss my arse, Hilde said again, skipping on, forgetting the game with the stick, forgetting the snake. She wore a skirt to her knees, a light one, and the jersey assigned to her team: number 4. And then the boys appeared—where did they come from? They were bigger boys but not so big, not much older than Hilde. Some Dorothy may have recognized, but maybe not. Who were these boys? Who? They were strong, she could see, athletes. They gathered round. Hilde had something they wanted. They wanted that, they told her. They wanted it.

No, Hilde said.

She wants us to say please, one said, and the others laughed but maybe they didn't; maybe she laughed. Dorothy can't remember. Why is she on their side? Why doesn't she save Hilde?

Run, Hilde calls to her. Run get—

But she doesn't hear what; she can't hear what before Hilde disappears within the team of them, swallowed whole. Dorothy doesn't turn to look. She runs. Her legs are sticks and her knees cranky. They are bruised. Her legs are bruised. She needs to eat more fruit, her mum said, and drink her milk and get her nose out of books so *run*, thinks Dorothy. *Run*. But what she saw, what she saw!

Dorothy remembers this in hospital, remembers Hilde swallowed whole and the feel of her own heart pounding, the sound of her heart pounding.

Or is that the church bells? These days they are always ringing. And always the rooks rest in the rookery or wheel above the steeple. It might be the end of the war or the beginning. The battles have been won or lost but soon they will be starting again, so much still to be discussed with Mr. Darwin.

DOROTHY TREVOR TOWNSEND

Wardsbury, England, 1914

The hospital attendant stands at Dorothy's door, staring. No one else is in the room, the hospital quiet, most of the doctors and nurses closer to the coast and the train station there, working in the makeshift tents with little more than scalpels and saws, a needle and thread, the attendant heard—cold coffee and a bloody bun to keep everyone alive. She turns to go, disgusted, closing the door as if Dorothy is sleeping but Dorothy is not sleeping.

Outside, the tree limb, a bare branch, ticks the window, and from somewhere church bells ring.

Dorothy could ask for a blanket but she would rather not speak. She is always cold now. She lies against the white sheet. It is a white sheet and a white room. Someone has hung a crucifix on the wall at the end of her bed. Thomas has drawn a picture—it is brutal, unimaginable, to think of what she is doing, what she has already done to the children, to think of what the children may grow into, given her absence, given their father's absence. Could she explain to them that she had no other choice? That she had nothing else to sacrifice but her life?

She will speak to Alexandra about it, propose explicit instruction on what should come next. She finds the sheet of paper someone has left by her bedside, not a sheet of paper at all, she sees now, but a menu of sorts, suggestions written in a neat column, as if all she need do is check a dish to have it magically appear—*sweet potato puree, creamed spinach*. She turns the paper over, thankfully blank.

Evie, she writes. *There are certain things one should remember,* she writes.

The paper blurs from so much staring, the words resurrecting themselves into points of light, or darkness, or nothing at all, explosions of color—what had Evie said? They had been at the lake not so far from here; the place in the park where on other days, colder days, when the children were little, they rented boats and rowed to the bridge where the cherry trees collapsed into the water, nearly rotted, their few blossoms browned and drained of color. Evie's lips were blue.

Warm me, sun, Evie had said, shivering, the thin towels Dorothy had packed too scratchy for Evie's taste, her colt legs pricked with cold until they found the good warm spot and Evie, flat as a gingerbread cookie, spread out and said, "Warm me, sun. Bring down your yellows and reds."

In her hand Dorothy holds the paper from her bedside table. She sees she has written something to Evie. She reads what and thinks that she could eat these words, *Dear Evie* or, *remember.* For as much as she will die—which she knows—she desires nothing more than to eat these words, to live, to swallow her life whole, her children, her compatriots, the memory of William in London before the war, a year ago, or two? Their affair had begun again as abruptly as it ended, as if its interruption—marriage, motherhood—were merely a child racing into a room and upsetting a vase. At the benefit for the suffrage fund, the tedious benefit, William had bowed when introduced. They had known one another years before, he explained to the host, as children, he said, smiling, his hair now gray, his handsome face lined. She could have touched it right then. She could have smoothed the skin.

She knew the arc of his life from the papers, his ambassadorships and recent decision to step back from public office, to return to England for good; it was strange that so many years had passed since they were in the same room. Once, she told him after the party, she had watched as he pushed a child on the Hyde Park swings, the ones closest to the fish pond where she was walking with her daughter, Evie. He told her he knew someone, an artist with an empty studio. They would be out of harm's way, he said. They would be safe there, and they were, bookshelves lining the perimeter, paintings stacked floor to ceiling or hooked on nails hammered into the fissured walls at random. The paintings were of women and men, nudes at all angles. William had a plan for her, she knew. He had anticipated undressing her, peeling her, her flesh, he said, because operatic William would love "flesh" more than "skin."

"And where is your wife?" she said.

"Occupied," he said.

"And the owner of the studio, the artist?" she said.

"Down the street," William said, "at the bakery."

Now she pictures tongs iced in crumbs and the young girls who plucked the croissants from their pyramids—their white hats, their white smocks, the fine earrings they wore, pearls or shells or even diamonds, presented from boys who were too soon dead. And the artist too in the bakery already dead. And her uncle. And her father. And most of the Cambridge men.

Dorothy is suddenly ravenous. Starving, she thinks. I'm starving, hunger just a purer form of desire—the world now flooded for her, saturated with color, sound, smell. She would try to explain this to William if he were to come, but he cannot, he says, or he won't, or he is no longer able. There are matters of state. There is a state of emergency. This is war, he says.

Dorothy looks up. She hears again the scratch of the tree limb, the bare branch, against the window. It is mostly quiet in her room. Quiet in the hallway. At the foot of her bed the crucifix hangs crooked on the wall. Someone must have brushed by. Evie? She looks down and turns the paper she holds in her hand to the other side. It is her mother's script, shaky, determined. *Creamed spinach*, her mother has written. It used to be Dorothy's favorite.

* * *

Nurse stares out the kitchen window, waiting for her milkman, Michael. Nurse should not be assumed dowdy; she is beautiful and young and is obligated to wear a uniform that cost her six weeks' wage, and must take care to keep it bleached bone white.

"Bone white," Dorothy would say, in a voice that had always reminded Nurse of dough left out too long, crumbly. It broke apart too easily, as if it never could quite take claim of its own sentences. Still, she did mean bone white, and Nurse took care to scrub and wash the now-thin cotton Sunday afternoons, her day off, Sunday mornings, as it were, devoted to Michael.

Evie breaks in, breathless, high color, raven-haired, the nursery rhymes would call it, though it has been some time since Nurse read either of the children nursery rhymes, Thomas engaged with music, Evie with mathematics, her passion, a form of which Nurse couldn't make heads nor tails of: something to do with logic in numbers. Now planes are the order of the day, or the one that flew across the Channel yesterday on its way to the Royal Naval Air Service, the crowd, Michael said, better than he had ever seen, come out to see the pilot, a Frenchman. Michael stood in the middle of it and got a crick in his neck, the streets full of persons rubbing their heads. The aeroplane arrived early.

Michael has been there with the news of Dorothy's death but Nurse still stands at the window as if waiting, staring at one point on the horizon, the orchard on the knoll beyond the dirt road where the trees, blighted with apple rot, twist toward the reddish sky. She pictures Dorothy there with her shears, how she cut out the rot, or attempted, furious, using the spade to bury it. On the rot's grave moss grows, a garden Dorothy cultivated with ash where Evie can be found most sunny days reading.

"Did he tell you about the aeroplane?" Evie wants to know. She stands behind Nurse, also waiting. Evie saw Michael come and go as she stood in the kitchen garden, her arms loaded with what Penny needs for the roasting fowl. The bundle made it difficult to run. "What did he say?" Evie says now.

Nurse turns, attacking the butcher's table with her steel brush. Dorothy would want her uniform bleached bone white, the kitchen gleaming like a hospital.

"Impossibly small, he said," Nurse says. "More like a giant insect. A dragonfly with a gun."

Nurse knows about hospital gleaming. Last time she went her mistress's face was afire, her bones lit with fever. She hasn't been back since and now, too late—Dorothy dead this morning, Michael said.

Evie takes her chair. "What else?"

Nurse stops and looks at the girl. Her breath catches in her throat.

"Apparently everyone's got the crick in their neck from looking up," she says. "It was fine and low and he thought he saw that French fellow, who? Smiling as he drove—"

"Flew—"

"—the contraption."

"Captain Junot," Evie says. "He's a war hero."

"Who?"

"The pilot," Evie says.

"I don't know anything more about the pilot."

Nurse crosses the room to the stone sink, aware of the girl staring, the tangle of herbs dirtying her butcher's table, the cock crowing. She squeezes the rag and returns to the window, the rag soapy, warm. She finds it difficult to look at Evie, who waits, shifting leg to leg, wanting to hear more.

"Mum said I could go," Evie says.

"Other things came up, don't you suppose."

Evie kicks out her leg, kicks it back again. She has done this since Nurse can remember, scuffing the floorboard Nurse will put right later. From the other room Thomas bangs his fists on the keys.

"He's going to break the bloody thing," Nurse says.

"What else?" Evie says. "What did Michael say?"

Nurse swirls the wet rag from pane to pane. There is comfort here in washing, comfort in the spotty sun, bright then dark this

odd, cloudy day, turning the dirt road a flooding river. She had
watched Michael pedaling toward the house so early this morning,
past the lilac and the rows of apple trees Dorothy paid the gardener
to plant, the stone wishing bench Dorothy paid the mason to build.
Her life's work, she laughed. This on the night that Nurse had
found her there, returned late from London, weeping. A full moon,
or something close to one, lighted the fresh shorn fields, and the
cypress cast bars of black shadows over Dorothy, dwarfed in landscape as she sat, a branch blighted by apple rot in her hand. She
had been to one of her benefits, though the war would soon put a
stop to them. Nurse had found her by the sequins of her dress, glit-
tering like a fish out of water, her suffrage sash looped from shoulder to waist.

"My life's work," she said, holding up the dead branch.

"Come to bed," Nurse said.

"I didn't sign on for this," Dorothy said.

"Didn't sign on for what?" Nurse said. They had always been
direct with one another.

She shrugged. "For you, for us. The children and you and me.
We're a team, aren't we? A music hall show. It's all so bloody predictable."

Nurse helped her stand and steered her toward the house and up
the long stairway, the children, thankfully, asleep. She unhooked the
back of Dorothy's dress and slipped it from her shoulders. She was
beautiful, Dorothy, her reddish hair the color of Evie's and thick. She
wore it high in a pompadour that Nurse unpinned and brushed as
she would a child's.

"Good night," she said to Dorothy.

"And what do we women do? We play our roles; we speak our
lines," Dorothy said. "Christ. We go along."

"Good night," she said.

"So what should I say next? I'm ashamed? Forgive me? I'm hope-
lessly drunk?"

Nurse turned out the light, her hand shaking. She would have liked to have told Dorothy that she hadn't signed on for this, either, but she simply said, "Sweet dreams."

Evie stares. Nurse can feel her staring. "What?" she says, turning too quickly, the dripping rag in her hand.

"What else?" Evie says. "What else did Michael see?"

"Oh, God," she says, sitting down hard. "Let's remember. He said the king arrived at Buckingham Palace in a balloon of the most fantastic colors."

Here Evie smiles. She has been waiting for the good part.

"And funny enough, he brought a baboon at his side."

"The orange kind?" Evie says.

"No, this baboon had a reddish cast, apparently. And the good men of Lloyd's came out of their offices just to see the hero for themselves, money bags hoisted to their shoulders."

"Did the aeroplane land?" she says.

"Directly atop the good men of Lloyd's," Nurse says.

Evie twists her skirt in her hands. At one time, she had been as talented at the piano as Thomas. Then she lost interest. "So it did land, then. There had been word it might continue if conditions were favorable."

Evie cannot bear the idea of not knowing, of missing the spectacle of the red plane, the Nieuport 10 with its bull's-eye wings, its sleek tail. Dorothy had promised to take her in the autocar to the staging area, where she might have caught a look at Junot. She drew him sometimes, in her schoolbooks. If she were as old and as pretty as Nurse she would have gone there on her own and introduced herself.

Nurse walks to the stone sink and twists the dirty water from her rag. "I haven't the slightest idea about that."

Soon neighbors will arrive, their hands raw from their own morning washing, or the cold clutch on the handlebars of the bicycles they'll steer down the rutty grooves, easier to manage when frozen in winter but now muddy from the rains. They'll track in footprints and ruin this hospital shine. Is it bone white? Are the tablecloths starched? Well pressed? There is no one else but her to tell the children, Grandmother indisposed in a darkened room, Alexandra in London.

Nurse turns to look directly at the girl.

"Evelyn," she says. "Go get your brother."

The neighbors come for Dorothy's viewing, everyone drunk on spectacle and news, the word spread fast. They walk, following the long rows of pin oak—circular, straight—leading into, then out of, Wardsbury, the village not grand though old and named and formerly off the Roman road, its market foundations held by iron pins to the ground. The town sits near enough to the sea to smell the gunpowder on certain windy mornings: this one of those mornings, and rain, the weather turned since the morning the Frenchman Junot flew in clear skies straight over the Channel to land in a field beyond. Then they had gathered as if to watch an eclipse, or the hole left in the ground by the meteor, Eros, its sulfur smell many could still remember, noting this and the eventuality of all things natural to mechanical: The primacy of the machine, they said. Combat waged in the skies, what next?

Now the starvation of a young woman, a mother in her prime; death brought on by modern ideas, pride, a certain vanity or rather, unreasonable expectations. This the neighbors say and more, huddled beneath umbrellas, riding along in carts, warming dishes on their laps, before they are silenced by the sight of Michael draping bunting window to window.

How appropriate, the rain, thinks Nurse. She sets the dining room table, spreading the cloth Dorothy would have liked best. Odd sensations with death; she can still hear Dorothy's voice, instructing, commanding, imperious at times and then not, then friendly or sad or crumbling. They might have been friends elsewhere, in a place like New York. Michael has been talking, again. Making promises. Now that she must—

A knock. Mrs. Jenkins from the apothecary in town, her big hand splayed on the glass. Nurse gestures but Mrs. Jenkins only knocks, again, her face a blur, pressed against the glass as if drowning beneath ice.

"I'm early," Mrs. Jenkins says, the door letting in the better smells; she'll take anything to chase away the incense Penny insists on burning through the viewing. This after Father Terrance sent word of his refusal to bury Dorothy in the family plot.

"How are the children?"

"Well as expected. Tea? I'm setting the table."

Mrs. Jenkins shakes off her coat and settles herself in one of the chairs arranged around the buffet. Michael helped her bring them in, the others from the various rooms, Mrs. Jenkins choosing the upholstered Queen Anne from Thomas's nursery, yellow trains and trucks.

"I have a daughter-in-law who carries on and I hope she takes this as a lesson," Mrs. Jenkins says.

"I don't know," Nurse says.

Mrs. Jenkins looks over the narrow buffet table out the long French window, the sole window left open for the purpose of the incense, or the spirit, depending. She'll have an unsteady path home with the weather, she thinks.

"My son acts as if she's hung the moon."

Nurse pictures Stevie Jenkins, his face flushed as she's seen it too many times as he walks between here and there, making his deliveries, his pants cinched with a belt he likes to finger when speaking.

"And Mrs. Trevor?" Mrs. Jenkins is saying. "Isn't she with the grandchildren?"

"Indisposed," Nurse says, remembering how Mrs. Jenkins once asked Michael to step out of her store, complaining he smelled of the cow barn.

"Lovely setting," Mrs. Jenkins continues, but now Evie is here, Alexandra behind her fussing with the flowers. There are flowers and more flowers.

"Hallo," Evie says to Mrs. Jenkins. She gives her a kiss as she has been instructed to do with guests, and curtseys. Then she walks into the other room to sit stone-faced next to her mother, her Votes for Women sash like some kind of badge from an undeclared war. Evie had insisted, though Alexandra said it would only stir the neighbors. Let them be stirred, Evie said, her eyes hard.

"What a beautiful dress," Mrs. Jenkins says, joining her. Mrs. Jenkins had meant to say, I'm sorry for your loss, or Your mother was a brave soul, but the thoughts had gone out of her mind as soon as she saw Dorothy in her box and the pretty girl next to her, so like her mother, intelligent face and those hands, pressed against her knees as if covering a scream. And in the far room the crippled boy—how sad—plays the piano.

The obituary in *The Times* includes an etched likeness of Dorothy Trevor Townsend, a reproduction hastily and sloppily drawn by the person paid for such things; it is boxed and inked and staring out from deep within news of other things, Dorothy Trevor Townsend, 1880–1914, widow of Sir Theodore Francis Townsend, Ceylon, mother to Evelyn Charlotte Townsend and Thomas Francis Townsend, ages thirteen and ten, respectively.

This is not the first news of Dorothy Trevor Townsend carried by *The Times*. Over the years, since she was denied a degree though she had placed in the first class of the Classical Tripos at Cambridge, there have been opinions registered of Dorothy Trevor Townsend, letters printed, and mentions, from time to time, of her various shenanigans in the name of suffrage and women's rights, though her pursuit of dying has been kept—given an edict from the editors—between the lines. This decision was made on the advice from certain persons familiar with the hysterical and copycat tendencies of

the Women's Social and Political Union, and of the precedence of the
war news above all else.

Still, the editors have instructed the artist to include the white
sash on his drawing of Dorothy. He does so reluctantly, acts such as
hers tantamount to treason, in his view, given male sacrifices of a
highly different nature. Hadn't she threatened all of them by suggesting there were other matters to consider? And what of her children
left behind? But he had followed his orders, the directive to include
the likeness of the suffragette Dorothy Trevor Townsend with those
of Sir William Whitehead, former chancellor of Bradley Ltd., a man,
according to all who knew him, who will be deeply missed on
Threadneedle Street, father to three grown sons employed at Bradley
Ltd., and husband of fifty-two years to Gwenyth, residing by the
seashore in Durham; and Alfred Branford, gardener of the high
estates and designer of the mazes and ha-has enjoyed by thousands
in the Yorkshire village of Quell. He has drawn them as a little group,
the two men flanking Townsend as if escorting her down an aisle,
which may or may not be true, thinks the artist, wondering, given
his work in the realm of the dead, if those who die on the same day
join one another on the journey homeward, temporarily forgetting
that Dorothy would not, by all accounts, be heading in the same
direction as the men, and that more than likely they have left her far
behind.

EVELYN CHARLOTTE TOWNSEND

Grayshead-on-Heath, England, 1919

The local soldiers returned, strangers and a few of the boys we knew from Top Hill. They came back somewhat whole, the all of them circling Madame Lane's like so many stray cats, released from the Red Cross station down the road and in no hurry, they said, to be home. They'd roll our cigarettes between dirty fingers, their nails black from rotted potatoes, blood blisters. Potatoes we ate, and carrots from Abigail's garden. Things had gone from bad to worse, though one morning Brigid yelled to come see the lad flying the kite. He held on to the string of it, its tail knotted rags and the kite itself made from a bedsheet, hubba, hubba, the soldiers said, and we said, bugger off then and watch. The kite chose this day to fly: blue and spotless as the bibs of our Mother Hubbards. It went up and up, the kite, though it did not make a straight line. It dipped. It swerved. This the perfect kite day, anyone could have told you. The boy held the string and the snot rags and did not let go. He stood on the little hill where Father Fairfield had taken the sled. There was snow that March before they drafted him. Impossible miracle. Father Fairfield stood on the top of the little hill with the sled and dared all of us before heading down. We waited in a cluster at the bottom frozen to the bone.

Go on, then, he said to us. Come up and have a try.

Brigid had never been and me only once, snow rare as beef.

We climbed the hill, the snow impossibly white. Go on, he said, in Christ, he said, close enough to wink. His hands were cold and the steel blade of the sled would have sliced his skin clear, too drained to bleed.

We went down and at the bottom of the hill we turned around and dragged the sled back up again. Some of the new girls were there and the thin one, Emma. She took a spin, too. She lost her breath on the fall and we ran to her and Father Fairfield bent over her looking like a sudden black hole dug in that white and looked up at us, smiling, and said, "Here lies poor Emma," and that was fine because we wanted her dead given his attentions. Him we wanted alive.

Now Brigid and I watched the kite fly where Father Fairfield had been and at the feet of the boy who flew it was a satchel of sorts in which he kept a knife and he used the knife to cut the string, more string, so that the kite could go higher, and now the wind pulled so that the kite stayed in an even line, a here-to-there line, and Brigid said it's a sign. He's giving us a bloody sign—as in the kite might stretch to Heaven where Father Fairfield would quick attach a little note, "weather's fine, wish you were here." Hah hah, I said, though I was hoping, knowing otherwise: him just a boy who had appeared from nowhere to fly a kite, we two girls still alive who waked to see it.

Father Fairfield is dead. Grandmother is dead. Thomas remains in America, in California with his new family, a musical protégé at sixteen, according to Alexandra.

Alexandra writes more often now; Buenos Aires like Paris only tropical, she writes, with flowering purple trees and gardenias the size of grapefruits and churches on every corner, their massive stone steps a pink stone polished to a gleam and crowded with beggars—the devout in a nutshell. Christ, God, she writes. When will we give up on Him? They have a neighborhood of the dead, their tombstones the size of mansions. She sends a postcard to prove it, though all I see is a collection of stone slabs and a lone black cat. On the back of the postcard she draws a picture of the Spaniard named Clemente, a man to whom she is apparently now married. *Muy bien!* she writes.

In Grayshead-on-Heath the rain has poured for weeks, I write back to her, the newspapers scrunched in our boots soggy, our toes blackened with headlines we have already read—but everything is fine, fine. The girls remaining, Brigid and me and Harriet, God Harriet, and Josephine and Abigail returned to life as we knew it, the war won and so too the vote if you're old enough. Soon they'll put Mum on a postage stamp, tah dah!

C'est la vie, says Miss Hammond, who once taught us French, meaning no vote yet for the likes of you or me, so why did we bother?

Brigid says the Bible makes things clear, but then she doesn't remember what things clear and she sold her Bible some time ago to pay for coal. We were near enough freezing then, after they drafted Father Fairfield, I write to Alexandra, after Father Fairfield died.

The local soldiers gather around, sitting on their haunches beneath our windows, lapping up whatever we lay out for them from the kitchen. Some are lame and some have gone off in the head. Some are just fine and pretending, says Brigid. Now we are running a charity organization *of sorts*, Madame Lane says, and we'll do what we must. She doesn't want the word out that we take them in for a while. We comb the village in the morning to see what we can find, buns thrown in the trash and moldy cheese. Some of the store owners remember us and offer what they have. We are just polishing rotten apples, says Madame Lane. God's work, but Abigail sells bouquets of peonies and iris and earns enough to court the butcher, and Josephine has been let out to a pub and brings home green potatoes on the fortnight.

We have nothing else to offer them.

The soldiers want to tell us stories but Brigid and I are not interested the way we used to be. It's too gruesome—gas boiling your skin and the smell of gangrene and the rain rain rain. They thought they'd never be dry nor warm again. We tuck them in. They stay a night or two at Madame Lane's, their Red Cross bundles beneath their arms. They stay for a meal and to tell their stories. They have heard that there's kindness here, they tell us, and pretty girls who will listen. They have heard that there are good empty rooms for sitting and that no one will turn them out. There are six rooms off the upstairs hallway and three cots in the attic and once in a while we make a bed in the kitchen, the men arguing for it given the heat from the stove. We do our best, we tell them. We're here to serve, but we are no Nightingales, just ordinary girls sent to Madame Lane's and stayed on. Still, they want to talk. There's the one who found his best friend's head in his lap and the one with no mouth, just a hole in his cheek, and the one with the line of thread that saved him, the miracle of it, nothing more than a line of green thread still wrapped around his thumb so tight it's cut the blood off, the thumb white as blue. If he unwraps the thread he will die, he's convinced. This thread has somehow saved his life, like a rabbit's foot in the pocket, or a mother praying back home.

A few wander in from the woods filthy. We wash them up and they tell us how they'd been walking, escaped from the Northern Command Hospital or from Auntie's house or from the wife, even. They said they were fine until the uniform rose up and saluted bedside or the cat talked in its sleep or a potato masher hit in the garden—sent from Jupiter, God willing, destroyed what little was left of the beets. Some of them are handsome when you scrub them off. One in particular had one blue eye and one brown. Jeremy, he said his name was, though you could never tell quite who told the truth and who did not. Jeremy said his mother had hexed him as a child and then he said no, he said his mother had the clap and so one eye went blind at birth. He said his mother was a whore, so. He said his father had given it to her. He said his little sister didn't make it quite. He twisted on the cot sheets we made up for him in the kitchen and asked we find some music and so we brought in the wireless and held his hand until he slept. In the morning he was gone, our wireless in the rucksack with him.

"Just a lying thief," Madame Lane said, "come up from Trafalgar." But Brigid and I had believed him.

And our Harriet rubbed the feet of a beautiful one named Dermot. "This will bring up the blood," she said, and no doubt: the two of them, Brigid and Dermot, were gone as the wireless in the morning. Lie down with dogs and get fleas, Madame Lane says. I am wrenched between morals and morale, Madame Lane says.

We sing whatever songs they have taught us; the men like to sing when the soup is thin. Even the dirty ones they teach Brigid and me to make us blush as we peel the green potatoes over the kitchen sink, the tickle Marie one. It would lift any heart to hear the band of us singing, Madame Lane says, pretending not to notice the words.

An American named Johnny stops for directions, flagging me down from the girls' garden as I'm picking peas. It's a cool morning. He's come from Dover, he tells me, and is bound for York to stay with a friend, a war buddy, who had extended the invitation back when it seemed impossible they would ever get out of the trenches. I tell him the way and then ask if he met any Hutterites in France and he says, "Hutter-whats?" and I laugh every time I remember.

Brigid hears from her sick mum and packs her bags, her brothers and sisters too scattered—brains and otherwise—to be reliable. Abigail and I wave her off, Madame Lane watching from the window as the autocar skitters gravel and disappears up over the little sledding hill. Three years have passed since she wrapped my toe the day I arrived and she is what I know of friendship, the best friend I have ever had. As a bon voyage I give her the silver I inherited from Grandmother, the ladles with the famous filigree wrapped in the brown velvet sack just as delivered. I don't intend to marry, I tell her. I'm done with family.

The soldiers have got us thinking about how we feel.

"Heavier than it looks," Brigid says, hoisting the sack to her cot. "Must be worth a bloody fortune."

"Might pay for your mum's health," I say.

"God willing," she says.

She takes out a tarnished knife.

"It was hers?"

"Whose?"

"Your mother's?"

"Skips a generation," I say.

"Toothpaste will take the stain off," she says, polishing first with the hem of her skirt.

We hear the men enter the kitchen downstairs, the new ones and a few Madame Lane has permitted to stay longer, knowing that Brigid is as good as gone, and that I too am leaving soon, news of my scholarship last week in the mail no surprise to her, she said, given my mathematical talents and the way I can argue like a barrister.

"That's the wrong way, to tickle Marie," they men sing loudly, stomping into the kitchen, hoping for Brigid and me to be there over the potatoes, our backs turned, potatoes skins stuck to our aprons, our bare arms. "That's the wrong way to kiss. Don't you know that over here, lad. They like it best like this!"

If he were young he would be dead, or maimed, or wearing greens, and so he must be older, much older than he looks. "Stephen Pope," he says.

"Evelyn Townsend," I say.

He has offered a mint julep I do not decline. I am on the prow of a ship, gone or almost gone, and on my way across the bonny sea. Brigid said, Write and tell if it's a bonny sea. I always picture it a bonny sea.

"Cheers!" says Stephen Pope.

He wears an odd face, slanted a bit and a shave not quite clean.

"Cheers," I say. "To Inverness," I say, because it would make

Brigid smile, though I have no idea why—the fairies she believes
live there in the dells, or possibly the monster in Loch Ness for
which they have now resumed the hunt. Anyway, I can say whatever I like, the sea not bonny at all but furious, a green the color
of dragon scales, I would tell her. It lies just beyond, over the railing and down. We churn through, crossing the Atlantic on our way
to the port of New York—the ship once a workhorse for soldiers
now put out to pasture though the ghosts of the soldiers still ride.
I hear them moaning when I'm half-asleep and I have seen their
faces in the water below, though that might be the phosphorus.
Alive it is—I write to Brigid—a living plant of light. And the moan
might not be a moan; it might be a "Mum." The dead might be
saying "Mummy."

The boat's name is the SS *Woodrow Wilson*. Most call it *Woody*—
obscene, according to Stephen Pope, given what that man did for
England, for Europe. Have you any idea where we'd be if Wilson
hadn't strong-armed the pacifists? he is asking now. He sits next to
me, though I have not invited him, in one of the bolted wooden
chairs intended for viewing, the telescope mounted on the railing if
you were interested in taking a look. I set down my letter to Brigid
and stand as if I am interested in taking a look. The wind is strong,
wrapping my too-thin cloak (Madame Lane's traveling cloak, purchased in Belgium before the troubles, she tells me, and going to
waste in the armoire) around my knees. I clutch the hat to which I
give all credit for good luck, or rather, the gummy partridge feather
tacked to its band. I do not want to lose my good luck to this wind
and the unfathomable sea.

No, I say, turning back to Stephen Pope. I have no idea.

"Fifty of our politicians voted against him. Fifty in the House of
Representatives!"

"Fifty?" I say, because I cannot think what else.

"Fifty!" he shouts above the wind. I imagine he has heard this
again and again from the pacifists who are here on board, the group
returning from the Viennese convention where they have, surprise,

surprise, slung the philosopher Benjamin Kidd upon their shoulders and paraded him through the streets, the poor sod now propped up in their history museum—next to Mum and H. G. Wells, the empty halls ringing out with the solitary steps of the guards and the occasionally curious.

Now they shout Kidd's famous lines as if they were their own. "Women are the housekeepers of the world!" they shout. "Look at the world!"

"Only women can end the manmade system of war!" they say. "Sign here for a constitutional amendment!" they say. They scurry about, delivering their pamphlets and buttons. They plan to march from New York to Washington on our arrival, to march straight up to the lawn of the White House where, reputedly, the First Lady still cultivates tomatoes.

"Townsend?" one asks. She has seen my name on the boat registry, posted in the dining room so that cousin might better find cousin.

"No relation," I say. I have sworn I'll start from nothing; that I am now no one's daughter.

Stephen Pope is still waiting. I gaze back at him to show my interest. "Pacifists," he says, spitting the word. "Communists of the highest ranking. They'll root them out, mark my words."

"Marked," I say, and Stephen Pope smiles then, or rather, grimaces, excusing himself for the bar. I remember my letter to Brigid and return to my bolted wooden chair, my "chaise," as it's called by the stewards, the word perfect and new, along with some of the others I've heard in the more formal dining room and have tucked up my sleeve for later use—"velveteen," someone said, referring to upholstery.

The mint julep Stephen Pope delivered burns. I haven't had enough to eat, my passage the cheapest ticket I could find—no doubt there is some regulation that would bar me from this particular deck. I must reach Barnard College on my own and pay for food on this boat—a luxury, even now. What would I eat if allowed? Roast beef at the Savoy, Yorkshire pudding and gravy, roasted potatoes. I am wiping my chin when Stephen Pope returns.

"I've been boring you," he says, resettling. He stares out toward the sea and I can see, in profile, that he was once a handsome man though his face is now etched and aged, worried. He may be forty, or older. He fidgets with something at his neck, an itch. It appears difficult for him to remain still.

"No, I'm writing," I say, returning to the letter.

"Mother?"

"Excuse me?"

"Your mother?"

I have to think for a moment.

"A friend."

"Boyfriend?"

Stephen Pope is an American.

I shake my head. "He passed on," I lie, though maybe not, maybe in saying it I am telling Stephen Pope of Father Fairfield, or one of the sick ones permitted to spend the night in the kitchen, or Brigid's lad who flew the kite. He had eventually wandered off like the rest of them, the kite left behind, stuck high in a leafless tree, its dishrag tail dangling down, wrapped in one thin branch, caught. No one could reach it and Madame Lane said we did not dare to climb. "We've come this far not to break our necks," she said.

Besides, Madame Lane had already had enough. Who did they think she was? The Chancellor of Good Deeds and Dispensations? Still, the soldiers seemed to bloom like mushrooms in the woods after a hard rain; they appeared out of thin air from the fields. Sometimes they were bold enough to bang on the front door and hold out their shaky hats, their Red Cross provisions inadequate, they would explain, given the appetites of the newly returned. Brigid sewed checkered handkerchiefs from the long tablecloth and doled them out, wrapped in each a muffin or something stale left over from the kitchen. "For sustenance," she said, quoting Miss Peach of Domestic Duties, who had already moved back to London. We were the ones who remained, Brigid and I, walking in the fields of heather that were once saffron. Occasionally, riders passed us and waved, hunters or schoolgirls in fresh uniforms—Top Hill had opened its doors.

Stephen Pope offers a hand down the long, narrow gangplank. He says the fuss is for the pacifists, and that normally few would have turned out to greet the SS *Woodrow Wilson*. By fuss he means the journalists—men and women in long, dark coats and hats, several with cameras. The pacifists pose on the viewing deck behind a gigantic banner, their gloved hands gripping it against the wind. "Peace Is a Woman's Job," it reads.

The livery are queued and at the ready and Stephen Pope offers to pay for my ride. I accept. I have not starved and I have crossed the bonny sea and I am on my way directly to Barnard College, where I will inquire, among other things, about a flat or rooms to share. In truth, I know very little of how I will survive, my letter of acceptance, the scholarship requirements, folded into the pocket of Madame Lane's traveling cloak. I have been given a meager stipend, a refugee provision for girls whose circumstances have been irrevocably altered by war. Madame Lane has included her own letter of introduction, addressed to whom it may concern.

> *Thank you for providing for Miss Evelyn Townsend. You will*
> *find she is a responsible and hard working young woman with*
> *an extraordinary talent for mathematics and the physical*
> *sciences. I have a great fondness for Evie, and wish her the*
> *best. Please watch over her with care.*
> *Miss Muriel Lane*
> *Grayshead-on-Heath, August 2, 1919*

Now Stephen Pope scribbles his address on a small white card. I take it and step into the livery, sitting back against the broad, hard seat, resting, and as the driver pulls away from the crowds on the piers the notion that I have come so far alone settles like a black crow on my shoulder and squawks.

Will You Engage in Academic Pursuit? Will You Reach for More? Will You Rebuild the Foundation of Your Dreams?

I find the brochure on the little table next to the leather chair. The door I entered, etched glass, says Office of the Secretary. I hold up my letter of acceptance, the confirmation of my refugee scholarship, to the woman behind the etched glass, a second panel, in from the first. "I've come from England," I say, inanely.

She slides the glass panel back, the words, Office of the Secretary, blurred, doubled. She wears her hair in tight curls, the way everyone appears to here. I have walked through a circle of girls, a circle of tight curls, on my way to this building, the redbrick one just beyond the ornate iron gates. They looked like angels, the girls. They were dressed in white and rolling large hoops with sticks, practicing, someone said, for the games. Are you in the games? they asked me.

The receptionist's face is not angelic; it is long and humorless, her neck triple-roped in dime-store pearls.

"Jolly good," she says.

"I'm here to enroll," I say.

"Hold on," she says.

She slides the glass shut then disappears behind it—rolling this way and that on her chair. I lean against the little ledge. Food smells drift in from somewhere. This is New York City, I now understand: the crowded, dirty harbor and the smells, mostly, or maybe I'm just hungry—diesel oil, exhaust, exhaust and exhaustion, sweat. I hold on to the little ledge, my legs still rocking from the boat, my head in a swell. I hold on and wait for the woman to slide the glass back, to see me, again. She is taking some time, and I might need to sit.

"What's this all about?" Mum says from behind. I recognize her voice though it's been years—has she been here all along? Did she follow me in?

"I am rebuilding the foundation of my dreams," I say. It is good to see her. "My foundation crumbled, do you remember?"

"I was there," she says.

"Then you crumbled."

"I'm sorry for that," she says. "I felt I had no other—"

"Despite us," I say, though I don't mean to sound so angry.

"Choice," she says.

She looks at me intently, as she always would—pale, beautiful, raven-haired, they would have called her, had she been a heroine though she was not, I could have told her; neither then nor now—not to me, not to anyone. No one will remember you, I want to say to her. No one. But I don't have the heart. Her wrists are so thin—is she already starving? She wears her Sunday gloves, the gray kidskin ones with the buttons that require a hook. Now she yanks one off and holds out her tiny hand. Was she always so small? Was she always such a slip of a girl?

"Forgive me," she says, reaching.

I dropped like a stone, the long-faced receptionist says. She says, First she didn't hear anything, and then she heard me talking and then, she says, I dropped like a stone. You'll have a bruise.

She helps me to my feet—I have somehow slipped out of a shoe—and says she'll get me into the anteroom, find some tea. I thank her, though my head pounds. Would it be too much to ask for an egg?

I may have slept. I don't remember. It is some time later when Stephen Pope returns, though I later learned he had followed me there in a separate cab. "I had a feeling you'd need me," is what he said.

"I'll take over from here," he says to the receptionist.

"We'll require forms before the semester begins," the receptionist says, handing Stephen Pope the packet intended for me.

"Very well," he says. "Very well."

* * *

I am quiet on the way to Stephen Pope's house, a brownstone on Gramercy Park quite a far distance, he has told me, from 116th and Broadway. Stephen Pope suggests I lean against him as I step from the cab and I do. He is thin and very tall, though strong enough to lean on. Still, there is little comfort here. He is like the horsehair mattress at Madame Lane's we had to beat in spring, Brigid and I, first lugging the weight of it out of doors.

It is dark, and late, the lamps of the brownstones burning, illuminating the shadows of the small gardens in front of the houses, each guarded by a gargoyle or stone lion. Beyond rise taller brick buildings crisscrossed by iron stairways that are like exoskeletons, I think to say, holding the buildings up.

Fire escapes, Stephen Pope tells me. In case of fire.

Stephen Pope carries my bag to the steps and unlocks the front door, wooden and elaborately carved. He has returned early, he tells me. The servants do not expect him until tomorrow. He suggests that I might bathe and change, if I like, into any of the clothes I will find in the room that had been his wife's dressing room on the second floor, first door on the right, unlocked, he believes, though he hasn't ventured in since she died. She had liked red, he tells me. Do I like red?

I must have guessed him a widower, he says.

He steps aside to let me in. A foyer domes over the two of us, rising to what looks like a peaked glass ceiling though it is difficult to tell given the dark. On the knob of the banister an elaborate lantern of colored panes glows, the faint light the only warmth. It is spooky, the all of it, though I am trying not to think of that. I am trying to stand on my own two feet and hear Stephen Pope, trying to understand his quick rush of words—that his trip overseas had been to visit the grave of his only son, killed in France, and to scatter his wife's ashes; she had made a request.

He should apologize for the abruptness of his introduction on board, his barrage of questions. He had been attempting to assuage his loneliness.

Kate Walbert

Later, it is the words "assuage loneliness," I'm thinking as I grip the banister, curved and smooth and polished to a gleam, a Lincoln banister, Stephen Pope said, dismantled and carried in segments from a mansion in the southern states, then pieced together here at great expense. His wife had loved the banister and his boy as well; the boy had more than once defied their objections to slide down the curve of it to land on the flourish of its base, the carved tulip beneath the lamp, did I see? Could I see it? Carved by an Italian, apparently, who had come to this country seeking something better, as so many of them have, the Italians. They live south of here, a mile or so, among their churches, massive structures made from their own stone. They ship it in from Padua, do I know it? Michelangelo's stone. You have never seen such luster, he says.

He has much to tell me, Stephen Pope, though he apologizes for going on so long when I turn to say good night, and thank you, and no, I'm fine, too tired to eat.

At the top of the stairs, I push open the door to find a room dark as pitch though Stephen Pope has already shown me the electric lights and the telephone and the shorter cord that can be rung in the morning to summon the housemaid and the longer cord for the cook, who will prepare anything I need.

I find the switch and for an instant before I see where I am, I imagine I might find his wife here waiting for him, waiting for me, even, on the edge of the bed in dressing gown and slippers, her thin feet sore from walking, walking, walking. She didn't stop, Stephen Pope said. She wouldn't stop, he said. She walked among them, the Italians. She felt it was her duty, her *calling* to serve those people.

There are so many sick children, she would say, ten to a room dying or near dead. Children, little children, she said.

But she is no longer in this room. She's been swept over the mound of her son's grave, her ashes more like tiny stones, Stephen Pope said, and with a weight he hadn't expected. "It was her wish," he said, "and so I complied, though I remain unsure whether it is within standard protocol or even legal."

96

The electric light scours. It is a pillbox of a room, lorded over by her tall, dark wardrobe—its oiled walnut doors opposite a trompe l'oeil wall of a road within a forest, the pigment faded, flaked off in places, though the painting seems so real one might easily step into it. Tree branches arch in a tunnel and the leaves, or some of them, have turned, are falling. It must be autumn there.

I open the wardrobe doors and find her clothes laid out shelf by shelf, the colors separated by sheaths of tissue paper. The smell is faintly of lilac or lavender, and crushed petals have been scattered in the drawers. I will later write to Brigid of this and, best I can, New York, so different from London, so daily reborn, the other Barnard students like the city itself, changing their names, their hairstyles, hustling into rooms and then out again. They talk and talk and talk, their cigarettes in long, ebony pipes. They might have always lived here, or they might have come from Poland. They might room with their parents or with friends in Morningside Heights. They might study English literature or they might switch to anthropology, the work of Franz Boas fascinating—did I know him?—given his recent travels and the clear evidence of matriarchal hierarchies in the Amazon Basin. Somewhere, right now, a female chimp is fashioning a better tool from a rock! Evolution! they rave, though no, on principle they have taken a strong position against forced sterilization however with Margaret Sanger they are in complete alliance on all other matters: No Gods, No Masters.

Look at us! they shout. Look at us!

It is a thrill, everything constantly changing, and I am nobody here, I write to her. I am a blank slate. Of Stephen Pope, I write, he is my friend, the tragedies that befell him, boom boom, too horrendous to recount—he does not like to talk about it, nor do I. The future is the point, he says. God bless America.

I tell her how we have settled into a boarding arrangement, a dressing room and the adjacent bedroom exchanged for conversation. I am just past his son's age, he said. Besides, you can't find a better rent, he said, no matter the distance.

Kate Walbert

A dollar a week, I said. I want to be fair and square. This is one of my new American expressions. I try them out on him, and on the other girls in Professor Browski's chemistry lab—eat your heart out, I say, or beat it, or what's this doohickey? And they laugh just to hear my voice, the accent they have heard on the wireless and from stage actors but never in person, they say, me their first Brit.

And you? I write. What of you?

The letter from Brigid arrives many months later. Mum is now with Christ, she writes. I've taken over the house and settled in. Joseph is a good man, a good husband. Nothing fancy, this life. Music on Tuesdays, neeps and tatties.

Twins! she writes the following Christmas. "We've named the boy after his father, and the girl," she writes, "we call Evelyn."

DOROTHY TOWNSEND BARRETT

Patagonia, Argentina, 2004

And wasn't it Browning who said, "All's right with the world; God's in his heaven—" etcetera, etcetera?

Charles found himself asking this—rhetorically, ironically—of their little crew in Patagonia, his soon-to-be ex-wife, Dorothy, else-where, at one of the extracurricular lectures delivered by those among them who felt they had something to add. He has been to several and proposed his own, on Browning, waiting to see if the req-uisite number sign the sheet outside the ship's dining hall before preparing anything in earnest. So far there are three names: his, Dorothy's and Chester Briggs, a biology teacher from Seattle who made their acquaintance early in the trip. It's to Chester that he addresses his question now; the two have joined a few others in the dimly lighted bar of the German hotel, in off the rough seas for a few days respite, the bar's Alpine theme strange after the endless flat landscape they have earlier crossed in their little bus, the dry, brown steppes interrupted only by windblown trash and the occasional group of guanacos, ears perked, in the distance. They had been on their way to Punto Tombo, to a vast colony—near a million!—of penguins, the only bird, they were told, to lack a natural aversion to humans, the penguins' minds on other things: the building and rebuilding of nests, the incubation of their dirty eggs. The fathers, even. Think of it! The women in the group had laughed. The fathers!

They had spent most of the day tromping around the penguins, stooping low to see the eggs, hurrying to get out of the birds' paths as the birds made their beelines to the water. Dorothy had found one covered "head to flipper" in oil, its mate nosing it along though the poor thing drowned once in the ocean, its feathers too clotted, its wings useless, this more and more common, given the way the wind was blowing.

Charles has told the story of the drowning penguin as if he too were witness to it, then added the various details he has read about the shrinking of the Antarctic ice, the predictions, the timetable, before finishing with Browning.

"Browning was a Darwinian, right?" Chester says. And Charles nods, wondering why he has introduced the great poet into this company of high school teachers and retirees, Dorothy right, as usual: he is an old snob. And if she were to return at this moment to apprehend the band of them slackly hunched together as if poised to plunge forks into a great bowl of melted Swiss cheese she would guess—from their various postures and the enervating silence—that her soon-to-be ex-husband has been boring his companions, quoting Browning or worse.

She would rather listen to Sachiyo de Pauling lecture on the art of Japanese floral arranging, or ikebana. Sachiyo was the proprietor, Dorothy earlier told Charles, of a shop in the suburbs of Rochester, where she found herself a war bride in the late forties. *Desperate,* Dorothy whispered, her look accusatory, as if he were somehow responsible for Sachiyo's misery. They were half-dressed for dinner in their little Alpine room.

"Frankly, I feel sorry for Sachiyo, though it seems as if there's a great interest in her talk," Dorothy said, her back to Charles, his thumbs on her necklace clasp, an emerald on a chain he had given her years before. It seemed especially cruel, given the proximity of the necklace and his helping her, that she would take this particular jab.

"And her qualifications?" Charles said, though she had already told him. Dorothy wheeled around, the clasp just catching.

"She's owned the store for nearly twenty years. She grew up in Kyoto, for God's sake," she said. "I think that accounts for something."

"I'm sure it will be fascinating," Charles said.

"I've always wanted to know how they do it," she said.

"What?"

"Put something here, something there. Take three stems, make a masterpiece."

"Ask her about the bamboo month. They have a month where everything they eat is made from bamboo. Even the hot dogs."

Dorothy narrowed her eyes.

"She's a lovely woman," she said.

"I know she is," Charles said.

"She's just lost her husband," she said.

"I understand," he said.

"How do I look?" she said.

Earlier, at the penguins, Dorothy wore boots up to her knees and a sun hat that shaded her face. Charles had taken her picture with the digital camera Caroline had sent to them announcing this trip; Caroline had booked the whole thing, of course, paid in full, meals and lectures included. She firmly believed, she said to her father—this in secret, out of Dorothy's earshot—that recent events suggested her mother needed a rest, Events which shall now go unnamed, relegated to that jar of History appropriately labeled Unmentionable, Not-to-Be-Discussed, At a Later Date, Plug It (and within the jar Charles pictures a young James in shorts, dirtied knees, sulking in the corner, his cheeks flushed and tear-stained, his fingers wrapped in twine: he's tying a cat's cradle or maybe the other one he could never get right; and now Charles sees his marriage there as well—what had Virgil said? There are tears in things. Fine, then, his marriage at the bottom of a glass jar: a lost penny, or a golf tee). These not-to-be-discussed Events have become more frequent now, Dorothy a fire sign, she will tell you, as if this explains it. It does not. In short, he no longer understands her. None of them understands her. She used to be happy with a steak and scalloped potatoes, a round of bridge. Now she seems like a different Dorothy, as if, during one of her secret excursions, she shed a skin.

"Beautiful," he says, realizing Dorothy is still waiting.

Charles found his bar friends out of desperation. Come for a drink and there they were, a few of the other men from the tour now bosom buddies. Chester Briggs had waved him over.

"Dorothy?" he said.

"Sachiyo's lecture," Charles said, taking the stool beside him. If Charles had bothered to ask, he would have found that Chester, too, felt a fondness for Sachiyo, this newly widowed tiny woman, a gray streak in her black hair, a habit of offering Kleenex. But he did not ask. He ordered a drink, disheartened by the image of the women over their individual containers, listening as Sachiyo explained the various symbols that the arrangement of the stems in their hands have historically represented: love, filial duty, friendship. Friendship? Hah! More like a coven, an exclusive club. They were all there together, Bibs Pierce, Ginny Donaghue, Gayle Schwartz, Madeline What's-Her-Name.

"I understand," Chester said, his voice coming out of the dark, "that Dorothy has settled on Florence Nightingale."

Charles had no idea what Chester referred to, though shook his head as if he, too, were baffled.

"She told me the great nurse is much maligned," said Chester, whose eyebrows curled in dramatic ways; at this moment they resembled the sea at its worst pitch.

"By whom?" Teddy Flamm wanted to know. Charles hadn't noticed Teddy before; he sat on one of the darker barstools, inexplicably distant.

Chester shrugged. "Schoolchildren," he said. "History books."

Charles ordered another drink. To find himself served in a true bar, albeit Alpine inspired, felt delightful. Theirs was not a grand ship nor even a passenger liner, but one of the smaller boats that could cut through the ice that might, if they lacked the equipment, maroon them. The bar on board consisted of the bottles they had purchased in Duty Free and carried to dinner.

"The one I always loved," Teddy said, joining their small circle, "was Mary Todd Lincoln. Didn't she walk the halls wringing her hands?"

"Ghosts, I think," Chester said. "She saw ghosts. Of course, her husband was a homosexual."

"Was he?" Teddy said, finishing his drink. "Well, I'm seeing ghosts. Last night my father sat on the side of my bed."

They paused, waiting, but Teddy didn't go on.

"So, when did Dorothy take on Florence?" Chester said, bringing it around again. Upstairs, in one of the junior suites, Sachiyo de Pauling demonstrated how with a simple piece of copper wire and patience, one could train bamboo to spiral upward, she said, like a dancer spinning to the heavens. The metaphor felt a bit hackneyed, or maybe, first generation, Dorothy will say to Charles later, but compelling nonetheless; this when he confronts her over Nightingale.

But for now Charles chooses to go along. "When did I take on Browning?" he said.

Charles must maneuver the narrow hallway to the door of their rickety, temporary room; within are the twin beds, a chest of drawers, and a mirror that reminds him that his teeth need cleaning. He removes them to drop into the fizzy water, watching as they bubble to an artificial white. James used to love to participate in this, flicking the wafer into the water, fishing out the whitened teeth though the boy could never understand why his own teeth wouldn't snap out like his father's. When he lost his first tooth Charles let him drop it in, the little pearl, where it sank to the bottom of the glass impossibly beautiful.

Charles startles and looks up. Dorothy looms behind him.

"So," he says, ineffectually frowning, tipsy. "Florence Nightingale?"

"Oh, you heard," she says. "I thought I'd give it a shot."

He will soon discover her sign-up sheet, boldly tacked next to his own in what passed on board as the lounge: bad coffee, donuts replenished in a box, some worn paperbacks. She has even stolen two tacks so that the corners of his flop while hers, which reads, pretentiously, he'd add, "Dorothy Barrett, A Discussion of the Works and Principles of Florence Nightingale," is neatly pressed to the cork. Though it has been posted after his, there are many names scrawled on the lines for interested persons—the women, of course, and Chester.

"I've been doing some reading," Dorothy says. "I didn't tell you?"

"No," he says, though without his teeth it is difficult to look doubtful.

"I'm sure I told you," Dorothy says.

Charles shrugs and sits on one of the twin beds to untie his shoelaces. He wears boots entirely out of keeping, sent FedEx by Caroline, who no doubt pictured her parents scrambling up rocky outcrops and crossing blue glaciers—not sitting on bolted chairs listening to lectures on penguins.

"Vivian gave me the idea," Dorothy says. Vivian Vivian, thinks Charles, because the names of all the women on board have run together into a swirl of muddy brown; Vivian now rises out of this swirl—a librarian or administrator of some kind from the Midwest—one of those smart women with an underappreciated profession who wears strange, square glasses and asks a lot of questions.

"Vivian?" he says. Dorothy has crawled into the opposite twin, covered herself head to foot in one of the wooly red blankets. She reaches over to flick off the light. The designers of these geriatric adventures have clearly ruled out making love as an activity—given this much exercise and twin beds and their age, of course. (He will be seventy-nine next month, and she, remarkably, is soon to be seventy-five.) Then again Dorothy is no longer his wife or intends not to be when they return to the Northern Hemisphere. They are roommates, perhaps. Bunk buddies. And it's been so many years, besides. The last time near his retirement, when Dorothy hula-hooped her toast a bit blotto, perhaps impressed by the number of speeches celebrating his success. Silly, crude things, but he believed they might have prompted her, just for that moment, to remember what had convinced her to say yes in the first place.

Yes, she had said, or rather, wrote. Yes, she wrote.

Simply that for a lifetime. It has been, for both of them, a lifetime. My God, he thinks. "My God," he says.

Dorothy stops talking and shifts—she had been talking! Damn ears. Now he hears the cold rustle of starched sheets as clear as a bell.

"Good night," she says.

"I was listening," he says.

"You're more than welcome to skip it."

"What?"

"My talk."

"I was listening," he says. Though it is pitch black, he sees her face, too angry to sleep, eyes wide open. She is lying there livid, regretting everything, regretting her life, regretting him; or maybe she's remembering James. He has no idea and besides he would rather not think about his son. He does not think about him, in fact, will not think about him. In his mind, James has gone with his Boy Scouts on a trip. They've ascended the mountain already and are looking down. James points out the general area where he lives—the development with its many neat houses in a row on the streets that wind and dip through what was once farmland, the trees grown large and towering (he can remember when they were planted!) since his family moved in when he was a boy, the ridiculous sign at the entrance, Thornbrook, and the garden of foxglove and black-eyed Susans, tulips and daffodils that his mother took the time to plant around its base. To lend the neighborhood some character, she had said, to spruce things up. James can see it all from there, or imagine it well enough to describe to his friends. He is surrounded by friends. He is on a mountaintop. He is standing beneath a brilliant blue sky. He is reaching for his canteen—

"She never married," Dorothy says in the dark. It is the steady Dorothy voice, the cool Dorothy voice: considered and one might even say dramatic. "She was tempted once. Apparently she fell in love. But she weighed the options. She wrote, 'I have an active nature that requires satisfaction, and that would not find it in his life.'"

It is the demon intellect that seizes him. "Vivian?" he says.

She sighs.

"Not your Browning," she says. "But a good line nonetheless."

Charles found it strange to see chaplains in the war: men who daily spoke to the pilots and gunners and flight engineers stationed on Tinian of the spirit of the bayonet, the bomb. The clergy had constructed makeshift churches: pews of horizontal cots. There the men prayed or slept, depending, and the chaplains preached. One they called Father Simple. "It's simple, boys," he would say whenever they'd approach him with what they believed were complicated moral questions. "Jesus wants you to kill Nips."

A boy named Frank Peterson, tail gunner when they dropped incendiaries on Okinawa, confessed that from his seat in the back he could see the way the fire ran like so many rivers of popping light. He said how it jumped in a school and the children flew out the windows, a flock of startled wrens.

Of course Peterson hadn't seen a thing. How could he from his place in the skies?

Father Simple started. "It's simple," he said, and Peterson interrupted him, a priest. He told him to go to hell. "Excuse me, Father," Frank Peterson said. "But you can go straight to hell."

By the time they passed Okinawa, no one cared about the complicated moral questions. There were no complicated moral questions. For months the orders were to bomb the islands, the airfields, the gun emplacements, igniting the targets and whatever else that got in the way, the thatched roof huts that served as homes to the poor souls unfortunate enough to have been left behind. There were caves, of course, there were always caves, but most of the Japanese were too sick to reach them and besides, they didn't have time. These were the days of orders. Command. Charles was still a young boy; his teeth unbroken; hearing, he would be the first to say, perfect. Hadn't he received the Army Air Corps appointment? Didn't his own representative write the recommendation? He could still remember the insignia on the letter, the raised gold seal of the State of Maryland, and how his mother had shined the thing before leaving it about wherever people might be passing. *We can think of no finer example of scholarship*, the representative had written. *We can imagine no young man better qualified than Charles Archibald Barrett to represent the principles and values of the men of the United States Army Air Corps*.

Mostly typhoons he remembered. The weather became their second enemy, everything conspiring against them. Or so said Father Simple. He preached nightly, wore a chaplain's white collar, the only one among them out of uniform. He came from the South and was the age of their older brothers. He had studied at Duke, then at the famous seminary in New York City. He spoke with an educated drawl, and often clapped his hands when he felt his audience drifting.

"Fog, currents. Mud, even," he said. "Certainly heat."

He clapped his hands; the few of them sat up straighter.

"If I could wear the greens—"

"You'd be dead by now," Tommy L. interrupted. He was a colored boy from Philadelphia who washed their potatoes and never missed Father Simple's lectures.

"And glorious in the Kingdom of God," Father Simple said.

So one must always consider the War, for obvious reasons, writes Charles, *and of course*, he writes, *what I'll call the Vagaries of Life*.

He scratches out *Life,* with a capital *L,* too highbrow, vaguely nineteenth century. Ditto *Vagaries.* Besides, he can already picture the other passengers on the boat smirking. We live in a cynical age, he knows. They'll have vague half-listening smiles. They'll hold off jiggling the change in their pockets and assume the posture of good listening, like with Terry Pinto's lecture on mollusks, Pinto an amateur biologist and a friendly enough man, but tedious to the extreme, a bore the likes of which Charles hopes he is not. Pedantic, yes; bore, no. He has asked this of Dorothy plenty of times in their later years, on certain moonless nights on the back patio, buffered by the now-towering walnut trees of Thornbrook and the sounds—distracting!— of crickets, cicadas, bullfrogs back in the swampy, wooded dead-end; they are well into their bourbons and conversation seems to take a turn to the one-sided and he wonders whether Dorothy is awake, much less listening. "Am I boring you?" he says.

And seated across from him, from the vague outline of a darker Dorothy, he'll hear her quiet, "Just thinking."

They've raised three children, which is the first thing: the girls, Caroline and Liz, and the absent one, James.

Is this then how he gets back to Browning? Via war? Time passing? A son's death?

He writes in the low glow of the Alpine lodge light, drunk and in some despair. If he were to look to his left, he would see Dorothy, her body curled in sleep. She has aged, his Dorothy. Her skin folds at the neck. Still, she doesn't give a rat's ass, she has announced. She will do as she pleases. She will trespass on government property. She will willingly break the law, bite a hand with full knowledge of the risks. At her trial on charges of trespassing and assault last year, the lawyer Caroline hired had begged Dorothy to keep her mouth shut, to save the words she had so carefully composed to be read before the judge for the *Rising Sun Times* editorial page, counsel Dorothy had refused, only to be silenced by the judge herself, who said she had thirteen cases on the docket and besides, the revolution was no longer being televised. Nobody would hear her.

Now Florence Nightingale of all things. When did that woman enter their lives?

Forget Browning, Charles thinks. Here is my story. I could write it as is: a soldier, an airman, is shot down over the Pacific. This is late in the game. This is nearly the end of it, spring of '45, early summer. The soldier is twenty, give or take. Call him Charles. There are days of floating in the salty water, lit in the nighttime by phosphorus so that the sea could have been the sky, the phosphorus stars, or so Charles thinks. He is, for all intents and purposes, dead, his crew at the bottom are fish food, though he, for some reason, is weightless. He floats along. Was he always lighter than all of them? Is he destined for greatness? He cannot help but be delusional; he floats, does he not? In the Kingdom of God. Beneath him shark shadows, or the shadows of larger fish cast from the light of the stars, of the phosphorus, slither by—he cannot get the phosphorus out of his eyes; he cannot sleep. He drifts as would a stick or a corked bottle until he is retrieved. Fishermen smart enough to know where to take him.

He would not call this place a camp, or a prison, or even a village. It is more a collection of cement barracks, man-made caves on a forgotten island. Within the concrete walls are empty bamboo cages—they've been expecting him, expecting others—and though he does not fit in the cage he is put in the cage for good luck. This is what his captors tell him: good luck, they say, folding him in.

They call him Good Luck. They think someone will come looking soon. He's their bait, their raw chicken neck, but no one is looking for him. They think him dead. Besides, the war is nearly over.

Rats live on the island and little else. The fishermen give him fish tails when he is close to death, drip water through a bamboo pole. He tries to bite his way out, but his teeth rot and the bamboo's too strong. His legs are bent in awkward positions. He licks his bamboo bars. "Good luck," says the fisherman who found him, the fisherman whose wrists are ringed in tattoos. The fisherman tosses Charles something gelatinous; there is blood on his fingers.

If the rats were to get into his cage they would devour him, Charles believes; he makes a strange sound they seem to despise. They circle and stare, their eyes phosphorous. He has come to the Kingdom of God, ascended to the Kingdom of God.

When the rain came, the thick leaves of trees elsewhere caught the rain and the tattooed fisherman appeared again at the entry of his concrete cave and opened the bamboo cage to unfold his arms to unfold his legs to pour the water on the sores he blows the ants from: all the insects want in.

If he were to say what he was thinking, if he were to know what he was thinking, he would say what Father Simple said, quoting the last book of the Bible, how in His mouth He had a sharp, two-edged sword. His sword was not in His hand, it was in His mouth. He too kept his sword in his mouth; he swallowed its blade, choked on its handle. But what did Father Simple know of this? What did any of them? You will fight the good fight, Father Simple said. Amen.

"Dorothy was a young woman of nineteen, working as secretary to some banking executives in San Francisco, her hometown, and living with two girlfriends in a cold-water flat near Chinatown. Anyway, this particular afternoon she was crossing the street on her lunch hour and found herself dodging the path of a runaway cable car. She collided with a lamppost, nearly suffering a concussion. I was just returned from the Pacific, Atsugi Air Base, where I had spent more time than I care to remember in rehabilitation and then pushing paper in a desk job for the Allied Occupation. I still weighed just shy of a hundred pounds. I later worked with the Japanese in polymers—"

"Plastics," Teddy Flamm interrupts.

"Shrewd, but decent enough in the end, the Japanese."

Someone has asked how he and Dorothy met and Charles is

happy to explain. They've been in the Alpine bar some time and Chester Briggs appears asleep, or at least half-dozing. Charles hears a distant clink of glasses and smells the sweet smell of cherry tobacco: Lionel Hughes, who steers the ship or stocks it. He protects them somehow.

"Dorothy," he continues, "weighed little more than I did—"

"Go on, Charlie," says Teddy Flamm, who has earlier confessed that as an overweight adolescent they called him Flab-Flamm.

"She held a small handbag, I remember. She was knocked out. There was a boy passing by on a bicycle who stopped."

Charles pauses to let them picture it, though he can sense inattention in the silence.

"I leaned over. I had just that morning had a shave.

"She opened her eyes. 'Who are you?' she said."

Charles excuses himself now because he knows he must. He is suddenly drunk and, in the words of their youngest, Liz, macho-nostalghoulic. Stop spilling the beans, she would have said to him; shut up, already.

But Chester Briggs, newly waked, implores him to go on.

"A crowd gathered. I worked up some nerve and explained to the police that as her just-returned cousin I had every right to tag along, which I did, sitting next to her in the ambulance. When they carried her into the hospital, she requested that her cousin not leave her side—"

"Then happily ever after," Chester Briggs says.

Charles swigs his drink.

"Essentially," Charles says.

"'Course Jeannie and I were set up by my cousin Bud. Took one look at her and wanted to ditch her but Bud said 'personality counts' in my ear and by God, we had a wonderful ride."

Chester lost Jeannie at the beginning of the year. Many of them on this trip lost someone at the beginning of the year, or the end of the last year, or sometime, long ago, in the middle. They are a ship in mourning and yet it's good to feel the cold air on their faces, it's good to be alive. This trip, Charles knows, is Chester's effort to move on. "And she was so brave through the whole goddamn thing," Chester is saying now, Charles finding himself patting Chester's hand a bit awkwardly. He's never been particularly good with friendship, but he feels a kind of kinship with Chester, who seemed interested in his story, and seeing that all the others have stolen away, he offers to walk his friend to his single room. The two stand shakily, pickled in booze. *"Auf Wiedersehen,"* they say, to no one in particular.

Cousin Charlie, she called him, in moments, certain moments, of intimacy, though these were fewer than he would have liked, given all their years together. He had learned to be patient. He had learned to come in from the garden with dirt on his hands, to not be quite so meticulous—she liked that. Once, they had studied dancing. Dorothy had come home from the club with the pamphlet. Wednesday nights, it read. Black tie. Wouldn't it be fun? she had asked, knowing, he knew, that he would not think it fun but pretending to believe him when he answered, "Yes." And it had been, he'd admit. They'd concentrated on the classics—foxtrot and Lindy, a Viennese waltz for which they won a prize. Even Caroline had sensed her mother's excitement about the lessons and urged her on, knowing her mother hadn't had much fun as a teenager—the remnants of the Depression, of course, and a father who had given her a rough time, a man who eventually succumbed to drink.

He succumbed, Dorothy would always say of him, as if drink were a particularly hard rain that could wedge loose what hadn't been firmly battened down.

She never liked to talk about her father to the children, or to him. Her father had been a sad man, she told Charles those first days, but he played the piano beautifully and was quite well known in San Francisco. His name was Thomas Francis Townsend, and he had been born in England to a woman who had passed away when he was just a boy, and sent here, to San Francisco, to be raised by the old people she visited, from time to time, in Sherwood Oaks. He had lost his job with the symphony before the war, but he played for years on weekends in the Ivy Room at the Fairmont Hotel and during the week gave lessons at the upright in their living room. He had just died last year, she said. In the veteran's hospital, she said, which was funny because he managed to miss all the wars. It's charity run, of sorts, she said. He was picked up off the street.

Her parents had separated when she was quite small, her mother remarrying and moving to the South.

Here Dorothy shrugged. "I've made my own way," she said.

"Into the path of cable cars," he said.

"Right," she said. "And you?"

"Me?" he said. "I don't know. A farm in Maryland. Cows. Tremendous heat in summer. We were poor, I guess, but everyone was poor. And then there was nothing but the war."

"Right," she said.

Where were they? He can no longer remember. They had extended their hours together to days, and then weeks, spending most of their time on park benches, or sipping tea at the restaurants near the Marina—perhaps they sat in the one where he would later propose, Dorothy, her hands in her lap, dwarfed by an enormous Dungeness crab on her plate and a red-and-white napkin tucked into her collar. A few months later they married—it happened that way then—their representative of the State of California standing before them with the Bible in his hand. He recited his lines, they recited theirs. Dorothy wore a sea green chiffon dress. Frothy, she said. Suitably turbulent.

Around her neck were the lavender pearls he had purchased as an enticement. She stood erect, her head slightly cocked. Her hands were sheathed in pigskin gloves, dyed gray, and had she turned to look at him it would have been through the web of stiff lace she had tacked to the brim of her favorite hat the evening before, her hands weaving quick stitches, her small, white teeth biting the thread.

There, she had said, displaying the hat for Charles's approval. He had been vague in his praise, buffed in silence (damned plane!) and distracted by his own project of copying Browning's lines onto sheaf after sheaf of parchment paper. He would announce his marriage to his father and brothers back home in this way—he never expected them to attend—with some lines of the poem he had chosen to read at the ceremony, no ceremony, really, just he and Dorothy and the witnesses provided by the civil office; a secretary and a clerk. He had loudly recited those lines, had memorized them, even, though he knew that they would consider this show-offy. His voice trembled, the sound amplified by the empty courtroom. The representative of the State of California appeared irked by the display, but the witnesses found it quaint, they later said as they signed the necessary papers and pocketed their honorariums. Dorothy, for her part, remained quiet.

In the blue hour of their wedding night, Charles suggested that they keep their clothes off and not hurry to dress, him still amazed by the birdlike weight of Dorothy. She was a corporeal ghost, he thought. She might have been air, silent through the all of it, though she had seemed pleased enough. She stroked his hair. She let him lift her, slightly, and prop the pillows. It seemed a reasonable enough request to linger for a while, to keep still, but she asked him then if she might please go, if she might sleep on the sofa in the other room of their suite, if he wouldn't mind terribly.

Charles took the robe he had purchased specifically for this moment; billiard balls against a green background, silk, and put it on. He had thought it rather stylish, or perhaps had been convinced by the salesman at the department store, the same salesman who chose his wedding suit and the tie to match. Perhaps the salesman was simply brilliant at his job, or perhaps he did indeed have Charles's best interest at heart. For whatever reason, Charles took the man at his word, buying the silk robe he said would be a "welcome relief," on this the most important evening of their lives, no doubt having guessed Charles a virgin. Perhaps he had seen it in the way Charles knotted his tie, or the way he spoke to this stranger, too excitedly, of Dorothy's beauty, telling him the way he had proposed the week before, hiding the ring beneath her tea cup rather cleverly, since he knew that she would order tea, that the waiter would bring her an entire pot as was the custom, that this would occur at the end of their meal when conversation generally abated, when they looked to the other diners. He had pictured it exactly the way it occurred, Charles had told this man.

The two sat in the comfortable chairs in front of the three-way mirrors of the men's department. The salesman listened with great interest.

"Just as I had pictured it," Charles said, shifting. He still wore his wedding suit, the one he had decided to purchase for the ceremony, and he couldn't help but steal a glance at himself in one of the mirror panels. "She turned over her teacup and there it sat."

"The ring?" the salesman said.

"The box," Charles said, "though she immediately knew."

"They always do," he said.

"She didn't open it at first. She took her time. She said, 'What's this, Charles?' but she knew."

The salesman nodded; he leaned over to pull a thread off the suit's lapel and then sat back in his own chair, waiting for Charles to continue.

"'Open it,' I said. 'I think you might be surprised.' The ring belonged to my mother. She passed on years—"

"I'm sorry," the salesman said.

Charles waved it away. "She left it to me. She had every faith I was still alive."

The salesman nodded.

"Anyway, Dorothy caught her breath. Literally. I told her we could have it adjusted for her ring finger. She said, never mind."

"She loved it just the way it was," the salesman said.

"Not exactly," Charles told him. "She said she needed time to think."

"Oh," he said.

"It seemed logical," Charles said.

"Absolutely," he said.

"She slipped a piece of paper underneath my hotel room door the next morning. I heard the swoosh. 'Yes,' it read. Just that one word. 'Yes.'"

"The girl knows what she wants," the salesman said, standing.

Charles stood as well, as if Dorothy had just then entered the men's department.

"I might suggest a deeper blue," the salesman said, referring to Charles's tie, and then excused himself to find the robe.

And here Charles now stood in the thing, his legs too thin, his arms too thin, his chest crisscrossed with scars. He understood immediately that she had sized him up, that her decision to sleep on the sofa had to do with a more general change of heart about the two of them. "Not at all," Dorothy said, though she offered no other explanation. She pulled the blanket off the queen-sized bed and dragged it into the sitting room, closing the door behind her. He removed his ridiculous robe, attempting to hang it on one of the hotel's wooden hangers though it repeatedly slipped to the closet floor. He intentionally left it behind when they packed their suitcases to go home a week later. Dorothy had kept her place on the sofa and Charles his in the queen-sized bed; he had, of course, attempted to convince her to trade places. It seemed the right thing to do. She refused, insisting that she would rather pay the consequences for her choice, that she felt sure she would eventually come around, that she did, indeed, love him. She needed time, she said.

On that first night, and on the others of their honeymoon, he couldn't sleep. He would, in the late hours, open the door between the two rooms to check on her. She looked remarkably similar to how she had looked the afternoon when he found her, eyes closed, head turned as if listening for a distant train. Permanent curls. Pale skin. Blue-veined lids he half-expected might fly open. He knew, if so, that he would once again startle at their largeness, at their remarkable green; that she would once again say, Who are you?

Due to the overwhelming volume of interest, Dorothy's lecture on Florence Nightingale is to be given in the more accommodating Trumbull Room, named for Louise Walcott Trumbull, the first woman to have done something so remarkable it's been completely forgotten. Apparently Louise-types flocked in great numbers to Patagonia at the turn of the last century, dressed in native attire, banging on drums—their husbands and children left behind in England. They were after Darwin or before Darwin. They lived a hundred years and grew scales.

Then came the other ones, the ones who arrived with their blue-patterned china and their silk dresses to build a community of small whitewashed houses in which they lived with their Bibles and pianos and servant girls, attempting to farm the impossible soil. The land stretched out for miles. These women in their good dresses could stand and look and see nothing and maybe this is what they were after, who knows? There are countless stories; Dorothy's coven loving nothing more than to recount the salient, feminine details—repression, depression, transformation, etcetera. The coven will be there for Dorothy's talk, several of them preparing hors d'oeuvres to serve afterward at the reception, a word she pronounces as if she's to appear before the queen. She roars here and there, back to the can-do Dorothy Charles remembers from her time with the children though years later she told him through much of it she'd been miserable inside. And not, she said. And not not not—did I say, miserable inside?

Yes, he had said. You said, miserable.

No, no, she had said. No, no, no.

This had been one of their late-night, back-patio talks, James at college, Caroline a teenager and out, Liz behind her bedroom door with her nose in a book. The two of them sat in wrought-iron chairs, face-to-face, across their wrought-iron table, its surface glass wet with condensation from their drinks. Around them the landscape had become dense, and wild; the towering, thick-trunk walnut trees too costly to take down, though Dorothy daily complained they were a dirty nuisance, blocking the sun from her rhododendron and azaleas. Perhaps this was the first sign: her impatience for gardening, her fury. The tulips and daffodils she had once so carefully planted by the sign at Thornbrook's entrance had doubled and tripled, weakening with each successive generation, and that spring Dorothy had taken her spade and unearthed the marred brown bulbs, tossing the lot into the trash.

These evening soliloquies had become part of the ever-constant Dorothy question, as Charles had begun to think of it, to himself, only, since to her he believed he showed nothing but compassion, or rather, empathy. "It is never too late to become what you might have been," he said, quoting George Eliot in a vague hope to articulate his understanding of the problem. (She had once called his empathy his strength. She supposed this came from his time as a POW on that island, she said, and his ability to befriend his fishermen captors, who saved him, eventually, by pushing him back out to sea.) A problem without a name, she stressed now, a solely female condition. "It's in our character," she said. "It's who we are, it's, God, it's our type, our lot, our cross to—" but she could tell by his silence that he was no longer interested—

"Of course I'm interested," he said.

"What shall I do?" she wailed—the "shall" alerting him to the fact that she had become, over the course of a few drinks and in the presence of night, the on-the-stage Dorothy, the one who saw herself in epic terms. She'd gone on, describing herself as a frightened child, describing herself as a metaphorical clubfoot ("my father's daughter," she says, as clink clink go the ice cubes, slosh slosh the gin), unable to keep up with the modern, liberated woman (she had earlier been to some sort of rap session, the details of which she swore would go to her grave), the Renaissance that was happening here, in this very town, in the houses that lined the streets of Thornbrook where so many of their neighbors, the wives, were dropping out, divorcing and fleeing to California. God, California. I was *born* in California, she said. I met *you* in California.

And still and still, she had promised she would stay with him, promised that she loved him—uncharacteristically wobbling over to sit in his lap, to stroke his hair, to nestle there within him in the dark.

"I am a hollow bone," she said.

"You are not a hollow bone," he said. "You are wonderful. You are my wife and the mother to our children. You are Dorothy."

"I am," she said. "That's right."

"And I love you," he added, because he did. He had always loved Dorothy.

A walnut thunked dangerously close to the patio chair.

"What shall I do?" Dorothy said. "I need something to do."

"You could kiss me," he had said.

"I will kiss you," she answered. And she did. And that had been a good evening, and there had been more since then, many more over the last twenty-five years. And they had survived it all for what? For this? For Dorothy pacing before him like something caged? Everything appears to take too much of her time. Where has the patience gone? Where has the mother gone? The blowing on skinned knees?

That he has suggested a critique of a run-through seems insane in retrospect, though, as Dorothy had said, now that they are soon-to-be-no-longer married they can be *honest*. They can be *brutal*. And he had seen the coven in these words; Florence Nightingale hovering ghostlike and shrill in her bloody, Crimean garb.

Now Dorothy stops and stands before him at the makeshift podium, a music stand, here in the Louise Walcott Trumbull Room, intended for more formal dining and, in an earlier time, dancing on board. The ship's ability to cut ice is a recent addition, and they are given to understand that in its former life the vessel was used to transport members of high society from Buenos Aires to the beaches of Uruguay. She wears her one suit, having opted last minute—and thank God! she says—to pack something besides her dungarees and boots.

"Don't lean," Charles says.

"I haven't yet begun," she says.

"I'm just reminding you," he says.

"Done," she says.

Charles takes a chair and crosses then uncrosses his legs. He's finding it difficult to position himself: he has a notepad and a pen and butterflies in his stomach.

Dorothy clears her throat; she wears half-glasses and her hair, he only now notices, has responded to the climate by curling in great, rolling waves. Or maybe it's that he's never witnessed Dorothy from this perspective: he the audience, she the lecturer. She looks entirely different, more formidable, for obvious reasons, though also wrong, her nose slightly shifted—did it always look so regal?—her eyes suddenly opaque, their brilliant green a dull jade: what in God's name is she thinking? What has she ever been thinking? All the years with Dorothy suddenly collide into a shut door. She breaks laws now, gets thrown in the slammer. She's lost all interest in bridge, and paddle tennis. She might have gone to the moon; she might be weightless. Has she always loomed so far away? (For right now, James does not occur to him; he remains with the Scouts on his mountaintop, earning badges, roasting marshmallows.)

"Can you hear?" Dorothy says, interrupting him.

"What?"

"Can you hear me?" she says.

"I can hear you."

"Good. Okay. Here goes." Dorothy clears her throat again.

"I'd like to begin my talk by giving you a little background, biographical, of our subject—"

"Dorothy," Charles says.

She looks up.

"Twain on the editorial 'we'?"

"Remind me," she says.

"To be used by kings and persons with tapeworms."

"I'd forgotten."

"Easy mistake."

The ship lurches and Charles grabs the sides of his chair, though he's bolted down. It's been smooth sailing since they got back on board, so this must be a random bump.

"Go on," he says.

"Biographical," she says, "of MY subject, Florence Nightingale—"

"Right!"

Dorothy glares at him over her glasses.

"I'm not a child," she says.

"I'll shut my trap," he says.

"Lock it."

"Done."

Dorothy straightens her shoulders, adjusts her posture, and begins, again. She has a stack of note cards on which she's written her lecture, and she flips through them efficiently as she recounts Florence's privileged upbringing, her well-to-do and well-meaning parents, their bafflement and disgrace at Nightingale's calling—so mystifying in its intensity Florence might as well have been a saint or a prophet with her visions of scaling mountaintops, a flag or possibly tourniquet clutched in her fist. ("My God! What is to become of me?" Florence wrote. "I see nothing desirable but death.") She had to steal her independence, Dorothy says, wringing the word *independence* for every drop of its blood. In her early thirties, she continues, when Nightingale was still searching for where she could place her intellectual energies, she wrote an essay she titled "Cassandra," in which she articulated the crippled life women had at that time. This was before nursing. This was before anything.

"What wonder if, wearied out, sick at heart with hope deferred, the springs of will broken, not seeing clearly where her duty lies, she abandons intellect as a vocation and takes it only, as we use the moon, by glimpses through her tight-closed window-shutters . . . Woman has nothing but her affections—and this makes her at once more loving, and less loved," Dorothy reads.

Charles, for his part, knows that there is nothing he can add. How can he comment? It is already past that, far past any of that. He thinks of Good Luck and how, from time to time, he might still see him on the street, or rather, the shadow of who he was in another man, someone passing by downtown, and though he's inclined to open his wallet he rarely does, believing the poor soul must have an addiction of some sort and that money will only worsen it. That the destitute look familiar, that they seem to sense a comradeship, makes it, oddly, easier for Charles to shun them: he might get fleas or lesions or worse. Charles walks on by, as the song goes, but not so Florence Nightingale. She ministered to Good Luck. She took all the dying in her arms and bathed them—

"Charles?"

Dorothy seems to be waiting for something.

"Were you asleep?" she says.

"I was listening," he says. "I couldn't hear, exactly."

"Did you actually fall asleep?"

"For God's sake, Dorothy."

Dorothy is packing up her index cards. She's stacking them neatly and popping a rubber band to hold the group tight. She's turning on her heels. She's folding up the music stand and clicking out of the Louise Walcott Trumbull Room, oblivious to Charles's applause because it's all he can think to do: applaud and applaud as his soon-to-be ex-wife's heels click down the narrow hallway and fade into the swells.

Charles Archibald Barrett, he told her. Charles, not Charlie. A typical name for a pilot? No, not a name for a pilot at all.

They were in San Francisco, in the eleventh hour, nearing sunrise, 5 a.m. or so. Early. She has been released to him, to her cousin

Charlie, and he has been instructed to keep her awake for twelve hours, that this would be absolutely essential to rule out the possibility of a concussion.

"Archibald is for my mother's grandfather, who grew potatoes in Ohio and had something to do with importing Clydesdales."

She leaned against his shoulder and he stroked her hair. He had never felt anything so soft. They were on a bench looking out to the bay. He had told her he would take her to the places where he often walked when he could not sleep, since he had found many places: they had already been to the particular back alley in Chinatown where the old men sorted the fish before dawn.

"Clydesdales?" she said.

"The horses with the furry hooves. You've seen them."

Was she interested? Difficult to tell.

From here they heard the sea lions barking. The fog, thicker now, poured in from the bay. The city had him backwards: West for east. North for south. Everyone upside down. The military doctor had understood his confusion; had prescribed new glasses and given him a certificate with which to purchase them. He had sought out a store for such things, having every intention of eventually seeing clearly. The optician said he should try the horn-rims, then the rectangles, describing for him the personality each frame suggested, since Charles, the salesman had rightly guessed, was newly returned and needed to start fresh.

That Charles had turned into an alley behind the store upon leaving empty-handed, heaving into a gutter as discreetly as he knew how, would have surprised the optician. Charles thinks the optician must have truly believed he had meant it, the business about thinking it through, checking at home with his wife, possibly returning in the morning. As it was Charles never returned, and walked the city streets in a literal blur, his retinas burned, frayed at the edges by what had been a beastly sun. That he had stumbled upon Dorothy at all, seen her crooked frame on the sidewalk, he still believed to be a bit of a miracle.

"What do you mean?" she said. She turned to him, her pinwheel curls flattened by his hand.

"About what?"

"The furry hooves."

"It's a fringe of some sort."

"Oh," she said, turning back to the view.

They had wound down to this. To nothing, really; to furry hooves. He thought again of the shop devoted to glasses, to the physician's note in his hand: a prescription, an explanation of whom to bill. Until that time he had not quite been aware of his own appearance; he had seen himself, of course, but he had not actually studied his face, nor taken notice of others doing so. In the shop devoted to glasses, he looked into a small, square mirror set on the glass counter for such things, a pair of brown tortoiseshell frames, their stems looped on either ear, across his nose.

"They complement your angles," the optician said. "Speak to who you are."

Who are you? Charles thought, looking at the man wearing the empty tortoiseshell glasses. His face looked as Charles's face had once looked, though now it wore a permanent bruise beneath the left eye, and his hair, once black as shoe polish, had lost its color. He wore it buzzed almost to the scalp, but if he were to let it grow it would have been thread white.

Charles blinked, his eyes still open. They seemed endless.

"These?" the optician said, another pair quickly swapped with the tortoiseshell; a black, nondescript form.

"You're a reader," he said. "I could tell the minute you walked in."

Charles nodded.

"These babies are lightweight. Better material. Frankly, they'll cost more than the last ones, but Uncle Sam's footing the bill." Charles imagines that he winked after saying this—he was that kind of man—but Charles didn't look to confirm.

"I could tell the minute you walked in. I said, a reader. Or maybe a college professor."

Charles smiled, the teeth he had fitted the day before so white as to look blue, though the swollen gums were a giveaway.

"Thank you," he said, removing the frames.

The optician stared at Charles, quizzical; he wanted more, Charles knew, could have guessed it from the way his left eye sagged a bit above the shadow-bruise, from the stiff walk of him, from the way he lisped with his new teeth. The optician wanted to know what had taken Charles so long to return home, after the heroes were already welcomed back, after the parades. Affixed to the optician's stare Charles saw the asterisk, read the notation: How has it been for you?

"'I was neither at the hot gates, nor fought in the warm rain,'" he said. Eliot, of course, "Gerontion," he nodded, somehow satisfied. A snob, yes. Always a snob.

They shook hands and Charles left, knowing that the optician watched him until he turned the corner, unaware that on the other side, in that narrow alleyway, he had retched until faint.

"I'm supposed to stand guard another hour," Charles told Dorothy. "Then you're a free woman."

His duties he took seriously, he said to her, but after that, she could either enlist him or send him packing. He told her this and some other things, how his captors had eventually had names, and how that was funny, since the island they occupied had no name; she took pity, she would later say. She had known immediately that he was a good man, a bruised soldier only recently returned. Besides, he couldn't see, she would say. He had no idea what he was getting into!

Afterward, in the crummy hotel room his government stipend covered, he did not undress her; the both of them too shy for that, and they were exhausted, besides, so fully close to the twelfth hour of his watch.

"I have been reading T. S. Eliot," he began. "A poet."

Could it have been his imagination? The smell of smoke here, the combustible sense of the room?

"Say that the end precedes the beginning, / And the end and the

beginning were always there," he said, because he hadn't had anyone else to say it to, and reading the poem again and again, as he
would, he had felt something close to prayer. Screw you, Father Simple, he would have liked to say. Screw you. They were in the dark,
the only light that of the flickering streetlamp outside the hotel. It
was dawn, or nearly: the end of the twelfth hour.

"Words strain, / Crack and sometimes break, under the burden."
He couldn't stop because he could say it, because she listened and
for so long no one had heard him. He believed she listened, then. She
was listening, wasn't she?

"Yes," she said. "Of course," she said. She crawled over to sit
beside him. They were on the floor, leaning against the bed. She
touched him, then, his shoulder. She leaned on his shoulder and
kissed his cheek and said, "Thank you for saving me," and said, "Go
on," and said, "I'm listening."

Charles stands with Dorothy on the prow of the ship, alone,
Dorothy's idea to escape the reception, to come out for air and to
hear the sloughing off of ice, the glacial shedding. An instinctual
retreat, their expert had earlier explained, a movement away from
the center of accumulation.

"You mean they fly the proverbial coop," Dorothy had joked, and
the small collection—some with notebooks, others nearly dozing—
had laughed.

A standing ovation! Dorothy repeats, flush, still, from the fire of
her talk, the many questions directed at her, the general good cheer.
She seems alive, again, softer somehow and restored to a depth that
Charles might step into, if he could; perhaps one of them will survive it, James. Besides, look at Florence! Look at all the death she
saw—the hardship! You had to admit she led a fascinating life and
that Dorothy had told it brilliantly—constructing a verifiable argument that all the roads that all women and girls now so blithely
travel led directly back to Nightingale or namely, her belief in female

saviors, her nursing school, and out of this, something called the National Association for the Promotion of Social Science, where women first got the opportunity to speak with men, eat with men—it was a club! And here, apparently, women delivered their first lectures: papers written from their own ideas about their own things. Indeed Florence, one of its first members, had fired their souls on The Woman Question—

"The what?" Chester Briggs interrupted.

"The Woman Question," Dorothy said. "It's what they called it then."

"What they called what?" Chester pursued.

"It. Us. The problem of us." An awkward silence ensued, punctuated by the satisfied looks of the coven. Charles attempted to ignore it, preferring to focus on Dorothy's clear command of her subject, on the way she delivered her exegesis with a daunting ease.

(Did it take that then? Losing him to find herself? She had told him she was not alone; she had told him this leaving she planned to do was in point of fact statistically in keeping with a growing trend, that three out of ten or possibly four out of ten women left their husbands in the dust either through widowhood or free choice, free choice far more common than generally acknowledged, she said; she had read it somewhere and besides, it didn't matter. She planned to do whatever the hell she wanted. "So you'll be one of those women in the red hats," Charles had said. They had, months before, stumbled upon a group of them in the movie theater, and though the rows behind had complained loudly at the start of the previews, the women had steadfastly refused, like Rosa Parks, Charles had commented, to move to the back.)

The coven turned to Dorothy; the men silenced.

And that led to her grandmother Dorothy Trevor Townsend. She had given her life so that women might, quite simply, do something, she said. She passed around the stamp then, the regal, blue-tinted, scallop-bordered proof of lineage, the original Dorothy a bit worse for wear, though preserved in a laminated sheath so that Dorothy could carry it with her at all times. But first, she is explaining, she should tell them that it is a replication of an engraving of a woman she had never met nor heard much of, her father not given to family stories—an only child, she believed for years—until learning she had an aunt (he a sister!) tucked somewhere in England, or possibly abroad, who could know? Once, even, she had written to someone named Evelyn Townsend, a chemistry professor at Barnard College in New York, quite accomplished, whom her daughter, Caroline, had read about. She never got a reply, the name common enough, if you thought about it.

The point is, she had researched the history, *her* history, as best she could, after Liz, her youngest, left for Cooper Union and the hours pooled at her feet like water. She might have drowned, she said, if not for finding Dorothy Trevor Townsend and those other women whose names you wouldn't know, women who came and went, their antecedent Florence, she said.

One must always look for antecedents, she said. You have to start somewhere.

The stillness in the room felt almost physical, like an animal holding its breath.

She went to the library, she said. She read what she could and her son—then across the pond on a Fulbright—helped out, tracking down this stamp from the ancient library at Trinity College, Cambridge University, the Rare Ephemera Collection, which, her son had noted, was a misnomer or at the very least a curiosity—the word *ephemera* a Greek term for things meant to be thrown away.

He described the collection as one of many in the library's archives, a rabbit warren deep underground and watched by hawks of the British kind. There were relics there, too—a strand of Mohammad's hair, Christ's tooth. They confiscated pens and you had to wear white gloves and show proof of scholarship and good bloody intention to descend, her son James had written.

Here Dorothy could not look at Charles; she could not. She kept her thoughts trained on her notes, momentarily allowing a lapse of eye contact with the audience in favor of remembering James and the look of that letter when she received it, scrawled on the blue airmail stationery that had once held such promise. News! she thought. James! she thought, finding the letter, slanted, propped, in the dark recesses of the mailbox.

The mailman's truck had come and gone. She had taken her time, walking slowly toward the mailbox at the end of the driveway, knowing that to be too eager would be to be disappointed. She passed Charles's garden, the long neat rows of tomatoes and pole beans, lettuce and even, this year, broccoli. She was tricking something, she understood, by walking so slowly, by pretending not to be too eager; tricking whatever it was she felt to be watching—to appear needy invited its disdain, "it" being, what? God? She thinks of the time James, home from nursery school, had announced that all things were made by God.

"She's blue," he had said. "Light blue. And her hair is down to here," he said, reaching. "And you can see straight through her."

Dorothy thought of this as she reached the mailbox, hoping for a letter from him, a blue letter, a God letter.

The physical silence in the room grows restless and shifts.

Dorothy looks up, suddenly aware she has been drifting.

"Where was I?" she says.

"The archives," Sachiyo de Pauling says, too eager.

"Your history," Chester Briggs adds.

Someone has returned the stamp to the lectern, and now Dorothy stares down at her paternal grandmother (her namesake!) who, in profile, looks like any of those turn-of-the-century types in profile, the hair piled high on her head in a pompadour, the collar, the eyebrows thick and arched, and the long nose and the slight downward curve of her mouth: Dorothy Trevor Townsend, it read, the name scrawled beneath the engraving, 1880–1914.

"Yes," Dorothy continued, tucking the stamp back into her notebook for such things, reminding herself to look up, to make eye contact. "I learned my grandmother benefited from Nightingale's crusade: she was admitted in 1896 to the prestigious Girton College, then a residential college for women at Cambridge University that had been founded more than twenty years earlier, ironically enough, by Nightingale's cousin, a painter and visionary named Barbara Bodichon. By the time my grandmother was admitted, the college had seen many extraordinary women pass through its doors and yet none were granted university degrees. They were awarded 'certificates' instead, certificates that amounted to little more than paper. The spring of the year my grandmother arrived, a vote was called in the senate to grant women degrees. Chaos erupted in the streets. Effigies of female students were hung from various college windows. It should not surprise you that the proposal was defeated and the status of the women of Girton remained unchanged.

"The young women still had to request permission to attend university lectures and laboratories, and were given, according to rumors, explicit instruction not to speak." Here the coven loudly shifted.

"From Girton she married unhappily," Dorothy said, peering over her reading glasses, "and gave birth to two children, my father's older sister, Evelyn, with whom, as I mentioned earlier, neither he nor I had any contact, and my father, Thomas Francis Townsend. Her husband, Theodore Townsend, an active member of the Explorers Club, was presumed dead in Ceylon soon after my father's birth, though my grandmother had what appears to be a rather public affair with a married member of Parliament, William Crawford, who later earned a degree of infamy for his secret dealings with the Germans and was placed under house arrest and tried for treason.

"Dorothy Townsend was an outspoken and active member of the Women's Social and Political Union, though she broke with them when they advocated more radical protests, and appeared not to have aligned herself with any of the myriad splinter suffrage movements, disillusioned, she wrote in one editorial, by how so many women stood in support of the First World War, their own demands aside. 'War is a man-made institution,' she wrote." Here Dorothy paused. "I read that in a footnote somewhere, mostly where I find her. Still, the reason she chose to starve herself remains a great mystery to me. She had two children she would leave as orphans. She was, from all indications, engaged in a love affair. She was respected, brilliant.

"But who can guess what a woman will do to stake her own freedom, even if, in the end, it costs her her life? No doubt she hoped, given her high profile and her association with William Crawford, that her death might provoke a Parliament no longer concerned with women's suffrage. The police had months earlier stopped force-feeding the jailed ones on hunger strikes, releasing them instead in their weakened conditions and—once the war began—granting them amnesty. But if her intention was to be heard then perhaps she succeeded," she said. "I mean, that's my best guess. She just wanted to be heard."

To this, there was an odd burst of applause from the audience, largely due to the clear emotion in Dorothy's voice and the fact that, though momentarily sidetracked by the tragedy of her son's death—known to all at this point on their collective journey—she had righted her stumble and finished.

Dorothy pushed through the applause, wiping her eyes and explaining how she had intended to end on an upbeat note. This talk was about Florence Nightingale, after all, not Dorothy Trevor Townsend, and she had many inspirational quotes she wanted to share, e-mailed to her in the Alpine office by her daughter Caroline's secretary, who had located a Florence website, a Florence fan club, and an ask-Florence blogger for desperate nurses considering leaving the overburdened profession.

"And you?" Dorothy asks, interrupting the silence that pairs them. "How's Browning coming?"

"Oh, him," Charles says. "I'm rethinking."

"All's right with the world," she says, and indeed it could be true, it might be true, here beneath the sky and the stars that pour out of it; but it is not, he remembers. It is not true: The world. Right. The two of them.

"Have you told the girls?" he says, a bit too suddenly.

"I only just told you, Charles," Dorothy says. "I'm not cruel, just unhappy."

The word, so simple, so unvague, so directly what it is, so Dorothy, somehow, completely upends him, and time folds in like a paper airplane to sail weightlessly away.

He had imagined standing before a crowd, or at least ten interested persons, with simply a few notes and his heart, he might have told her. He would recount the story of Browning and that poet's love for his muse, Elizabeth, a tale so well-known it is too rarely told, he would say. He would look directly at Dorothy and describe for the gathered audience their meeting on the street in San Francisco, refraining from mentioning his battered condition, or the rats, or the prisoner he once was, the man known as Good Luck, or the smoke that sometimes blinded the pilot, the greasy smoke of Tokyo. He would speak of their life together, his and Dorothy's, and try not to think of James on his mountaintop. He would think of something new; something wholly beautiful, a new Charles with white teeth and fresh eyes and a walk that could easily shift to a trot, a full-scale gallop. An athlete, he'd give Dorothy; a hero of the mind. The dazzle would be so brilliant, so blinding, so nurse-like and efficient—a clean slate, a *tabula rasa*—that she'd ask for him back. Then they'd be together again in a world without history, a world without end.

"Dorothy," Charles says, though she has already turned away from him to listen to something else—the blue cacophony of sound, the hollow thunk and whoosh as a glacier cracks, fills, and splits in two. She alone must have heard the start of it, felt the nearness of the spectacle; this the fate of all glaciers, they were told, unbudgeable until divided.

DOROTHY TREVOR

William at the window did not surprise her, his clothes ripped, his eye swelling, bloody nose. Bloody hell, he said. The assailant had come from behind, out of the shadows. The assailant, he said, had something sharp in his hand, or blunt, or singularly hard and piercing, a knife? The assailant must have gotten in through the bloody gates when some bloody first-form idiot forgot to watch his bloody back and now look, criminals here for Christ's sake, of all bloody places to have to pat your bloody pockets—

Dorothy ministers with a bowl of soapy water she brings from the kitchen, careful not to wake the others, tiptoeing. The water sloshed in the bowl, a sturdy blue ceramic used for scrambling eggs, kneading onion into pork—she helped out, from time to time. Now she squatted on her knees to wipe William's face, to dab just so. They said you bled most from the face—nose, brow, forehead. She wrung the dishrag and the blood went brown in the water.

"There, there," she said. That sounded right.

"There, there," she said, again.

She thought it better to get to the infirmary, to use her key to hold the lock so that it would not click shut, to step back into the dark to guide him—dishrag against the blows—down Huntingdon Road and through the various gates and courtyards to the infirmary where the university doctor, or master for such things, slept in his tiny box of a room, a cat at the window. The night dark, William said. First thing to notice. He couldn't see his bloody hands. A fool to walk alone after midnight. A bloody fool.

The doctor said, "It happens all the time now." They have waked him and the doctor is tired and still a bit drunk—the cat his one friend, his companion, his captain on his lonely ship. To hear him think it, the cat jumps down and curls upon the doctor's lap.

"And who are you?" he asks.

"Girton," William volunteers. "One of the Girton girls."

"Pretty," says the doctor, looking not at Dorothy but at William. He gestures for William to sit down so that he might swab William's eye and bandage his nose. He unwinds gauze from within one of the glass cylinders and scissors tape: the box of a room an orchestra of instruments with which he works, steady, mute—antiseptic, cotton, string. He is a good doctor who, years from now, will become a hero of sorts, a World War I medic and witness to the Christmas truce at Ypres. He will write of it, one of the few to describe the miracle—the way the German soldiers lined lit candles along the parapets of the trenches and then climbed out of the mud in the dark like so many rising shadows, some quite good with English and friendly enough, he wrote. Autographs were exchanged and black bread and ham traded for cigarettes, the night moonless as this one.

The universal thinking, the doctor wrote, *could be described as the thinking men do at times when they set aside force to engage in power, or by that I mean, power of game, of friendship, of camaraderie. It is female, this power; the power of the next generation, a power given solely to women. Indeed, it is a power stronger than force—everlasting, self-sustaining.* (He had been reading the philosopher Benjamin Kidd. He had been thinking of absolution. He had considered God. He had made a silent pledge that upon his return to England he would work with the pacifists. He was no H. G. Wells, he understood, and yet, as a doctor, he might have something to add.)

The doctor wrote of the Christmas carols and the game playing and how all the men clutched their lucky things and dragged the dead ones, those "gone west," back to their holes. Like ants dragging crumbs to their anthills, he wrote.

The next day the men waked to kill or be killed, again, the doctor among the dead, though his letter remains like a button or a leather boot, a testament for generations donated to the British Museum by the family of the librarian to whom it was addressed, the librarian a small man with spectacles who had managed to walk past the war as a child past bullies. He had asked the doctor to please write and the doctor had promised he would.

I'm no poet, the doctor wrote in his famous letter to the librarian. Besides, the shit is knee-deep and the stench impossible to describe. I amputate limbs with a wood saw and iodine, straddling the wounded in the back of an ambulance that must maneuver shells and the already dead. Still, the doctor wrote, he hoped the librarian knew how much the thought of him cheered even this life. If he returned, which he doubted he would, he planned on making a house of it—the two of them—they could be masters to the boys and whatnot. See? he wrote. Whatnot. I cannot even say it.

That same Christmas the librarian sent the doctor an extra pair of socks and cigarettes and some chocolates he had received earlier in the week from his mother, pilfered from the house she cleaned, one of those places filled with artists who painted flowers on the walls and didn't fight. Conscientious objectors, they said. Pretentious objectors, she said. They were all snobs, eating sweets, drinking absinthe, smoking God-knows-what. Who will notice if I snitch a few? God help me if this is stealing, she said.

It is and thank you, Mum, the librarian said.

The librarian received first the doctor's letter of the Christmas truce, then the news of the doctor's death (an announcement issued by the university). He pressed them both between the pages of Oscar Wilde's *Intentions*. He, too, had been aiming for self-improvement.

*   *   *

But the doctor is a young man now, newly installed and alive. It's nearly fifteen years before the fighting at Ypres.

"Cheers," he says to William, pouring something and raising his glass. William inexplicably salutes. Does he already see the ghost of the medic rising? Too many ghosts and Dorothy wants out. She stands and walks to the door, waiting for William to finish his drink.

"Good night," she says to the doctor, when he stands. "Thank you."

In her rooms, later, she smells a cinnamon smell in William's hair, something unfamiliar. The doctor had finished with iodine, the stain of orange where ash would have been if it were Ash Wednesday, though William, like the rest of them, has sworn off God.

Now, he must reconsider, he said. Everything has suddenly been upended, the all of it suspect. Perhaps there are rules to follow. Certain rules. If one can't walk safely through the Commons on a given night, what could happen next? He had prayed for his life, he said. He had begged the assailant, Please God don't hurt me. He had said a few other things he could not repeat and is ashamed remembering. He needs to be gone, he said. He needs to go.

She watches him leaving out the window, latch locked, the watchdog fast asleep on her bed in the other room. He limps a bit, though she knows he'll be fine. He is a tall man, William, and from here, in the moonlight that has suddenly appeared out of nowhere, he seems taller, his shadow falling back to her. There is something defined in this, in the manner of his leaving, so that when she turns to find Hilde waiting, Dorothy is not surprised. Hilde sits in the corner of the room, just behind the piano, her face bruised, her nightgown loose. She smiles and fades into the pattern of the wallpaper, twisting vines and leaves too large and somewhere, here or there, a parrot.

"I see they've stuck the ladies in darkest Africa," William had said upon his first visit. God but he was handsome then.

DOROTHY TOWNSEND BARRETT

Silver Spring, Maryland, 1973/2006

The women, new *friends*, are gathered in the home of Mary Chicka-rella, or Chick, as she's known—one of the faster set, formally introduced to Dorothy at the club ballroom-dancing finals. There, Chick and her husband, Georgie, had Lindy-ed to First, while Dorothy and Charles took a Second with a waltz. The two had occasionally golfed since then, though Chick's handicap, she'd be the first to tell you, was in the single digits—Mary "Chick" Chickarella one of the more frequent names engraved on the trophies and silver bowls in the glass case outside the ladies' lounge, even the huge regional championship cup with its ornate handle and tiny, 24-karat gold woman arrested in midswing on the top.

"It's going to be a rap session," Chick had said when she called Dorothy. "You know, about what's going on."

"Vietnam?" Dorothy had asked.

"The war? Are you into that?"

"No," said Dorothy, who wasn't, truly, though James's long hair and POW bracelet kept it close.

"My friend Jean's coming from Philadelphia," Chick continued. "She's a facilitator there—what they call a Big Sister. It's quite a scene. She says you won't believe what comes up. Scratch the surface, she says, and it bleeds."

* * *

143

Kate Walbert

Dorothy arrives with flowers. She couldn't think what else and Charles's garden is in full, June bloom, iris and delphiniums, the geraniums that reseed and grow wild in the paths and those poppies he adores in red. These are the days he disappears within it, Liz like a small, turbulent shadow at his side. The other children are gone: James at college, Caroline backing out of the drive too quickly on her way to flag-twirling practice, or a student council forum, or one of the endless clubs she has recently joined, anticipating, she says, the brutalities of admission in the fall. Only Liz remains, her glasses smudged and sideways, her knees bruised and scabbed. According to Piaget, she's in an exuberant cycle—nine to ten—though to Dorothy she remains a puzzle: restless, skinny as a twig, given to writing notes of apology or despair, often in verse. At times, Dorothy has found them slipped beneath their bedroom door, as if an urgent message has just been delivered from the front desk. The last one, a poem, had been scratched in ink on the corner of a notebook page, lined and blue, then torn out and folded many times over. It was something about the earth tilting on its axis, she later told Charles. Get her a Feelings Jar, Charles said, him still of the opinion this had helped James and Caroline and their constant squabbling.

God, don't remind me, replied Dorothy; she knew a Feelings Jar spelled disaster.

Chick's house is as Dorothy would have guessed, an interesting color, set off from the other houses of the development for its suggestion of purple and its festive summer wreath—pussy willows, these, and a tiny tarnished bell attached to a dangling ribbon. A cement animal—a narrow, long-snouted dog with a gaping mouth—stands hip-high, within its jaws someone has wedged an ashtray and what looks like a plastic rose.

Dorothy knocks and Chick immediately opens the door; she wears a golf skirt and matching top, her hair newly cropped and bleached.

"Dorothy!" she says. "*Entrez!*" she says.

Chick turns and leads Dorothy into the foyer's darkness; Dorothy follows, a bit off balance. She had expected light and air, houseplants, but here is a hint of the Orient and the smell of something new—she might well turn the corner and find women sprawled on silk pillows, the air thick with a druggy, opiate smoke. She has read about this kind of thing—in Maugham, mostly, back when Charles studied at the kitchen table and she had the time. Then they had lived in married-student housing—Quonset huts!—in that bleak, Midwestern state where Charles was getting his business degree and where she spent her days first in a knitting circle, and then, preferring solitude, on long walks in the woods. Oh, how she loved Maugham! His exotic women, his prostitutes and troubled girls who would sooner eat their young than find themselves in ordinary lives, but no, now Dorothy has turned the corner to find the women gathered in Chick's living room looking remarkably familiar, friendly enough, even eager to begin, as if she has just entered the introductory meeting of the Links Beautification Committee at the club. These women sit on folding chairs pulled into a circle within a recognizable living room: its floral-papered walls hung with prints of wildflowers, its mantel clustered with photographs and semiprecious stones carved in the shapes of jungle animals, if she were to look.

"Sissy," Chick is yelling into the adjacent room, the dining room, where a black woman in a white uniform appears intent on polishing a gleaming mahogany table. "Here's the last of us!"

"Am I late?" Dorothy asks, turning back to Chick. "I couldn't find the—"

"You're fine," Chick says. "Perfect."

She claps her hands.

"Ladies," she says. "This is Dorothy. Terrific dancer. Three children, I think. Three?"

Chick looks at Dorothy, who is suddenly aware of Charles's flowers in her hands.

"And a husband," Chick adds.

"Here," Dorothy says, offering the bouquet to Chick.

"Gorgeous," Chick says, sniffing. "Sissy," Chick yells, though Sissy has magically appeared, drinks on a tray and the polishing rag slung over her shoulder. Chick passes Dorothy's bouquet then turns back to the group, who remain fixed where they are, as if waiting for someone's attention to animate them.

"Say hello to Dorothy, ladies," Chick says.

"Hi, Dorothy," they say, released in unison.

"Hello, everyone," Dorothy says back. "Hello, Laura," she adds, recognizing Laura Rasmussen, a younger woman from the club, good golfer, who smiles and waves, mouthing another hello.

Chick pulls an empty chair from the circle and gestures for Dorothy to sit; the rest of the women, now distracted by Sissy's return, accepting drinks from the tray and passing a mother-of-pearl bowl of cocktail nuts. The drinks are gin gimlets. The nuts an assortment, shelled and salted.

"So," Chick says, clapping again. "Knock-knock?" The women quiet and turn toward her.

"Should we review?" Chick says. "To my left is Jean, our Big Sister."

Jean nods as she's introduced. She looks nothing like the other women in the circle—her thick, graying hair has been tied into two braids with a kind of rainbow yarn and parted so evenly down the middle she might have used a knife. She wears overalls and a patterned blouse, the sleeves rolled past her elbows as if earlier she had been kneading bread.

She looks at all of them and smiles. "Hello," she says.

"Hello," they say.

In truth, Jean reminds Dorothy of some of the female musicians who would gather in her father's house, women with strong hands and heavy shoes who lugged extraordinary cases up and down the San Francisco hills, their determination written across their foreheads in clear, unspoken sentences—Do you know how many hours I had to practice for this? Do you know what I've given up? They always addressed Dorothy slowly and in half-tones, as if, when talking to a child with a crippled, brilliant father, one must speak in whispers.

"What are we here for?" Jean begins. "Has it been explained?"

"Let's get the names down first," Chick says.

"Oh," says Jean. "Right."

"I have the ball," says Chick, reaching beneath her chair to bring up a tennis ball.

"Fun and games?" Laura S. says.

There are two Lauras, Laura S. and Laura R. The women's names are spelled out on sticky labels and stuck over their breasts. Everyone has had a drink and been apprised of the following, known in the movement, Jean explains, as our pledge of allegiance: There are no rules; There is no bad idea in a rap session; Everything goes; Jean is the boss.

"So," says Chick, looking at all of them and crossing her legs, muscular, she'd be quick to tell you, from preferring to walk her daily eighteen holes, carrying her own bag. "Since I have the ball, I'll go first," she says.

"Great!" a few of them say.

"I had an abortion," Chick continues, her tone relatively unchanged. "No, I had two abortions. Both before I was twenty. Both before I met Georgie."

Jean tilts over to rub Chick's back, though it doesn't appear to be in need of rubbing. Chick bristles a bit. If her eyes are filled with tears, she hides it well.

"Sara?" she says, tossing the ball to Sara.

"Me?" Sara says, catching it.

"Yup," Chick says.

"I go next?" Sara says, holding the ball.

"If I throw it to you, you go next."

Sara, who sits directly across from Chick in a skirt and top more customarily found in South America, turns to Jean. "I thought there were no rules in a rap session," she says.

"Speak your mind," Jean says, and her voice booms out and settles over all of them like a heavy parachute.

"I hate rules," Sara says. "That's the first thing. And I feel like—God, this is hard—I feel like we always have to live by this bullshit protocol, these rules—"

"We?" Jean interrupts.

"Yeah. Us," Sara says.

"Here? In this circle? Or do you mean women in general?" Jean says.

"Is it a rule we have to state the obvious?" Sara says. Jean bites her lip and fingers a strand of bright yellow yarn unraveled from her braid. Dorothy watches and thinks, not for the first time, that they all lie in wait of something, something unnamed and unnameable and yet as present in this room as the tray of drinks, the bowl of nuts. They stalk the thing like prey, are fierce in their desire to attack and devour it, but then again, they are instant friends, aren't they? Here to buoy spirits?

"No," says Jean. "No rules."

Sara is the one woman among them with a graduate degree, and though she had once believed this would elevate her above the noisy din, the degree did nothing more than require her to waste a few years in Boston, prolonging the inevitable.

"The inevitable?" Jean asks.

Sara's look could kill.

"The inevitable," Sara repeats. Then, more brightly, "Dorothy?"

"I'm sorry?" Dorothy says. She's heard her name but she'd been thinking, trying to picture Sara in the snows of Boston, her dungarees frayed around ragged sneakers, her coarse shirt tucked into a waist cinched with a bright, handmade macramé belt. Dorothy had met women like Sara before, certain older friends of Caroline's, teachers Caroline brought home, requiring role models, she said, of a more appropriate kind.

Dorothy had been imagining Sara in the Boston snow. "Oh, yeah," Sara says, tossing the ball to Dorothy, "and I had an abortion, too."

That Dorothy is here and not at her weekly bridge game, that she has made several telephone calls to reschedule this and that, to find a fourth, to arrange a babysitter, is a bit of a puzzle to her. True, she had been flattered when Chick called, Chick a woman who turned heads when she walked into the clubhouse, her golf shoes clicking the flagstone as if she were dogged by maracas. (Chick rarely went without them: either worn or dangerously slung over one shoulder, laces cinched, spikes down.) Yet Dorothy has little to no idea what is now expected of her, what she is supposed to add to the conversation. This is what Jean, the Big Sister, had said: We've come here today to have a conversation, she had said, to rap our experiences, to find the words to our collective history.

It had been a stirring introduction, only dampened by the fact that Jean read from prepared notes and would pause on occasion to bite the end of one braid, her shoulders cattywampus, as if they were originally cast in a defective mold. Still, the word *conversation* bloomed when Jean spoke it, unfurling endless possibility of talk of a richer kind: words packed into sentences as ornate and complicated as those found in Maugham, words that zinged and zagged, bumped and ruptured, words she could crawl out of or maybe into— "conversation" a forest thick with evergreen through which lay a suggestion of a path where light, tempered and soft, beckoned her forward.

"Where are we going?" Jean had said in conclusion. "Whence did we come?" And to this Maggie Sykes had spontaneously applauded, though she stopped, immediately, shifting in her hard, straight chair then patting her nametag as if comforting a baby at her breast.

* * *

It's a good feeling, Dorothy thinks, to catch a ball, a camp feeling, though she had never been, a summer feeling, regardless, something of promise in it—she might win!—the ball new and firm. She thinks of the pleasing sound of a tennis can being opened, the release of that air, the sigh of it.

"Dorothy?" Jean says. "Your turn."

"Oh, right," Dorothy says. "Right," she says.

She sits in a ring of unfamiliar women and they are all of them staring at her, waiting for her to say, what? She is unused to such attention; unused to being watched or rather, seen. The ballroom dancing lessons, offered by Ginger Foxe—who once, apparently, lived in New York and studied with Martha Graham—would be an anti-dote to this, she had told Charles, an attempt to break out, to twirl and dip, to have *fun*, she had said to him, fun, something they had once had in spades, or at least occasionally, hadn't they? Besides, the children would get a kick out of their parents' dancing and, why not? Black tie! Club championship! She had shown Charles the mimeo-graphed page with the specifics: limited space, couples only, come as you are (in formal attire), strap your dancing shoes on. Calling All Freds and Gingers! it said in big block letters across the top.

The night of the first lesson they had dressed in their fancy clothes: Charles in his military tuxedo, Dorothy in a sequined dress she had found years earlier at the Junior League Stop & Swap and bought on a whim. It had been a dark night, predictably, with a blue-ish March moon, too chilly to forget a wrap. Charles had linked his arm in hers and led her down the flagstone walk, breaking away only to open the station wagon door, to bend with a flourishy bow as if earlier the station wagon were a pumpkin and he a mouse. The chil-dren, or rather Liz (Caroline had something else to do, though she wished them well, she said. "Have a wonderful time!" she said. "Break a leg!") clapped and clapped, watching. She stood silhouetted with the babysitter against the light of the hallway chandelier, the front door open, the two flanked by the ghoulish shadows of twin rhododendron. Dorothy looked up to see Liz raise a shaky hand good-bye, the babysitter's arm tight around her thin shoulder. Earlier, when Liz had heard they were going, she curled into a soft ball beneath the dining room table, refusing to budge, so that it did not entirely surprise Dorothy to find Liz's crumpled note crammed into her beaded clutch before they reached the club, as she searched for a cigarette to calm her nerves. The note, written on a tear from a brown grocery bag, took some time to unfold.

"I am a hollow bone," it read, the o's shaped into sad smiley faces, so that, in the dark of the automobile, Dorothy had to read it twice to be sure.

"Dorothy?" This now Jean.

"Yes?"

"Remember our pledge of allegiance?" she says.

We are all of us the same; we are all of us sisters.

"I am a hollow bone," Dorothy says.

Jean leans forward, craning around to look Dorothy eye-to-eye. "You are a hallowed bone?" she says, the room deadly silent, though Maggie Sykes, the unanimously elected recording secretary (there had been no challengers) scribbles minutes, good for history, for giving voice to the collective, for articulating the void.

"Hollow," Dorothy says, louder. "Hollow bone."

"Oh," says Jean, pulling back. "A hollow bone."

"I mean," Dorothy says. "It's as if I echo, or rather, feel in myself an absence. The days spill out. They're frantic, really. There's so much to do! But at certain times I feel as if I've forgotten something, as if there's a question I've forgotten to answer," Dorothy says, looking around though most of the other women seem to be doing something with their hands. "I don't know what I'm saying. I don't really know what I mean."

Jean smiles, sitting straighter. "Did everyone hear that?" she says, looking to Maggie. "Did everyone hear Dorothy's contribution?"

Maggie nods, although the other women seem distracted by a sudden grating mechanical sound—a backhoe? a dump truck?—out the opened bay windows.

"Sissy!" Chick yells, but Sissy is already there, cranking the levers closed, drawing the draperies across the light. She circles the furniture, clicking on individual lamps: a floor one with beaded glass; a large hooded bottle containing a ship; a small antique, its shade fluted into pleats. In the gradual dawning, the women turn back to Dorothy to hear what else, their eyes deep and unblinking, as if carved from wood or cast in bronze and gilded.

The tennis ball rests in the cradle of Dorothy's lap, furry and uncomplicated and impossibly bright. Don't rush into silence, Jean had said. Our history, she had said, resides in silences.

Sara had snickered at this, but then again, Sara had snickered at nearly everything until Chick asked if she were allergic and should Sissy put the dog out?

"Dorothy?" this now Chick, impatient.

"Yes?"

"If you're finished, you might want to toss the ball," Chick says.

"Oh," says Dorothy. "I guess I am. Should I pass to you?"

"It's your choice," says Chick. "Equal rights."

Dorothy picks up the ball.

"I could go again," Chick says, leaning forward, hands reaching. "There's no rule that I can't."

The first thing you would say about her husband, Georgie, is that he's a natural dancer, slim-waisted, broad-shouldered, a bit of a resemblance to Gene Kelly, if you were looking for that. Suffice it to say, he has a kind of feminine style. By that I mean, Chick adds, he's a dresser. Likes his spats, his trousers pressed. "I've never seen the man in jeans," she says. "And also, he's easy to talk to."

The women cross their ankles, their flats kicked off and carried by Sissy back to the foyer, where they are paired and lined in rows: Pappagallos in various colors, sandals with daisies chiseled in the cowhide, or bright, artificial flowers attached to the straps. Now in the soft glow of the lighted room, the women's feet, bare and colored at the toe, caress the Corsican rug. They have had another round of drinks; they are trying to think of what to say next.

"We married the day after graduation. You know, everybody did that sort of thing then. Georgie had a certain light in his eyes. I won't say I didn't fall head over heels. I did, God help me. Head over heels. So he popped the question and we got married. The day after graduation, I already told you. The day after that, I mean, *the day after that*, he told me he prefers boys. Mary, he said—I was Mary then, a good Catholic girl, you know—he said, Mary, I must tell you. I prefer boys. Which is not to say he couldn't, you know, with girls, or never had, just that he preferred the other. I mean, he wanted to make his preferences known."

Here Chick pauses as if to take a sip of water, but there is no water, only a pitcher of gin gimlets, and they've finished that and so she holds out her empty glass. "Sissy," she yells and Sissy is there, her bright white uniform stark as she leans down to refill Chick's glass from a new pitcher.

"Jesus, would you give her a break?" Sara says.

"What?" Jean says.

"I'm talking to Miss Diarrhea of the Mouth. I'm saying, tell Sissy to sit, already. Let's invite her in. Let's see what Sissy has to say."

The women in the circle turn from Chick to Sissy to Jean to Sara, who reaches over and plucks the ball from Chick's lap, tossing it too quickly in Sissy's direction. It spins then plonks the pitcher.

"Game point," says Laura S., lighting a cigarette.

"I could take a rest," Sissy says.

"Take a rest," Sara says, standing up and offering her chair. "Sit here, Sissy."

"I'm Sister," Sissy says.

"Sister," says Sara, pointing to Sissy, "and Big Sister," says Sara, pointing to Jean.

"Never were there such devoted sisters," sings Laura S. She smiles and blows some smoke out.

"We're getting off-subject," Jean says.

"What's happening?" Chick says. "I'm not finished."

"Go on," says Jean.

"I was telling you about Georgie," Chick says.

"We're listening. We're still listening," Jean says. Someone asks for the nuts and the mother-of-pearl bowl is passed.

"I feel Chick is in a lot of pain," says Maggie Sykes. "I feel we all are."

There is a collective silence through which the nuts continue to circulate; everyone suddenly declining. Chick attempts to begin again, and then she goes quiet like the rest.

"You were talking about Georgie's preferences," Jean says, encouraging. She has tied the yellow strand of yarn from her braid into a bow, which she unties and reties as if determined to perfect the loops.

"As per boys," Sara says, "as in, not you."

"Let's be kind," Jean says, looping the bow, face down in concentration so that her voice seems to issue not from her, but from a whisper somewhere at the center of us. "Kindness costs so little. Why can't we, at the very least, be kind?"

The afternoon waxes and wanes—the ball lost, eventually, dropped in one of Chick's sneakers by Sara on her way to the powder room.

Now it's Faith's turn, her voice issuing up from the living room, rising and falling as she describes her delivery—how she was strapped to the bed and cinched tight with buckled leather belts; how she was held down as if she were insane. No one ever said that they would do that. "I mean, no one ever said," she said. "Did anyone ever say that?"

"They don't tell you," Laura R. adds. "They don't tell you any—"

Jean clears her throat. "Ruptions," she begins, "come from interrupt—"

"They gave me a shot of something," Faith continues, "then they all left the room. Like they had a train to catch, or a curtain. They shut the little door and no one was there at all. I couldn't move. They left the lights on, all the lights, and the shot made me sweat and shake and the baby—it smelled like garlic. Not the baby but the whole room. Someone must have had it for dinner. And when the doctor came in he was whistling and he didn't even look at me, say hello—"

"God, when Michael was born, I swore like a trucker. I mean, the language!" Chick has slipped off her chair and sprawls on the Corsican rug, an ashtray at her elbow. "And of course Georgie was off somewhere, with some orderly, no doubt."

"Chick," Jean says.

"Or maybe a male nurse."

"Chick," Jean says.

"I'll shut it," Chick says.

"Button it," Jean says.

"I'll button it," Chick says.

Sissy laughs. She sits Indian style on the folding chair, the mother-of-pearl bowl in her lap, the white uniform stretched above her knees. She's untied her shoes and slipped them off her feet. She has had a drink, and she might have another. "Being off-duty," she had said in Chick's direction. "Being invited to participate," she had said. Sara sits on the floor in front of Sissy, leaning back against the legs of Sissy's chair, toe-to-toe with Chick. Earlier, they played footsie—PhD Against Married-to-a-Homosexual, Sara had suggested, though it was an unfair match, really, she said, Chick already up two abortions to one. At that Jean called a break, suggesting a moment of silence and inviting all to please stand and hold hands—shoulder-to-shoulder, as it were, bone-to-bone.

"Let's hear how far we've come," Jean said. "To hear your words in the voice of another is extraordinarily empowering," she said.

Kate Walbert

"Let's celebrate our commonalities," she said. Then she asked Maggie Sykes to step forward to recite—in random order, please—the minutes, Maggie Sykes making what appeared to be a unilateral decision to push through the circle to stand bull's-eye in the center. She raised her notepad to an easier reading distance and cleared her throat.

"Beverly P.," she boomed, "having to do with invisibility, childhood in fort, circumstances of mother's hospitalization; Chick— abortions, Georgie's homosexuality, self-esteem?, undermining, like a trick knee; Laura S.—the questions asked in the workplace, molestation by older brother appropriate vis-à-vis boys will be boys, or not, maybe criminal?; Laura R.—laundry, etcetera; Margaret— definition of frigid?, what is considered normal?; Laura S.—we are our own enemies, listen to us!; Sara—graduate degree bullshit?, academy bullshit?, abortion, entire discussion bullshit?, our privilege to ask, our privilege of speech, our privilege of voice re: look at Sister; Sister—industrial/military complex (son in the marines), Christ Ethiopian; Dorothy—hollow bone."

The words *hollow bone* were the last read before Maggie Sykes lowered her notes, the o's dissipating like smoke rings, wafting over the group as they were instructed to sit down and resume their former positions.

"I thought I was dead," Faith continues. "I thought I had come to die. I did die. I was out of myself. I was in a corner shouting and no one could hear me and then I screamed and screamed and screamed and no one could hear me, and it was only after they took me off the stuff, I mean, took the needles out, Annie in the nursery, that I saw they all had plugs in their ears—every one of them. Plugged ears."

How the day ended is a bit of a fog, though Dorothy knows she lined up with the rest to thank Jean and to shake her hand, and that she had inexplicably hugged Laura Rasmussen, feeling a sudden kinship and promising to invite Laura and her husband to dinner. Sister she tipped five dollars. "Unnecessary," Sister said, though she folded the bill and tucked it up the sleeve of her uniform.

Dorothy walked out into the June day, the brightness disarming, assaulting, even, as if all of them had been huddled in a cave. Chick bent just beyond, dead-heading a pot of daisies, flicking the dried blossoms into the yard like so many spent cigarettes. Beside her, the dog gnawed the tennis ball.

Perhaps Chick had already forgotten her guests, or maybe they had just disappointed her and she was glad to see them go. Hard to tell with Chick, hard to read that face—she was pretty, after all, and a terrific golfer: practically a scratch handicap, regional champion three years running. She would win several more local tournaments before being asked to resign from the club, its rules firm on the question of divorcées. Still her name remained for years on the trophies outside the ladies' lounge before, one by one, her titles were defeated.

Why Dorothy remembers all of this now, more than thirty years later, she has no idea: it seems inappropriate to daydream here, beneath this makeshift tent, the cemetery stretching out for miles around them and the minister now at the lectern reading from the Bible. Charles lies in the closed casket before her, Liz and Caroline returned with their own families, sitting like so many supplicants on either side of Dorothy, reaching for her hand at certain difficult times, as when Charles's younger brother read the Browning poem that Charles had sent to announce his wedding, the happiest day of his happy life, he wrote to his younger brother. That's the kind of man he was, Charles's younger brother said, ending his eulogy, tucking the slip of paper on which he had written his remarks back into his coat jacket pocket and bowing his head. Many spoke to the kind of man Charles was: a few of Charles's business colleagues, his golfing buddies, a long-lost pilot friend who limped up to the lectern to tell stories of Tinian, where they both had been stationed during the war; how the two had flown planes over the Pacific, strafing the hell out of the ground targets, he said, like a couple of cowboys.

Kate Walbert

The minister drones on, reading predictable passages. She will be the last to address the gathered, it's been decided, though for the spouse to speak, says Caroline, the *ex*-spouse, adds Liz, is entirely against protocol.

She is happy to break protocol, she tells them. Entirely delighted. Just take a look, she says, and it's true, she's evolved, as she says— how can they not see it? She wears her hair gray and short, *sheep-shorn*, Caroline had commented, and she's invested in what she calls her uniform: white shirt (tailored, pressed, starched) and black pants, occasionally a long black skirt with knee socks and flats. The rest—the colorful ensembles of skirt and sweater or blouse, the cock-tail dresses, the trousers and matching silk and linen jackets, are gone—dropped off in a cardboard box to the Goodwill, a few furs mailed to Liz, who asked first, and some jewelry packed and in a safe at the bank, the key sent FedEx to Caroline for safekeeping until her death, she had written in her still-loopy script, resisting the urge to punctuate with a smiley face. Bad habit. Along with the clothing, she had packed their former belongings. The knickknacks. The col-lectibles long past caring. The framed prints. The carved stone ani-mals. The letter openers.

Charles had never wanted anything. For Chrissakes, he said, he had lived in a cage, did she understand? The retirement community he had found would be a cakewalk, he said.

In the two years since their divorce he had shriveled to nothing, according to the girls, moving into assisted living just last month. So be it; his choice to give up, to let go, to wait for doomsday. This is how she thought of it: she too had only so much time and there was a lot of work to be done. She needed to read. She needed to think. She no longer cared what she ate for dinner—a bowl of cereal, a peeled orange. She could slice some cheese and crackers and have a glass of wine alone in bed. She could fall asleep with the lights on.

Yet for this, for now, she would like to stand, she tells the girls, she would like to say something about their father, to speak to their many shared years together, complicated as any marriage but not without its glory days. "Who but I," she asks, rhetorically, "can recall that your father was a terrific dancer?"

"Now here's a talent!" Vivian Foxe had barked. "Absolutely terrific!" she shouted, as Dorothy and Charles waltzed in the way that she taught them.

But first, Vivian Foxe introduced the couples. There were a few who looked familiar, and Chick and Georgie, of course, whom everyone recognized. They were led into the club ballroom and told to form a circle. Vivian Foxe held up a finger for silence, then clicked over to the stage and unsheathed a record album, fitting it onto the turntable. She lifted the arm as the record revolved, timing the needle to the groove. In an instant, scratches etched the otherwise quiet—then, remarkably, the music. The music! There were chords and phrases, refrains, rifts and solos filling the voluminous ballroom, sweeping them up as a tide would to spill them onto a different shore: Charles in his military tuxedo, she in sequins and gloves.

"Let's begin!" Vivian Foxe had shouted, clapping her hands. "Ladies' choice!"

But as she reached for Charles's hand, the note she still held— she had forgotten!—slipped like a secret message to the polished ballroom floor. "I am a hollow bone."

EVELYN CHARLOTTE TOWNSEND

V-J Day, New York City, New York, 1945

I'll walk from here to Gramercy Park, I tell Stephen Pope.

The buses and subways will be impossible, the entire campus a zoo—the Columbia boys from naval training and the Teachers College girls in an improvised parade: around the tennis courts, up the quad to Milbank, down Trumbull steps. I've seen more than one Betsy Ross, an Eleanor Roosevelt, Carmen Miranda, Myrna Loy. There's a Red Cross nurse in a cardboard ambulance and a cluster of Florence Nightingales, one with the British flag draped in a cape around her neck.

Stephen Pope, predictably, says this decision may be unwise, that I should stay where I am and that he will send someone to escort me, although this might take some time. The buses have completely stopped, he says, the crowds too thick and dangerous; one bus near Times Square apparently pushed on its side, the revelers swarming it like ants at a picnic, out of their minds, he says, drunk. He's heard all about the Japanese surrender on the radio, he said. But is he alone of the opinion that this party is entirely premature, that we are fools to make light of the Chinese? Has anyone even bothered, he says, to look at the Asian peninsula? It's too early for this mayhem, he says, and dangerous to boot. From all accounts the subways are near to bursting, certain lines completely shut down.

I describe for him all the wonders I have seen: girls in their costumes parading about, the radios blaring, propped in the dormitory windows, the streamers and the horns and the general pandemonium. I picture him in his chair at the window, the square, plaid blanket he keeps on his knees though it is August and hot. He is always cold.

"Everyone is dancing," I tell Stephen. "It's a *celebration*," I tell him. "I'll be fine."

"Walk straight home," he says.

I have worn my conference suit and lucky hat, though my talk has been cancelled given the extraordinary news of the day. There was to have been a dinner to celebrate the publication, my first *Science* cover, and for once Stephen Pope had agreed to join, knowing what the assemblage would mean. This is it, I told him, imagining them hoisting me to their shoulders, carrying me out of the auditorium to thunderous applause. From there I would have heard Nurse's voice in my ear: "What's it like in the clouds, Lady Jane?" she used to say. "Do you breathe the same air as the rest of us?" Nurse was of the mind, as she expressed on several occasions, that I tilted my chin just a bit too high. If a cold wind blew it might freeze my expression that way, me forever looking down my nose at the rest of us, she'd say. It was the mathematics she couldn't make heads nor tails of, though there were times we both sat down at Penny's kitchen table, covered between meals with the oilskin I liked to crease with my nail. Show me, then, Nurse would say, I want to learn. And for a minute she claimed to understand, though the numbers, she said, just as quickly flew out of her head.

But Stephen Pope! He would have been proud to walk through the doors of the restaurant to find me seated at the head of the table, thick in speculation, although the events of the last few weeks would have dominated the conversation, the study of chemistry forever altered by the bombs dropped on Hiroshima and Nagasaki, the magnitude of which none of us could have imagined. There would have been wine and interruptions, an argument or two and a certain intellectual comradeship that issues out of these occasions. For this I am grateful to Stephen Pope—who has given me, beyond his affection, a base on which I can somehow stand and be heard. He is all I need of family, held at a distance, present yet removed, our lives cleaved out of circumstance and need. In this way we remain something other than what is normally accepted between men and women—compatriots of an entirely different order.

I leave the mimeographed pages of my talk stacked on my desk and lock my office against the mayhem. Earlier today Professor Browksi, who recognized the inevitability of the bombs, she said, given her knowledge of the Manhattan Project and past governmental shenanigans, wandered in, lingering only when I asked her to sit down. I like a comfortable office. In the corner is an armchair I found on Broadway and had recovered. There's morning sun there, and a thriving potted bamboo that Stephen Pope gave me on my fortieth birthday. (Impossible to defeat, he said. It reminded me of you.) Just this past June I painted that particular wall a shade of blue identical to the color of the room I had as a child, the Blue Room, Mum called it.

Professor Browski seemed agitated. She said she had made her contribution to the physical sciences and look at the consequences. "I have always been drawn to the secrets of chemistry, the mysteries of what cannot be seen. Suddenly," she said, "I am terrified."

She's become an old woman, Professor Browski, bowed and practically disappeared within the chair, her thin, veined legs sheathed in scratchy stockings, her suit the wrong material for this season. She wears the same ensemble to campus every morning, and her faculty apartment is the one that was assigned to her by the college when she arrived before the First World War, the scientist daughter of a Polish refugee who had raised her as if she were a son. The apartment is a living room and a kitchen, side-by-side, the kitchen unused and the living room bare but for the outline of a Murphy bed, a sofa, and a round coffee table. There she stacks the professional journals she receives, given her memberships and associations, and the day's newspaper folded into a neat column as if she later intends to swat a fly. She's alone, of course, this one of the many sacrifices she described to the six of us, the chemistry core, as it was called in those days, on that first class our freshman year. We sat around the soapstone laboratory table staring at the table of elements, its blanks, she said, our possibilities. You might very well be the one to fill Element Seventeen—the chance of another Madame Curie here in this room, she said, just as real as another Madame Curie anywhere.

We were in the "science wing," a series of bunkered rooms deep beneath campus constructed out of cement blocks and painted a putty yellow. (It is now our college bomb shelter, and fully stocked with cans of soup and dried noodles, I'm told.) No natural light could reach us, and little sound. Occasionally we smelled the smoke from the cigarettes in the girls' lounge just above us, but apart from that, it was as if they had put the chemistry students in a separate galaxy, like electrons circling the nucleus of campus, away from the breezy chatter of the quads, the lectures in the humanities spilling out of open windows, the other girls and the Columbia boys and the Friday night dances and the chaperoned Tuesday teas and the Etiquette and Fine Living and Good Manners clubs. I see Professor Browski there as she once was—fifty at most, a female professor in wool suit and pumps, her accented English brilliant and clipped. She stood at the head of us and doled out rules.

"You must be fast," she said. "You must do things that much quicker than the boys do. And you must understand that you will do them alone, that no one will pay attention. If they do, they will not be pleased."

Professor Browski held out her old hand. She needed help getting up from the chair.

"I'm late," she said. She no longer taught, but spent most of her time in her carrel on the third floor where on any given day or night you could find her. No doubt she'll eventually turn to dust, and Diego, who cleans after midnight, will sweep her up.

* * *

"Professor Townsend!" someone's calling as I reach the stairs. "Professor Townsend, wait!" It's Helen, of course, always Helen, though in past semesters it might have been Marilyn, or Sadie, or Joyce with the complicated question they forgot to ask in class. They're stumbling on Heisenberg's Uncertainty Principle, or in need of a more general pep talk or even someone with whom to share some news. They are good girls, good students, and I am their mentor, I suppose, though it is in my nature to wish for a bit more distance, a more formal arrangement. I know what will come next, how each will move on and be replaced by other girls with similar names and faces and questions, an endless line of them stretching out these ornate gates to the Lower East Side, to Brooklyn, to Queens, girls waiting for something better, patient yet shifting as the carriage horses will who wait for passengers in Central Park, hoping for a fare so they might, at the very least, stumble forward.

Helen hurries down the marble hallway toward me. She appears to be spruced with rouge or maybe she's just excited. She looks as they all look these days: thick reading glasses and a sleeveless blouse. Her heels click the marble as she rushes—Does she actually believe I haven't yet heard the news? Everyone has heard the news, I could tell her. Confetti is falling from the sky. Explosions of fireworks light the piers, the Hudson, the stones of the Cathedral of St. John the Divine where earlier, after Professor Browski went on, I walked to find quiet—my mood sour and jubilant, hard to pinpoint. I wished to be alone. I wished to speak to Thomas, wherever he might be. Dead, for all I know, or on the next block. In the first years here, I thought to contact him, to send a letter or even to board a train and track him down. He had no idea where I was—I thought perhaps I should remind him. But what would I say? What could I possibly say? No doubt he too wanted to erase our history. It is the *Principia Mathematica*, I told Stephen Pope, grounded in Russell, in logic, quantifiable by numbers, I said, and the arrangements of the elements, the all of it as invisible to the eye as hydrogen and helium. I spoke incoherently on that first night he took me in. He gave me his dead wife's dressing room and asked for nothing in return—I was her size, after all, I even resembled her, he later told me.

"Are you going?" Helen says. She's caught up. "Professor Townsend?"

"I'm going home," I say.

"No, no," she says. "Professor Weinstock's party—you're not going."

"I'm walking home," I tell her.

"I'll come," Helen says.

"I'll be fine," I say.

Helen looks at me, her cheeks inflamed, her eyes dark behind the thick glasses.

"All right," I say, and give her my arm.

It is a singular day, a momentous day. Earlier, in the Cathedral of St. John the Divine, I thought I would have liked to call them—Nurse and Penny, Mum. I would have liked to console Thomas in his weeping over the peacock, its plumage stained with blood, its thin neck ripped by the fox. I would have liked to carry Thomas up the stairs to bed in his yellow room, piggyback. I would have liked to answer Mum's constant questions, to put my book down to look up and speak when spoken to—Thomas my brother, after all, and she my mum, and I nothing more than an ordinary girl who loved books, the piano, aeroplanes, even—the fireworks I heard from inside the stone vault, set off from the piers, putting me in mind of the war hero's flight across the Channel, the glorious spectacle of that as I imagined it, though Michael said it wasn't quite: the cloud of the tiny plane had shadowed them as it passed, leaving them all afraid, a collection of men and women staring up at the bull's-eyes painted on its canvas wings.

In the Cathedral of St. John the Divine, in the apex of the stone vault where every candelabrum was lit and burning, I prayed for Professor Browski and Stephen Pope. I prayed for Father Fairfield and Mum and Thomas. I prayed for all of them and this new strange jubilation, this new peace, as I knelt with the others in that necropolis, the sheer height of it swallowing us whole.

Helen pulls me through the throngs of students in the quad, several of them shouting hellos, their hands held in victory signs. We push toward the looming gates of the college, the guards, according to Helen, soon to padlock the entrance against the rowdy festivities and issue a curfew. She heard it somewhere, she shouts back toward me. We should get out as soon as we can, she shouts.

Helen believes her mission to be purposeful. She cuts a clear path leading me, though she's jostled, suddenly, her butcher's satchel slipping from her shoulder, her books and papers spilling to the brick path. She squats, flustered, her knees bruised as a child's. "I'm sorry," she's saying as I stoop to help her. "I'm such a klutz," she's saying.

What I know of Helen is what I know of any of the scholarship girls, or have guessed. They are close enough to what I once was though entirely different—their mother is a seamstress, their father a shopkeeper or teacher. They come from the Lower East Side, or Queens, or parts of the Bronx to which I've never been: there's a community there, apparently. There's always a community, and she, the girl, is somewhat known within it. She's the smart girl, the girl in glasses—chicken or egg, thinks the poor thing. What came first? The smarts or the glasses?

After school she reads on the top step of the stoop or she works in the shop, a book on her lap, and during school she keeps her knees locked tight beneath the wooden desk, pushing her pencil point into the lines of her paper when the others are roughhousing. They will get demerits, she has said so many times she no longer says it and she could cry she wants so bad to make things right. She has already finished her report, besides, and now carries it with her secondhand books in her satchel, the glue-paste still wet from the discarded *National Geographic*s and *Life*s she had found—a whole stack!—next to the garbage cans. She had been doing her brother's job, again, taking the trash out.

At Barnard she wears her scholarship on her sleeve, sewn in the coarseness of her cotton dress, a hand-me-down from a mother who thought she might just sew a satin bow, or a felt poodle to spice it up. Please, she had said to her mother. Don't.

These scholarship girls have summer internships on campus—typing, filing—every hour repaying what has been given them in tuition. They loiter about with their dark hair and thick hands, their foreign-sounding, clunky names. During lunch they sit in circles on the newly mowed lawn, or they sit alone, like Helen, reading beneath the maple. They carry brown bags with hardboiled eggs or sliced tomatoes or, occasionally, a meatloaf sandwich, salt folded into a slip of cloth, and a thermos of sweetened tea. They read dimestore romances and take a bite of an apple, chewing slowly to make it last—the apple and the good parts, crossing their legs as they read so as not to fidget.

In the school year these girls move like dark shadows within the gleam of the others who will arrive next month, the blondes who are already pinned to soldiers they write to on perfumed stationery and for whom they sit at the back of the class knitting socks, girls who come armed with trunks on wheels and dresses for dances. There will be dances, again. Dances upon dances.

"Wouldn't you rather go to the party?" I ask, returning the last sheath of paper to her.

She pushes her glasses to the bridge of her nose, then gathers up her satchel and stands. "I hate parties," she says.

"As do I," I say.

Beyond the gates the sound is deafening, down Broadway to West End, where the SROs have emptied onto the streets, the veterans and merchant marines and sailors still in their pressed whites. Someone plays a trumpet. The negroes and Italians have set up stands and are frying meat, the smells delicious. I haven't eaten, I realize, and neither has Helen, so we stop and I treat us both to sausages. She says the music makes her feel like dancing, but she's never been good at it and besides, everyone somehow has learned the Lindy Hop, and where was I? she asks me, when all this was happening?

In the library, I tell her, because she is that kind of girl and, I realize, none too pretty, her eyebrows grown thick above her eyes, and dark circles beneath them, as if permanent shadows cast from all that reading, that looking down, that sewing, because she tells me now that she is as fine a seamstress as her mother, and that, before the scholarship, Mr. Levine, who owns the factory and for whom her mother has worked for twenty-seven years, had suggested her mother take home a few pieces for her talented daughter to fiddle with. Her mother had said her talented daughter was too busy with her books and working toward her degree, and Helen pronounces *degree* in a way that sounds familiar, in the way I once would, years ago, when it was the one important thing I felt I had to say.

We sit on the bench in the little park at the fjord of Broadway and West End. We have paper plates in our laps, and for dessert, we have decided, we'll stop at Grossman's for a slice of chocolate cake, all the shops opened, the business men and women slapping their customers' backs, money slammed down on the counters stranger to stranger—everything free or a hundred dollars, it doesn't matter. Nobody cares.

Nagasaki, a city she never knew before, Helen says. The name as beautiful as *chrysanthemum*.

It's been nearly an hour. Somewhere in the Forties, Helen is wrenched into a kiss and afterward takes my hand and holds it tightly, her glasses lost, one lens crunched by a heel before they're retrieved. It's an interesting perspective, she's shouting. "I'm left-sighted," she's shouting. "My father's going to kill me."

We head east at Times Square, passing the crate poet shouting fifty cents for an epic; ten cents a haiku. Who could possibly hear him? He's bobbing on the sea of revelers, everyone chanting, "Over! Over! Over!" The word itself building like a wave, a rumba line. A sailor exchanges his hat for my own and sways before me, saluting before being swallowed back into the maelstrom, his breath too close and lingering, rank. It is all I can do not to abandon Helen and pursue the sailor and my hat, my good luck, into the surging crowd, but I don't.

Everyone has a drink, or a flask of something, or is pouring. Beyond Grand Central the sidewalk clears and I catch myself in a shop window, the sailor's hat on my head, my gray professor's bun coiled and hidden within it as a snake would be, sleeping. I am just my own face reflected in the glass: Evelyn Charlotte Townsend, professor of chemistry, Barnard College. Bear witness to this. Bear witness, I think. This day, this hour, momentous for other reasons—for what might come next more than what has been: the city at dusk newly bright and cleansed, the joy of being alive writ large.

I reach out to Helen, grabbing her into a whirl.

"It's over!" I say, Helen laughing, blind, saying, "Yes! Yes!" We find a place at the next bar and I tell Helen that I too was a scholarship girl and that I began my life again in this country and that I have a brother in California I haven't seen since I was thirteen. He could be dead or alive, I say. I tell her that I was often scared and that I made my bed, as my grandmother would say, and that there but for the grace of God, as she would also say, and that I often wished for more, or rather, other things, and that was it, wasn't it? The wishing? And that this day has affected me oddly, a historical day, as if all of us are passengers on the same boat knowing soon we will be asked to get off—

Helen can't hear a word, I know, nor can I because the crowds wash in and out, surging, receding, the entire city a stormy sea. We hold on. A radio on a high shelf plays a big-band tune or repeats the news of the Japanese surrender, of Hirohito's disgrace, the entire country bleeding and ruined in two magnificent strokes, says the announcer. This is history, he shouts, as if, even from the perch of his stool in his soundproof booth, he is well aware of the volume of the crowds, the complete pandemonium.

The long bar has been polished to a wooden shine: bottles like so many tenpins mirrored back to us. We shell peanuts and pop them in our mouths, waiting for quiet, again, to be heard. Helen says she's getting used to not seeing, though she squints a bit. It makes her feel brave, she says.

"What?" I say.

"Brave," she shouts. Then, Was I ever in love? Did I ever love? she wants to know, and what can I tell her? That I loved my mother, once, though I did not cry when she died and that I believe I loved Father Fairfield, his thin wrists and beautiful lips and the scarf he insisted on keeping around his neck, presents in his business so few, he said. I have loved numbers since before I can remember and the click of the mind and the bloody smell of ink, and I do love Stephen Pope, and even Helen and the other girls for all they do not know nor yet can understand, though what I love is not the love of which Helen speaks, is not what a woman's love should be or look like, absent, as it is, a family, a husband.

What Helen means is have I ever married. And what she wants to tell me is what has happened to her that very day, and that it's still hard for her to believe but just this very day, this afternoon, in fact, he had proposed. It was the news she had been coming to tell me in my office. The news! she said. He's not going after all. The time is right, he had said, and I picture Helen's young man, confetti on his shoulders, in his short hair, on his polished shoes. "Marry me," he had said.

"What happened to medical school?" I shout, knowing, as I do, what propels me.

"What?" she says.

Kate Walbert

"A doctor," I shout. "I thought you were going to be a doctor."

"I am!" Helen says, squinting.

To Helen I am a blur, the vague outline of a woman too old to understand.

I raise my glass. "Good luck," I say, drinking, as Helen, blindly, smiles.

ELIZABETH "LIZ" ANNE BARRETT

New York City, New York, 2007

Matilda's mother apologizes for calling so late but she wonders whether Suzanne might be free for a playdate? Like, tomorrow?

"Matilda's had a cancellation," she says.

Liz searches the kitchen drawer for Suzanne's Week-at-a-Glance. It's ten already and she's had her wine; down the hall the baby nurse, Lorna, is asleep with the twins and Suzanne; Paul's out of town. What the hell is Matilda's mother's name, anyway? Faith, Frankie, Fern—

"We could do an hour," Liz says. "We have piano at four-thirty."

She can picture her clearly: a single woman who hovers in the school hallways wearing the look that Liz has come to associate with certain mothers—a mixture of doe-eyed expectancy and absolute terror, as if at any minute they might be asked to recite the Pledge of Allegiance or the current policy on plagiarism; the school one of those places where mothers are kept on their toes and organized into various committees for advance and retreat, their children's education understood as a battlefield that must be properly assaulted. Didn't she just see her last week at the enlightenment session? A talk given by a Dr. Roberta Friedman, professor of something, entitled, "Raising a Calm Child in the Age of Anxiety: Or, How to Let Go and Lighten Up!" But now, for the life of her, Liz can't remember whether she and Matilda's mother exchanged two words, just the way Matilda's mother balanced on the edge of her folding chair taking notes, the intentional gray streak (intellectual?) of her cropped hair, the fury of her pen.

"Oh, God, that's great," Matilda's mother is saying. "I just need to keep Matilda from losing her gourd."

"I understand," Liz says.

"Do you?" says Matilda's mother. "You do?"

Her name is Fran, apparently. Fran Spalding. Liz has looked her up in the confidential, you-lose-it-you're screwed parent-and-faculty directory. She and Matilda live across the park on West Eighty-sixth Street. Does anyone not live uptown? Liz wants to know, but she asks the question only of herself, so there's no answer, just the relative quiet of her studio—a big loft in what was once considered Chinatown. Liz spends most mornings here spinning clay into pots and teacups and dessert plates. At this hour there's little interruption, the occasional rumble of a garbage truck and the low chatter of the radio and her own mind: Fran Spalding, daughter Matilda, West Eighty-sixth. They'll go today after school. They'll cross the park in a taxi, mothers and daughters, and aim for the apartment building, 340-something, where Fran Spalding and Matilda live, and go up to the fifteenth floor, 15D, she knows—the address listed in the second section of the directory, the front pages clotted with emergency numbers and please-put-in-a-place-of-prominence evacuation routes.

It's a playdate; Suzanne duly apprised of the plan this morning as she and Liz waited for the school bus on Lafayette. Around them, Cooper Union students bunched up like black flies, bluebottles in window corners, at every "Don't Walk."

"Who?" Suzanne says.

"Matilda. She's in your class. You know. She wears striped shirts."

"Does she have a cat?" Suzanne asks.

"I have no idea."

"Does she want to play My Little Ponies?"

Liz looks down at her daughter. "Who doesn't?" she says.

Suzanne shoves her hands in her pockets and swings one leg. She leans against a filthy meter tattooed with stickers advertising things: 800 numbers for important advice; someone staying positive with HIV.

"I'll go," Suzanne says, as if going were a question.

"Great!" says Liz. "Here comes the bus!"

The school bus is the big yellow kind, exactly like the one Liz once rode to elementary school, in that faraway place, that faraway land known as rural Maryland. Here, in Lower Manhattan, the bus seems too large, a dinosaur lurching through the veering bicycles and throngs of pedestrians, the construction cones and smoking manholes; a relic of a thing, a dirtied yellow shell, an empty chrysalis whose butterfly has flown the coop. Inside, a handful of children are spread front to back, their expressionless faces gazing out the smeared windows, their ears plugged. Her own school bus had burst with noise and the boys who wouldn't move over and then, later, would.

The bus stops; its doors open. Liz releases Suzanne's hand and waits as she ascends the high steps and disappears down the aisle. In an instant, she reappears in the window seat closest to Liz, her backpack beside her like a twin. Liz waves and smiles; that she has refused to buy headphones and the machines into which they fit remains a constant source of outrage to her daughter, though on this morning Suzanne seems happy enough, smiling back, crossing her eyes and sticking out her tongue as the doors close and the school bus lurches on.

"First, the golden rule: Never compare your own childhood experiences with those of your children," Dr. Friedman had said, her glasses pushed to the tip of her nose. "This is a particular parenting no-no to which women are more prone. Stop gnawing the bone, ladies. History is behind us, or at least it's over, and besides, this is a fruitless exercise, unhealthy and counterproductive. Best to live in the now, to look forward. Yes, you must remain alert; but you must also, whenever possible, accentuate the positive, express joy. Who

Kate Walbert

but we women can smooth the surface? Who but we can make things nice?"

Liz pounds the clay on the wheel and straightens her miner's cap, a figment of her imagination but one that works relatively well in focusing her thoughts away from the business of children and onto the clay. The twins are presumably in the park with Lorna, sleeping in their double stroller or being pushed, side by side, in the swings meant for babies. Lorna is a pro. She will have bundled them up and thought to bring nourishment—formula or the breast milk Liz pumps every evening; her breasts have hit their expiration date, she thinks. And Suzanne is safely in school, repeating the colors of the vegetables in Spanish or sitting at a small round table having what's known as Snack: individual packages of Cheez-Its (they've all complained!), or free-of-hydrogenated-oils-and-corn-syrup-though-possibly-manufactured-in-a-factory-traced-with-nuts animal crackers. The point is, Liz has five hours before she needs to take the subway uptown: five whole hours. It is nothing and everything. It could stretch out before her like an eternity if she has the will, or it could evaporate in a single moment.

Concentrate, she thinks.

In the bright light of the cap, Liz sees the spinning clay take form and her own hands, aged, fingernails bitten to the quick. She has written Fran Spalding's cell-phone number across her knuckles, in case she forgets, or there's a problem, or the world blows its cork: a possibility, a probability, apparently, but for now she's going to concentrate. She's not going to think about that.

"Ladies and gentlemen, this is an important message from the New York City Police Department," says the subway voice over the loudspeaker five hours later. Liz stands half in, half out of the subway car, a new habit; she always waits until the last passengers have pushed past before she fully commits to sitting down.

"Keep your belongings in sight at all times. If you see a suspicious package or activity on the platform or train, do not keep it to yourself. Tell a police officer or an MTA employee.

"Remain alert, and have a safe day," the voice adds as the doors shut.

Now they are on their way to the West Side, the taxi barreling across Central Park, through its odd scattering of tunnels; blocks of stone rise on either side of the road as if the taxi were plummeting through earth. Above loom the barren trees, leafless and gray, or the blotched white of sycamores; once, eons ago it seems now, before the twins were born, orange flags were unfurled along this same route. Then, thousands of people, all of them vaguely smiling, had wandered the paths like pilgrims in a dream. No one appears to be smiling now. They hurry along, wrapped in their coats, the day leaden, darkening; an *Ethan Frome* day, Liz used to say in college, to be clever, though she wasn't, particularly, unable to decipher the strange manners and customs of the Northeast. She hasn't thought of that in years.

Fran pays the driver, while Liz, in back, unbuckles Suzanne and Matilda, leaning over them to push open the door. "On the curb," she's saying. "Watch your step," she's saying. "Grab your gloves." Fran gestures for them to follow her into the building entrance, where two men in uniform hold open the large glass doors, bowing slightly as Fran passes.

"Partner!" one of them says, high-fiving Matilda. "Who's your buddy?"

"Michael," Fran says, arrested at the "WELCOME" threshold. "This is Matilda's friend, Susan."

"Suzanne," Liz says; she can't help it, raw nerve.

"Of course," Fran is saying.

"Buddy bear," Michael says to Matilda. "Look at you."

They look. How can they not? Everywhere there are mirrors, reflecting them, reflecting Michael and the other guy, reflecting the bounty and the grandeur of it all—potted green plants with white lights, garlands, a cone of poinsettia and even, on a pedestal between the elevator banks, an elaborately carved stone urn containing—what? Liz wonders. Dead tenants?

"This is lovely," Liz says.

"It's home," Fran says. She rings for the elevator, the girls crowding next to her. In an instant there's the ping, and then the doors slide open. Another man in uniform smiles as they step in; there is a small chair in the corner for sitting, though he clearly prefers to stand.

"Hey, Matty," he says. "How's the Go-Go?"

Go-Go, Fran explains, is their cat who recently contracted a hot spot. A hot spot, she tells them, is an itch that can't be scratched.

"Wow," Liz says.

They rise in mechanical wonder and then stop, abruptly, on eleven, where the elevator doors slide open to no one.

"False alarm," the man in the uniform says, releasing the doors and driving them onward, upward. They all stand stock still.

"Are you allergic?" Matilda says to Suzanne.

"The cat," Fran says to Suzanne.

"Are you allergic to cats?" Matilda says. She wears pink plastic barrettes and a striped shirt underneath a pink jumper.

"Suzanne," Liz says. "Did you hear—"

"No," Suzanne says. She hunches beneath her huge backpack, carried solely for fashion, or just in case. In it now, Liz happens to know, is a palm-sized notepad on which Suzanne draws the details of her day and a purple-lipsticked Bratz doll that she treasures, received on her last birthday from Paul's mother, who, Paul said, meant well.

"Lots of people are," Matilda says.

The elevator stops.

"North Pole," says the man in the uniform.

"Thank you," says Fran.

"Thank you," says Liz.

"Thank you," says Matilda.

"Thank you," says Suzanne, walking behind Liz and tripping her, accidentally on purpose.

"Suzanne," Fran's voice soars in from ahead. "How do you feel about strudel?"

But neither Suzanne nor Matilda is listening, or hungry, for that matter; released from the grip of the elevator, the girls run down the poorly lit hallway playing some sort of imaginary game, knocking into doors and taking corners at high speed.

"Matilda Beth," Fran yells after them. "That's one." She pauses. "Don't let me get to two."

Matilda stops and grabs Suzanne's hand, pulling her toward what must be D—an unassuming door with a child's drawing taped over its peephole. It is always the same, Liz thinks, in these pictures: the mismatched ears, the round eyes, the name scrawled across one corner. The girls are six years old and braided, the days of the week stitched on their underpants. They wear seamless socks and rubber-soled shoes, and both are missing two teeth, though not the same ones; each has been read *Charlotte's Web* and *The Boxcar Children*, the first a story of a pig on a farm and its friendship with a spider, the second a story of children, orphans, living happily alone in the woods, making do with rusted spoons pulled from the dump and the occasional cracked cup of milk.

"Suzanne," Liz says. "Is this a gold star day?" She has spied Suzanne twisting her finger up her nose and refers to a deal between the two that sometimes results in better behavior but more often does not.

Once in the apartment, Matilda leads Suzanne to her room, where they settle beneath a green canopy of gauze playing My Little Ponies. Liz returns to the living room with Fran, whose gray streak, she learns, is natural and who works at home during school hours, copyediting and proofreading documents for a legal firm. From time to time, the girls interrupt them, flying into the living room in leotards or ballerina skirts and, once, nothing at all, at which point Fran calls Matilda aside and speaks to her in a voice that Liz has heard only from single mothers or from mothers with numerous children—women who simply do not have the time or the patience for the monkey business that everyone else puts up with, they have told her; once, even, she heard the voice from a mother who said she just placed herself in the hands of Jesus. So maybe it's the voice of Jesus, Liz thinks now, admiring it; her own, she knows, entirely lacks authority, as if she were questioning each verdict she might pronounce.

"More tea?" Fran asks.

"Thank you," Liz says, following her back into the kitchen, where they wait with great anticipation for the water to boil, watching the kettle's curved spout, its shiny, smudged lid, as if they had never seen anything quite so fascinating in their lives.

"We are living in the Age of Anxiety," Dr. Friedman said, "and here we sit at the epicenter, the Ground Zero, if you will." She looked up and over those glasses at all of them, the throng of mothers, the few stay-at-home dads or those fathers whose schedules allowed them to be flexible—men in T-shirts, shorts, and sturdy boots, their hairy legs oddly comforting, as if, at a moment's notice, they could sweep the whole group onto their shoulders and hoist them out the window. Many of the women in the circle appeared to Liz to be close to tears, though some were more difficult to read, writing with expensive pens, their briefcases balanced against their slim ankles, their hair blown smooth. Dr. Friedman surveyed the room, clearly attempting to make eye contact with the closest suspect, unfortunately Janey Fitch, wall-eyed and so shy she looked ready to faint.

"Everywhere we go are the reminders of where we are, reminders that New York is no longer the place it once was. I don't think the reminders need to be chronicled here. The school has briefed you on contingencies, and your emergency-contact cards have been filed in triplicate. Each child has an individual first-aid kit and a protective mask.

"Still and still, you might say, the question remains: What can you do right now, on this day, at this hour, in this moment?"

Here Dr. Friedman looked up again and smiled, the smile so studied as to be disarming, as if Liz weren't really looking at a woman smiling, but at a portrait of a woman smiling.

"Take a deep breath," she said, exhaling loudly. "Smell the roses," she said, inhaling loudly. "Relax."

The women slouched a bit in their folding chairs, attempting to follow Dr. Friedman's advice. Liz imagined that if Dr. Friedman were next to suggest that they all stand and do a few jumping jacks, most would leap to the job.

"Now," Dr. Friedman said, wiggling her shoulders. "I'm going to give you all some homework. This is an exercise that I've found works very well with my patients. It's simple, really. How many of you keep a journal?"

A few hands shot up, Marsha Neuberger waving as if desperate to be picked.

"That's fine, that's fine," says Dr. Friedman. "I only wanted to get an idea. Anyway, what I'm going to suggest is that you all try keeping what I call an anxiety journal; just like if any of you have ever tried to diet and kept a food journal—"

Anxiety journal like food journal, Liz would have written in her notes, if she had remembered paper and pen. *Bemused laughter,* she would have added.

"—where you wrote down your caloric intake. Your anxiety journal will be the place where you write down everything that makes you feel nervous, or anxious, throughout the day. Don't worry about how it sounds. This is an invitation to look inward, to think of no one but yourselves, to access, perhaps, who you really are and how you really are—no cheating. Truly. No one is going to read the journal but you." This Dr. Friedman said *emphatically,* Liz would have noted, whipping off her glasses and looking up, avoiding Janey Fitch but generally trying to reassure each and every one of them.

"Promise," she added.

Liz looks from her steaming tea to Fran. Fran is describing her terrific luck in finding the apartment, falling into it, desperate, after fleeing San Francisco with Matilda and a few pieces of luggage. Now, as a single mother, she keeps a tight rein on things, she says. "Have you noticed?"

Liz is unsure what she should have noticed, so she blows on her tea and shakes her head.

"There was a burglary," Fran says. "In San Francisco. After that we felt like we had to get out. I mean, I did. I left Matilda's father. Richard. And moved back East."

"Oh."

"Strudel?" Fran says, sliding a plate across the counter.

"Oh, gosh, no thanks."

"I've sliced some apples for the girls."

"Great," Liz says, knowing Suzanne won't touch them—the edges, minutes after being sliced, too brown.

"What about you?" Fran says.

"Oh," Liz says. "We moved from Boston. We were in graduate school, Paul and I, and then we moved here—Paul works in television, children's television—and then we had Suzanne and now the twins, James and Colin, but I'm getting back into it. Art. I'm a potter, actually. I work with clay."

"In vitro?" asks Fran.

"I'm sorry?"

"The twins," Fran says. "In vitro?"

Liz nods.

"Your eggs?"

Liz blows on her tea. "Nope. We had to shell out twenty thousand dollars; we did it through the alumni association."

"Smart eggs," Fran says.

"I didn't really care. Paul felt strongly about that, you know. He didn't want to adopt."

"Men rarely do."

They sit in the living room, on opposite sides of the sectional.

"I think our girls really get along," Fran says.

"Yes," Liz says.

"After the burglary, you know, Matilda had trouble making friends. I mean, she played by herself most of the time. Made up stories. I'd take her to a birthday party or something, and all the other children would be running around and screaming and playing tag or smacking the piñata, that kind of thing, and Matilda would be sitting by herself involved in some fairy-tale game. It was embarrassing, frankly."

Liz can't help thinking that taupe is the entirely wrong color for this room, high as they are above the city. Excellent light, the listing would say. Light and air; airy light; sun-drenched, sun-gorged, sun-soaked, rush to your sun-kissed oasis! There are windows everywhere, and those radiators that line the walls. Fran should clear them off and paint the place—something dramatic, terra-cotta, or saffron yellow.

"This was in San Francisco, where everything is, well, healthy, do you know? There's always someone talking about loving-kindness. I couldn't stand it after a while. We just got on a plane and flew away. Anyway, that's it. I'm here now for good. I mean, I grew up here, in the city, but it's different now, of course."

There is a bit of a pause; comfortable enough, Liz thinks. The truth is, she's enjoying herself. It's a playdate, she finds herself thinking; I'm on a date for play.

"Would you like a drink?" Fran says. "I'd have one if you would. Carpe diem, or whatever. Anyway, screw tea, we're grown-ups, right?"

"OK," Liz says. "Sure. Great. Yes."

"Excellent!" Fran says.

From behind Matilda's door comes a shriek of giggles.

"Besides, they're having fun!" Fran says.

"So are we!" Liz says.

Fran disappears to the kitchen and Liz stands to stretch a bit, to look out the windows. The apartment faces west, she believes, though she gets turned around at these heights. She still isn't used to apartment views or high floors, and the ease with which you can see other lives: how even now, across from here, a boy sits reading at a dining-room table while an old woman—a nurse? a grandmother? a nanny?—moves around him, straightening up, stepping in and then out of Liz's sight. A diorama, they are; what you might see at the American Museum of Natural History: early twenty-first century, NYC, USA. They're dead, actually—stuffed mammals, the old woman on some sort of moving track.

And what of Fran in the kitchen? Liz in the living room? Urban/suburban women circa 2007 participating in/on playdate, an urban/suburban ritual intended to alleviate boredom/loneliness among children/women while encouraging/controlling social engagement—

"Chilled?" Fran yells.

"Wonderful," Liz yells. She turns away from the windows; pokes around the taupe room. On a wide bookshelf are the usual histories and paperbacks and framed photographs: an infant Matilda; an earnest-looking boy in mortarboard and gown, Richard?; a teenage Fran standing before a fountain, her hair not yet streaked with gray but solely black, her posture sophisticated, worldly—she's in college, possibly, or a Manhattan high school. I live on a narrow island, her posture says. I live at the center of the world.

On the secretary are bills and Post-it notepads and loose receipts and whatnot. Liz has a strong feeling, a hot spot, an itch to be scratched, and, sure enough, there it is among them: Fran's anxiety journal. It's as she expected, a steno notebook generally used for reportage. Liz resists for only a moment.

"Voila!" Fran says. Liz turns to see her carrying a tray, the TV-dinner kind; it makes Liz anxious.

"What have you got?" Fran says. She's now pouring and doesn't notice.

"Oh, nothing," says Liz. "Your anxiety journal."

Fran stops. "You were reading it?"

"Oh God, no. Of course not. I just saw it here and picked it up. I mean, I was thinking, Good for you, and remembering that I've been meaning to buy one. I'd write, 'TV-dinner tray.'"

"What?"

"'TV-dinner tray.' Like the one you're holding. It makes me nervous and I can't tell you why."

Fran looks down. "It belonged to Richard. He liked to eat in front of the news."

"Exactly."

"Maybe it's the news you associate it with."

"Maybe."

"See? She had a point," Fran says. "Cheers!" They toast and sip the wine, red, which is delicious, Liz says—she never thinks to drink it chilled. "You should," Fran says. She takes the anxiety journal and tucks it beneath one of the sectional cushions. "To playdates!" she says, toasting again.

It's near dinnertime and Suzanne and Matilda are getting hungry; they haven't heard a peep from their mothers. Pinky Pie and Sparkle Dust have been to the castle about a zillion times; they've flown in the blue balloon, late for the costume ball, and then arrived, the My Little Pony theme song playing as Pinky Pie and Sparkle Dust twirl on the special pink plastic revolving disc within the castle walls. Suzanne lies on her back, pedaling her legs in the air, her finger working her nose. Matilda is reprimanding her imaginary sister, Beadie.

"Get down from there," Matilda says. Beadie perches dangerously close to the window ledge, threatening to jump, and even though she has wings on her back and little ones at her ankles, Matilda pleads with her to stop.

Kate Walbert

"Good-bye, my friend," Beadie says. "Good-bye!"

Beadie takes a tremendous leap and falls, tumbling, toward the street. Matilda screams an imaginary scream, though Beadie, she knows, won't splat; she'll fly with her little wings right back to Matilda's room. Still, Matilda feels scared.

"Help! Help!" Matilda yells. "Thief! Help! Thief!"

The door swings open.

"Do not even start with that," Fran says. "It makes me insane." Behind Fran, Liz looks in. "Suzanne," she says. "Gold star day, remember?"

Suzanne pulls her finger out of her nose.

"Are you girls happy?" Fran says.

"We're hungry," they say.

"We're staying for dinner, how's that!" Liz says.

The girls hop up and down holding hands; they wear only their underwear.

Fran wades through stuffed animals and clothes and artwork and books, to the stack of pillows and blankets in the center of Matilda's room, excavating until she finds the small table buried beneath. They were making a fort.

"Jesus," she says, flushed. "Can you believe all this crap?"

"Yes," Liz says.

Fran sets down a tray of chicken nuggets and calls the girls over. "OK, ladies," she says. "Which princess?"

"Jasmine," Matilda says.

"Oh, for God's sake," Fran says, rotating the plates.

"Ketchup?" Liz says. The girls nod, and she lurches toward them, ready to squirt.

"I can't say that anything really *happened* with Richard," Fran says. "It was just, you know, the feeling." She lies on the floor in the now

190

dim light of the apartment, balancing her wineglass on her chest, her feet propped on the sectional. "The elephant-in-the-room feeling."

Liz can't remember the last time she drank so much wine in the afternoon; usually, she waits until Suzanne's asleep, the twins with Lorna in the nursery, Paul back at the office (the demanding life of a children's television executive!) before pouring her first glass. Then she might have another, and another, enough to erase the day, or the parts of it she doesn't want to remember: Suzanne standing with her backpack on Lafayette, the neon-scrawled windows of the gay bar next to the bus stop, the public-service poster showing an unattended bag, like an old-fashioned doctor's bag, shoved beneath a seat.

Fran rolls over on one elbow. "Did you ever ruin your life for a feeling?" she says.

"I don't know," Liz says. "I hope not."

She has closed her eyes to watch the tiny red pricks of light behind her eyelids. It's a trick she likes to do, a habit. She counts them, pretends they're sparks. She's combustible, perhaps—she's burning up.

"I miss Richard," Fran is saying. "I miss him every day. There's nobody to tell anything to anymore."

Liz opens her eyes and the sparks die out; she is back where she was, things reassembling around her—bookshelf, secretary, radiator, carpet, floor lamps.

"I mean, there never was anybody to talk to, really," Fran is saying. "But I thought there was. For a while I used to. Do you know what I mean?"

"Yes," Liz says, closing one eye and then the other; it changes her perspective. "I think so," she says. She is a highly trained artist, she could tell you. She has training up the wazoo. She got a fellowship and there were many, many applicants.

"Do the others look like you?" Fran asks.

"What?" Liz says.

"The twins. Do they look like you? Or, you know, like the smarter, younger egg woman?"

Liz laughs. She doesn't mean to, but she laughs and tips over the nearly empty wineglass that she forgot she'd balanced beside her. She's a well-trained klutz is what she is, a social miscreant fluent in art history, trained in art history. "Sorry, sorry," she says. "I did it again."

"Forget it," Fran says.

Liz blots the wet spot with her shirtsleeve. "Not at all, is the thing," she says. "The twins don't look like either one of us. They're blond and blue-eyed for one. I mean, adorable. Absolutely adorably wonderful, but people think they're adopted."

"That's so funny," Fran says.

"I forgot to laugh," Liz says.

"But you're lucky," Fran says.

"God, I know," Liz says. "I am in the ninety-ninth percentile of luck."

"You tested out," Fran says.

"I am among the gifted and talented."

From Matilda's room there's the sound of a thud.

"You guys happy?" Fran yells.

"We're OK!," Matilda yells back.

"Suzanne?" Liz yells. "Are you still there?"

"I'm here," Suzanne says.

"I thought she might have disappeared," Liz says. "Sometimes I think she'll just disappear."

"They're fine," Fran says. "More?"

"Just a skosh," Liz says.

"A skosh?" Fran says.

"Japanese for 'a little,'" Liz says. "*Sukoshi.*"

"Oh," Fran says. "Do you speak it?"

"My dad was in the service. POW. I used to think it was Yiddish. He'd say, 'Just a skosh' whenever someone offered him wine. He was like that. A little, I don't know, snobby. I miss him," Liz says.

"Your dad?"

"Yes."

"And your mom?"

"She left him for Florence Nightingale."

"The nurse?" Fran says.

"Please. Don't say, 'nurse,' say, 'visionary' or something. Say 'rabble-rouser.' Apparently I'm from a long line," Liz says.

"Cool," Fran says. "Here." She pours; they've finished one bottle and opened another; what they are celebrating they have no idea.

"Lemme at it," Liz says. She crawls along the sectional on all fours. She hasn't been able to locate the floor-lamp switch, but it doesn't matter; she's a cat who can see in the dark. "It was here, I saw it. You took it away from me."

"Oh, God!" Fran shrieks. "The whole thing is so stupid. Please. You're going to hate me," Fran says.

"Are you kidding?" Liz says. "You're my new best friend."

"You have to promise," Fran says.

"I promise, I promise," Liz says.

"Not to laugh. Really. No. I mean it. Don't laugh. You're going to laugh. I know it. I can just—"

"Bluebirds honor," Liz says. "Bluebird, Brownie, Girl Scout. God, can you believe me?"

"Wow," Fran says. "Are you serious?"

"I'm always serious," Liz says. "I'm never not serious. I remain alert."

"Do you think if we lived like, in Montana or something, things would be, I don't know, different?" Fran says.

"Ta-da!" Liz says.

"Shit," Fran says.

"You said I could."

"Go ahead, just please. You promised."

"I'll be dead serious," Liz says. "I am a deadly serious, dead-serious, never-not-serious person. I repeat. I remain alert."

What is she saying? She has no idea, really, though it feels good to speak, the words tumbling out of her mouth and knocking around in the darkening room, high above the city where she has spent the afternoon with a new friend, a sophisticated friend, a woman who grew up here, a woman with a streak of natural gray, a divorced single mother with a legal, razor-sharp mind. And now look! The promise of the journal in her hands! Fran made notes! She caught all the things that Liz missed—the meeting room overheated and crowded, the acoustics so bad it was impossible to concentrate. And afterward—this is now Liz talking, Liz babbling—Dr. Friedman had been so mobbed, so impossible to get to, that she had actually waited in the school lobby and followed her out, down Madison then over to Lexington, the subway entrance there, Dr. Friedman walking with such robotic purpose that she quite literally couldn't catch up before Dr. Friedman descended down the stairs to the subway.

Liz turns to the journal. "It must be done," she says.

"OK," says Fran, who has moved to sit cross-legged on the floor in front of her.

Liz opens the journal to read, but the truth is, it's difficult to see what's written in the near-dark, and her eyes have started to go. She brings the page to her face, and squints:

1. *Thieves*
2. *Crowds*
3. *School*
4. *Shadows*
5. *Playdates*
6. *Lunchrooms*
7. *Helicopters*
8. *Anniversaries*
9. *Night*

"What?" Fran's saying. "What? Oh, God. What did I write?" She moves closer to Liz, scoots in, so that Liz imagines Fran might crawl into her lap as Suzanne does to practice reading in the way she's been instructed at school: Read It Once to See; Read It Twice to Comprehend; Read It Again to Fully Absorb Its Meaning.

Go-Go appears from nowhere. He scratches and scratches, gnawing at the hot spot on his leg. "Stop!" Fran says, clapping her hands. "Stop!"

Liz closes the journal and stands up a bit unsteadily. "Jesus, it's dark," she says. "I can't believe it got so late." She hands the journal back to Fran. "I promised Lorna I'd be back earlier."

"Right," Fran says, taking the journal. "God, I'm sorry."

"Oh, no. This was fun. I mean, this was really fun, and the girls—"

"They seem to hit it off," Fran says.

"Suzanne!" Liz yells in the direction of Matilda's room, the shut door. "Shit. We had piano. I totally forgot."

"Oh my God. I'm really sorry," Fran says.

"Don't apologize. Suzanne hates piano. Anyway, it wasn't your—are these my shoes?"

"Here," Fran says. "They're with Suzanne's backpack."

"Suzanne!" Liz yells.

"It's impossible to get them—"

"Suzanne, now!"

The door opens slowly and the girls, or what looks like shadows of the girls, drift out, fall out, into the hallway.

"Are Thursdays better?" Fran is saying.

"I'm sorry?"

"Thursdays. We could do Thurs—"

Liz feels a kind of draining away, as if the ebb of the twilight has returned to the night all that is loose, unmoored. She has always fought the feeling of this time of day, when her father would remain in his garden and her mother did what mothers did then—in the house, at the club. Caroline was gone, or almost, driving here and there, permit first then license. James had left for England and Liz, the youngest by far—a mistake, her mother once admitted, born out of momentary indecision, an uncharacteristic recklessness—would ride her bike up and down the driveway, waiting for her father to call her, to tell her to come quick, to see the misshapen gourd, or the earthworm, or the potato bug before it got too dark, and she would. She would pedal like the wind to get to what her father held: a miracle, he would say, no doubt quoting Browning or some other poet no one read anymore or even remembered. Look, he would say. Life, he would say. And this placed her squarely in the world, kept her from being sucked down.

Liz ties up Suzanne's sneakers, yanks the laces tight. "I'm sorry about Richard," she says, straightening.

"Oh, it's fine," says Fran. "Really. Matilda and I are a team, aren't we, Matty?"

"Rah rah," Liz says.

"Thursdays," Fran says. She has found Suzanne's jacket beneath the coat rack and now holds it out for her. "We're going to do Thursdays!" she says to Matilda.

"Let me check at home," Liz says. "I never know which end is up."

"Oh," Fran says.

"Thank Matilda," Liz says to Suzanne.

"Thank you," Suzanne says.

"Thank Fran," Liz says.

"Thank you," Suzanne says.

Liz clutches Suzanne's hand on the subway platform. There is work being done somewhere, and the trains are running intermittently, though a taxi or a bus is out of the question—the traffic insane. The twins have had their baths and are sleeping, Liz has heard from Lorna. Everything is fine, she has been told.

"Did you have a good time?" Liz says, squatting so that she can be eye level.

"Uh-huh," Suzanne says.

"Is Matilda nice?" Liz says.

"Uh-huh," Suzanne says.

"Does she like to play My Little Ponies?" Liz says.

Suzanne pulls on the loose straps of her backpack, a filched Pinkie Pie, its tail braided, its eyes pocked by a pen point, now zipped into one of the many compartments.

"I don't know," Suzanne says. She turns away from her mother and stares out over the empty tracks. "No," she adds, quietly, though who could hear anything for the screech of the approaching train. In the rush, Liz teeters, grabbing Suzanne into a hug, her hands gripping Suzanne's thin shoulders for balance. "But it was a gold star day, baby," she says as the crowd swells over them. "Wasn't it?"

DOROTHY TREVOR TOWNSEND

Wardsbury, England, 1914

Hilde comes more often now to Dorothy, appearing out of nowhere to sit in the corner of the hospital room, to stare, her bruised face and pretty hands, her large eyes—once, even, she rose from rain, drifting in with the breeze of it; someone had propped open the window with a stick.

"Hilde?"

"Yes, Mrs. Townsend?" The attendant shakes Dorothy's shoulder.

"The lilies," Dorothy says, blinking Hilde gone. "They reek."

CAROLINE TOWNSEND
BARRETT DEEL

Caroline discovers her mother's blog during one of those middle-of-the-night nights when she can no longer sleep and thinks that she should just read, or go online and research Dora Maar, for Christ's sake, her daughter Dorothy announcing earlier on the telephone that she had been studying the poems of Picasso's sad, troubled mistress and that she would like to be known, henceforth, as Dora.

"You know, Mother," Dorothy-now-Dora said, "as in *Woman with Two Faces*?"

Caroline knew the picture: the large, almond-shaped eyes and the nose askew and the long, long neck and the face coming out of the face—weren't there often two women's faces?—in profile and not, listening and not listening. She could remember a long, long neck, she said, but then, didn't everyone Picasso painted have a long, long neck?

"Are you kidding me?" Dora said. "Knock-knock? Hello? Gertrude Stein? A rose is a rose is a rose?"

"What?" Caroline said.

"Stein looked like a frog," Dora said. "She was beautiful. She had about a million lovers—"

"Stein? I thought she loved Alice—"

"Dora Maar! Mother!"

"Oh, right."

"Forget it," Dora said, and followed this with that voluminous silence well known to mothers, the everything-you-should-have-understood-and-did-not-guess/intuit/deduce silence. With Dora at college, Caroline knew she had to be careful. The silence could sift down too easily, like molten ash, and solidify to rock with a hard rain: no phone calls, no e-mails, just the unbearable weight of a daughter's absence. Hadn't the young dean of students warned them exactly of this?

"Your children might be here," he had said, standing at the lectern in the Orientation Room and speaking, from all indications, extemporaneously, "but don't let them be *gone*. This is CC time: critical communication. And you're, like, Ronald Reagan. And they're Gorbachev." The young dean of students wore a dark suit and a lavender tie and, according to the Parents First program scrunched in Caroline's sweaty hand, had just last year received a master's in communication with a minor in juvenile rhetoric from Harvard University. Really? Caroline had found herself thinking. Juvenile rhetoric? Harvard University?

Caroline sits at her desk, the dim glow from the computer screen lighting her face to a ghoulish mask. Around her the things of her study—paperweights, framed photographs, filing cabinets, a lucky hat, seem arrested in their forms, as if, at any minute, someone might flick a switch and release them.

Dora Maar, Dora Maar, Dora Maar, Caroline reads, scrolling down a long line of Doras: the history of, the significance of, the importance of, the papers letters biographies articles theatrical works representations of; there were 341,288 entries for Dora Maar and if she so chose, Caroline could narrow her search to look for even more, including a recording of Dora Maar reading a passage of Cervantes. Everything linear, organized, boxed and squared, and titled. She thinks of her own time at college and the quaint little entries on the yellowed cards of the card catalogues, plugged straight through, spined with a steel rod. There had been randomness then, but didn't that lead to better things? Jesus, Caroline thinks, class of '77 for

God's sake. *Our Mothers, Ourselves*. *Ms. Magazine*. The Second Wave. Well, that did all of us a lot of good. That really knocked our socks off.

Dora Maar stares up at Caroline from the Feminist Arts&Letters: Essays on the Obvious website, her gorgeous dark eyes—stranger in the Man Ray photograph—insistent, somehow, as if Dora Maar has grown impatient with Caroline's lack of interest, her general drifting. I am not a woman accustomed to being kept waiting, Dora Maar might have said, had she been alive and not just a constellation of pixels. I would like a little consideration, she might have added. She is used to adoration or, in the words of the scholar who wrote this entry, objectification, but the truth is Caroline is no longer interested in researching Dora Maar. She finds herself typing something else: Wiliam Deel. It's a bad habit, she knows, like an itch to scratch, and still she waits, anxious for the split second he takes to load.

Do you mean William Deel?

Christ, yes, you asshole, she says to the screen, adding the missing *l* to her ex-husband's name. She hits return harder, staccato, and there he is: Bill, materialized in suit coat and pressed trousers, squared at the top of the page like a Lilliputian. He appears to be engaged in conversation, this the most recent post, from someone's journal and photographs of a company function held at a resort in the Bahamas. There are 12,297 entries for William Deel, though Caroline knows from past nights that only a few are her Billy and tonight she sees there's nothing new. She might type her own name next. She often does, rereading certain accomplishments she finds pleasing to review—scholastic honors, professional accolades, articles from the company newsletters in which her work is mentioned, the all of it, she supposed, adding up to evidence that she's done something.

Instead Caroline types in the original Dorothy. She's memorized the dozen or so entries already—her suffragette great-grandmother's place in the various footnotes of current scholarship (though she

Kate Walbert

always hopes to find further mentions, a recent book from some feminist press in Iowa or Kentucky). Perhaps for this reason she doesn't immediately notice her mother's name there among the listings, similar enough to her great-grandmother's but quieter, somehow, like a hand raised from the unlikeliest student in the back row: "A Proclamation: Ruminations on Florence Nightingale, Old Age, and Life by Dorothy Townsend Barrett, aged 78."

A Proclamation

You don't know me but that's fine. My story is not so dissimilar to yours, if you're a woman of a certain age, with children. I am a fire sign, but I have passed the point of rage and now stand on the other side looking back and wondering why I wasted so much time being angry. Why Florence Nightingale? Because she was, first and foremost, BRAVE. She made a different life. She got blood on her hands. She did not accept what she could not abide. When she finally understood that her bonds were made of straw, she broke them, or bent them, or whatever you'd do to straw. This is what she wrote in her seminal essay, "Cassandra," which I would highly recommend to those of you who have an interest in self-expression. I am seventy-eight years old. I have lost my only son. I have divorced after a marriage of fifty-odd years. I have been arrested for disorderly conduct, trespassing, and aggravated assault and were it not for my eldest, and most responsible daughter, I might still be in the slammer. I have little left in the way of me, or who I once thought I was. I am pulling myself up by my bootstraps. I am an old lady. I am moving on. I am trying to name "it," whatever "it" is. I am doing my best.

Oh, and Florence traveled, which I find admirable.

I cannot promise stellar prose, but I now value honesty of a particular kind and will reach for that and accept nothing less of myself.

—DT

Liz answers the telephone in a low whisper. Caroline hasn't thought to check the time—there's some light in the sky, she can see out the window, and she's already heard a few birds. Besides, she knows that her sister rarely sleeps, and when she does, she leaves a hand free, just in case she hears again the cacophony of sirens, or the drumming of the helicopters at such close range.

"Did I wake you?" Caroline says.

"What time is it?" Liz says.

"I thought the twins were up early."

"It's five thirty in the morning," Liz says.

"Mom's blogging."

"What?"

"I'm looking at it right now. She calls it 'A Proclamation,' like she's Patrick Henry or something."

Caroline hears Liz breathing, a mumble of something and then Liz again.

"Okay. Start over."

"Mom has a blog. Did you know? She started it three weeks ago."

"No idea."

"She has a picture of us up. The whole family. And Florence Nightingale."

"Which one?"

"In front of the tent with all the wounded. You know the famous one."

"No, us."

"The rocking chair one, where we look like the Kennedys and Petunia's at her feet."

"That's so *depressing*."

"Animals die."

"I'm talking about Mom." The heavy breath, again. "Can I call you back later? The twins were up at like two. I'm sorry. I was awake, you know, but not."

"Sure."

"I mean, thanks for calling me."

"I'll call back later."

"After seven, okay?"

"Gotcha."

"A blog. Jesus."

"She misses Dad."

"It was her choice."

"Yeah, but then he died."

Caroline hangs up, turning back to her computer. The screen saver has kicked in, and Dora stares at her from the front seat of a rented convertible, her smile barely concealing her annoyance. She'd clearly rather not pause for a photograph before driving in heels and gown, before zooming—stag!—to the prom. "They don't even call it stag anymore, Mother," she had said. "Get real."

Caroline hits the keyboard and the page appears: the family photo tagged with their birthdays and, in the case of James, their father, and Petunia, the word *deceased*. Beneath it is the famous photograph of Florence Nightingale in her peaked white hat, her uniform, by all indications, starched.

It is perhaps her tenth time reading "A Proclamation," written by DT, a woman once her mother, a blogger who has traveled through rage—Rage!—and arrived on the other side wearing black pants and pressed white shirts, serious shoes, feet firmly planted in honesty of a particular kind, her bonds nothing more than straw. A flurry of posts follow, uniformly beside the point—clearly no one understands what her mother is trying to say; what *is* her mother trying to say?— and then, nothing.

September 24, 12:20 p.m.:

Yes, I liked the thing about rage in "A Proclamation" and I too admire nurses! How would we get by without them? My question is, Where has the time gone? Is this what you mean? I too wonder

about self-expression vis-a-vis being alone and/or getting older.
And why everyone these days seems to medacate instead of
motivate! Here is the problem. When you and I were young—I too
am seventy-eight next June!—there were porches and less
expectations and we understood the value of a dollar. Keep up the
good work!

—*LuvMyKoffee*

September 27, 12:47 p.m.:

In other words, it's a bitch getting old. FYI. "Med-a-cate" is spelled
"med-i-cate."

—*Mackie45*

September 29, 1:03 p.m.:

At last! Thank you for this. The Lady with the Lamp has many more
charms than the popular interpretation gives her credit for—you
might even say that she alone dispelled the myth of women as
helpless, hapless, anemic beings confined to Victorian drawing
rooms. She refused, she wrote, to be nailed to a continuation. And
did you know that she has many hidden, devoted fans, including, if
you can believe it, Joe of the radical sixties band Country Joe and
the Fish? P.S. *Mackie45*, you are a P I L L :)

—*Confabulator*

September 29, 3:52 p.m.:

It's good to hear voices of all kinds!

—*DT*

"What's LuvMyKoffee got against medication?" Liz is asking. "I
mean, Jesus, if it weren't for Xanax, I'd be insane. She loves her coffee, doesn't she? The whole thing is nuts, actually—all those people
knowing Mom's personal details."

"Are you kidding?" Caroline says. "There's no personal anymore."

"Still," Liz says. "It's creepy."

Caroline hears a baby in the background, and then what sounds like a plate shattering on the floor. "How's things?" she says.

"Fabulous," Liz says.

"Do you have to go?" Caroline says.

"Lorna's with the babies," Liz says. "I think."

"Listen," Caroline says. "We should post something. I mean it's pathetic how nobody has said a word in weeks. I hate that she's just sitting there peering into the void. We don't even have to say it's us. We can just play along. Make up some names or handles or whatever it's called. Get the conversation going."

"What?" Liz says. "I'm sorry. Colin just spit up all over the couch."

"Never mind," Caroline says.

"Listen, let me call you back. Paul's on his way out and I've got to feed—"

"Bye!"

"Don't be pissed off."

"I'm fine. Bye!"

Caroline hangs up the telephone. Time was when she too felt that busy, when there was much to set straight before catching the train to the city. Now she has all the time in the world. She might take a bath; she could paint her toenails; she might think of her dinner and pull something out of the freezer to thaw. The train departs at 8:12, give or take, and she'll play cards or read or maybe this morning she will write Dorothy-now-Dora an old-fashioned letter, tell her that she's been thinking about it, the new name, and that she thinks it has a good ring, sophisticated, exotic, calling to mind a woman with a certain tragic artistry, or perhaps this is only what her Dora had told her, that business about Dora Maar slicing her fingers, discreetly, with a block printer's blade as Picasso and some famous friend watched from an adjacent table, this, apparently, the reason both men were drawn to her: the mutilation of her fingers, the red blood staunched by the white napkin.

The birds have started up in earnest and she can hear some kids shouting, a few of the gang heading to the school-bus stop at the bank of mailboxes near the end of her neighbor's driveway. She will wave when she drives by on her way to the train station and perhaps one or two will wave back. They are teenage boys, mostly, or appear to be, though she has no recollection of when they were younger or whether they were ever young at all. Were they her Dorothy's friends?

Thinking of her Dorothy, Caroline feels a gnawing. Or maybe it's simply loneliness. Empty Nest Syndrome, according to the young dean of students, who tossed out the wretched seventies lingo as if it actually meant something new, the all of history coming around in the width of his dorky tie and the length of his hair and the ease with which he leaned against the lectern and addressed the women gathered as Moms. She stopped listening then, though in truth she could barely hear him, pushed toward the back of the crowded Orientation Room and drifting within its collegial grandeur, its warmth.

On the walls hung portraits of previous deans, identically framed and lit by trendy, incandescently correct bulbs; dust motes floated like fairy glitter, metallic and suggestive of other worlds, around the grand Gothic windows. There, before the lecture began, Caroline watched as all the students hurried to and fro, their strides purposeful, grown-up, as if they knew they were already late for something. She had hoped to see her daughter, to catch a glimpse of her through those panes of wavy, tinted glass, the bronze sashes crisscrossing her view. A hydraulic gesture, she remembered her aged classics professor called it, the sashes similar to the swirls on Corinthian columns, prone to disappear, he said, in the swiftness of a current. A weak attempt to elevate the status of both worshipper and worshipped, he said, his face illuminated by the overhead projector, Corinthian columns reflected on his craggy cheeks.

Had the class been taught in this very same room? Doubtful, though the crisscrossed windows all looked alike at Yale, here or in any of the other rooms carved out of the labyrinth of residential colleges, each behind wrought-iron gates with elaborately rendered symbols—the hieroglyphics of men, someone called it—and tucked off of quads and corridors and stairways leading up or down.

Kate Walbert

The History of Arts and Letters, it was called, or The History of an Idea. No matter. As an undergraduate, she had been completely taken in by that ancient professor. "Professor Edwards is God," she had written in the margins of her notes. He is the Omniscient Narrator of My Life, she wrote, though his later, pronounced and, truth be told, clumsy flirtations baffled her—he was her father's age, older!—and she couldn't quite place whether his behavior was acceptable in a kind of medieval, Ivy League way, or entirely repulsive. Among her friends, there were differing opinions—they all knew the other one, who deposited the occasional rumpled freshman back onto campus early mornings. No one seemed to be particularly bothered by him. But Professor Edwards was different—more discerning, Caroline had imagined, more discreet—so that she eventually felt chosen by his attentions, or at least acknowledged as more than an ordinary senior. The irony wasn't lost on her. She was reading Susan Brownmiller. She spent Wednesday afternoons counseling rape victims in New Haven. She was no idiot about sex and power, she had told herself then. She had made it into Yale, after all, one of the first class of women to be allowed, and was soon to graduate magna cum laude. Yet here she was, wasn't she? Exactly no one her mother would have imagined she would become: an undergraduate spread-eagle on the floor of his emeritus's office, a scratchy, Tibetan prayer rug against her bare skin. Their first and only coupling had been furtive and doomed until she took matters into her own hands. She felt sorry for him, actually, the genius with his pants shoved to his ankles, his cock "in retreat," as he put it; and though he often invited her back she never went, dropping his class during the requisite post-midterm period in which to do so, citing the reason as "conflict" in the appropriate line.

"What I'm talking is detente," shouted the young dean. "I'm talking breaking down the Wall. You must think of me as the bridge—the link, and by that I mean *interstitial* between generations."

"What did he say?" someone asks her.

"Interstitial," she answers. "*He's* the interstitial."

"Oh," they say, Caroline noticing that this woman's face no longer matches her neck, as if she'd erased the years she could afford and then, short on cash, figured to hell with it and left well enough alone.

Several days have passed since Caroline's discovery of her mother's blog. She has done her best not to keep constant tabs on DT, but it is like a hot spot, an itch to scratch, and she finds during certain slow moments at work and in the late evenings that she cannot resist the pull to check in on "A Proclamation," to read again her mother's declaration of passing through the point of rage and the posts that follow. Who were these people? What else did they have in their lives?

It all felt a secret business, furtive and seedy, as if Caroline were once again a child of twelve, rifling through her mother's underwear drawer, digging beneath the silky folds of lingerie and scratchy hosiery to get to the beaded clutch at the bottom where she knew she'd find the diaphragm, a flesh-colored ring in a hard, pink plastic case. The instructions for its proper care and application were creased and folded within, but she had already memorized them: the drawing of a woman squatting over a toilet, pushing the diaphragm into her vagina, the ring a way to staunch or suffocate something, Caroline suspected. The day her mother walked in on her in the powder room trying to follow the directions, her scabbed knees shaking from holding the position for so long, her mother had cried and cried. "First your brother," she had said. "Now you."

A few weeks earlier, James had run away to the woods at the dead end, refusing to live under the same roof as their parents.

"Why don't you just cut it, for God's sake?" Caroline said, James enlisting her to follow his instructions at all costs. She had stolen a tuna fish sandwich folded in wax paper from the refrigerator and snatched a banana from a bowl in the kitchen, though their mother was nowhere in sight, serving at the time the less fortunate in the downtown soup kitchen, her Junior League pin affixed to her scarf.

"I told you," James said. "Principle. Charles and Dorothy will just have to deal with it." James had been the one to come up with the idea of calling their parents Charles and Dorothy, as if the family were just a collection of friends who happened to live under the same roof. It had taken her some time to get used to it: Charles and Dorothy, she used to whisper when alone, practicing—the very names of her parents daring somehow, entirely illegal for reasons she couldn't express. But these days she said Dorothy's name as often as she could.

"It's supposed to get cold tonight. Freezing or something." She picked at the place on her knee where she always picked. "Besides, I miss you," she said.

"I only just left."

"Dorothy is driving me crazy," she said.

"Isn't she with the biddies?" he said. He had moved on to the banana.

"Dorothy will soon drive me crazy," she said.

"Just ignore her," he said.

They sat in the little clearing he'd been working on; she'd brought him a bucket of water earlier so that he could wet the saplings and he had already bent a few into an arch. He was making a teepee; something he'd read about.

"Bring me some books, will you?" he said.

"All right."

"And matches."

"Okay."

"And another banana."

"For God's sake."

He had remained there for four or five days before their father conceded defeat and dragged him back in. James could grow his hair as long as he liked, provided that he wash it regularly and tie it back from his face during school and that he stop mumbling when spoken to. "I've returned," James announced later that night. He stood in her doorway.

"I know," she said. It was very dark in the room and she might have already been asleep. "Welcome back," she said, but he was down the hallway in his own room, the door already shut. Before, they had slept tiered in a bunk bed, his crumpled bag of penny candy stashed beneath her bottom bunk, where their mother never seemed to find it, ringed, as it were, by a posse of plastic soldiers, guns raised. She would climb to the top to sit across from him, Indian-style, her back to the footboard, diving, from time to time, for the peppermint or butterscotch he tossed her way.

"This is the part," he would say, "when the X-Men kick collective ass."

"Let me see," she said, and he turned the comic book, teacher-style, to show her, though she could never clearly make out the tiny figures, too complicated and jagged on the distant page. Still, she said, "cool," as he read it too her, quizzing her from time to time to test that she was listening.

"Someone's got to teach the girl," he said, his long arm reaching into the crumpled bag they had fished up.

"What's left?" she said.

"Jawbreakers," he said.

"Fork one over," she said.

"Cyclops's ne'er-do-well brother?" he said.

"Havoc," she said.

"Caroline the Magnificent," he said. "The girl's got more brains than we give her credit for." He had short hair then—a crew cut of sorts, and freckles, and the glasses that he couldn't keep straight, that he called his spectacles, that he unfolded, every morning, from the small table next to her, where he would ask her to put them for safekeeping just before lights-out.

He tossed something in her direction and she caught it, slipping the jawbreaker from its cellophane wrap and popping it into her mouth. Could she have been any happier then? She sat across from her brother, her mouth full of sweet. Beyond their windows the world stretched out with all its elaborate complications, mysterious and uniformly drawn: house, tree, lawn; house, tree, lawn. They could

do anything with it that they wished, she knew, just as soon as they
grew up and sailed away.

But in the powder room, still holding the diaphram, she stood
and hugged her mother as hard as she dared, caressing her mother's
hair in its tight chignon as if she were the grown-up, and her mother
the child.

"There, there, Dorothy," she said. "There, there."

October 10, 9:45 p.m.:

The Proclamation continues:

I have been thinking of my life, trying to put together the pieces of
it. Initially, I did what I was told to do, or rather, what I believed was
required of me. I had a distant father who would be recognizable to
many of you. He was terribly bright and refused to speak about
much more than the weather and what we were eating for dinner,
and as a musician (the piano) he was frequently away from home.
My mother had remarried and moved away when I was still a child.
She was no match for him, he said of her. I left the house as soon
as I was able, moving into a small apartment with friends for a few
months before I met my husband. He used to joke we were set up
by Fate, which was true—we came together in a freak accident—
and that the Gods had insisted on a blind date. He was a romantic,
my husband. He spoke of the Gods, and Fate and the Furies as if
they were dining in the next room. I don't know if I ever actually
loved the man, but I will say that I admired the depth of his soul
(now listen to me!) and the courage he showed (much like Florence
Nightingale) in the face of war—he survived the Pacific Theater as
a POW and wasn't released until years later. Life followed its
course after our marriage. And thank you, Confabulator, for the
contribution of the idea of being "nailed to a continuation." I was a
continuation, you might say, a housewife of the sixties and
seventies, and though I had many friends, we'd rarely talk of more

than our children and our husbands' jobs. I don't know if we were capable, honestly. There were times in the middle of the night I would wake and walk into my children's room. It's the one place where I felt whole, somehow, and I would often just sit on the edge of one of their beds, thinking. This I remember from those years, which seem so lost, now, in a flurry of mittens and coats and shoes outgrown and orthodontia and student council meetings.

When I think about it, I think how long it takes to clear your throat, and by that I mean, to say anything true. What am I trying to do with this? I am trying to find my OWN VOICE. I am trying to SAY WHAT I MEAN. I am BEING PRESENT. Here is an exercise for anyone interested, I read this somewhere and thought at first that it sounded ridiculous but then it actually made some sense. Write down 3 true things every day. By that I don't mean, My hair is brown, but rather something like, I am happiest when I help others. Florence did exactly this and we're talking about the 19th century, give or take :)—maybe she was our earliest self-help author! She asked the soldiers to record a happy thought. One happy thought, no matter how ill they were, and do you know she said it improved their health?

But one step at a time. Look at us, for instance, talking and listening this way. Expressing. And we have such a road ahead! It is only at the brink of death that we are truly present for our life. And isn't that an outrage?

Liz is eating when she answers the telephone, Caroline can hear. Caroline sits at her desk in her study, shuffling a stack of quarters—this her bad habit since quitting smoking.

"Have you read it yet this morning?" Caroline says. "There's new stuff."

"Good morning," Liz says.

"My question is, who the hell does she think she's talking to?"

"I don't know," Liz says, chewing. "There are lots of women out there like her, women stalking the elephant," Liz says.

"The what?" Caroline says.

"Forget it," Liz says.

"Did you read it this morning?" Caroline repeats.

"Are you kidding me?" Liz says. "Read Mom's blog? It's a good day if I can take a shower."

"How are the twins?"

"Perfection."

"And Suzanne?"

"Awesome."

"You should check it out."

"No," Liz says too quickly, then adds, "no time," and Caroline suspects, by the silence that follows, that Liz is leafing through a catalogue, trying to get a jump on Christmas, or possibly spraying and sponging the kitchen counter. "I mean, Mom's entitled to a private conversation, isn't she?" she says.

"Suit yourself," Caroline says.

"I won't tell her if that's what you're worried about," Liz says. "I won't say a thing."

"Believe me, I know."

"What do you mean?"

"I mean, I know you won't say a thing. You never say a thing. You just, God. You have the kids and Paul and blah blah blah. Don't burst the frickin' bubble is the point. Don't step outside of the awesome, candy-coated fun mobile for a—"

"Gotta go," Liz says.

"Of course."

"Have a nice day!"

"I will," Caroline says, though Liz has already hung up the phone.

October 11, 8:23 p.m.:

Hi, DT. Enjoying your self-expression. You asked about one true thing, or maybe three, but here is one: I'm lonely. First, I wasn't. I mean, I wanted him to leave the house. I asked him to leave, or

what I mean is, when he said, should I just leave then? I said yes,
because at the time I wanted him to go. It hadn't been great
between us for years. I think he had affairs. I KNOW he had affairs,
but then I did, too. We'd kind of agreed that would be okay. But
then I changed my mind. We had a child. I earned more, too,
which always bothered him. Now I guess you could say, I feel
scared. I am still Miss Responsibility, only terrified. That's the point
in a nutshell. Do you think all of our actions are motivated by fear?

—*Robinsnest*

Caroline logs on several times through the evening to see what her
mother has to say about her post. That she could pick up the telephone and call her mother directly, that she might say, Hey, lady, the
jig is up!, that she might actually pose these questions face-to-face
over tea or a glass of wine or even one of those new drinks her
mother likes, the ones with the grenadine (God!), doesn't escape her.
The whole business begs some kind of postmodern, existential question no one bothers to ask anymore.

Caroline turns from her computer to pick up the telephone. She
dials Dora's number with deliberate effort. It is past midnight, and
for a split second, Caroline thinks she might just hang up. Then she
remembers that every dorm room is now equipped with caller ID
and the telephone is already ringing.

"Sweetheart!" she says when Dora answers.

"Mom?" Dora says. "Are you okay? Is everything all right?"

"It's fine, honey. It's fine. Nothing's wrong. Everything's great."
Caroline pauses. "Great."

"Oh," Dora says.

"And you? How are you?"

"Mom? It's late. I was sleeping. What is it?"

"Nothing, really. I mean, nothing big. I just wanted to hear your
voice, I guess."

"Well, here I am," Dora says.

"There you are," Caroline says.

Kate Walbert

"Can I hang up now?" Dora says.

"No," Caroline says too quickly. "Not yet. I mean, wait," she says.

There's a long silence in which Caroline closes her eyes and wills something that feels like calm, or happiness, toward her daughter. Goodwill. It is a trick she first tried when Dorothy blew through the house, furious at a grade, furious at a slight, furious at what she couldn't name. Caroline would have been just home from work, still in that ridiculous suit with the little tie and the man's shirt they used to wear. She had curled her hair at 5:30 a.m. but now it drooped as if exhausted. Her briefcase bulged on the side table; she might steal a few hours before bed. Too much to do. There was too much to do. For, what? Money? Yes, and no. It was beyond that—it was something she couldn't name: pleasure, of course, intellectual engagement, of course. And she had talents, for God's sake. She had been named a VP only a few years out of business school. She was one of the best and she needed to use her noggin, she used to say, when Dorothy was just a little girl and asked why she had to work.

"I've got to go," Dora says into the telephone. "I've got to go."

The click is as clear as the sound of a lock, catching as a door is pulled shut.

October 12, 12:47 a.m.:

I find it is the dark of the night when you least expect it—whatever this thing is—regret, perhaps, but not, it is bigger than that, more epic, somehow, padded and full and weirdly historical: this restlessness, this discontent. You've done it wrong, again, and you were going to do it perfectly. You've lost the forest for the trees. Now it rises up to knock your breath out. Was this what you felt, DT, when you sat on the edge of our beds? Is this the same feeling for any of you?

—Robinsnest

DOROTHY "DORA" LOUISE

BARRETT-DEEL

New Haven, Connecticut, 2007

●

Dora Barrett-Deel

Basic Information

Network:	The Whitewood School '07 Yale Undergraduate Student '11
Sex:	Female
Interested in:	Men/Women
Birthday:	August 3, 1989
Looking for:	Whatever I can get
Political Views:	State-of-Terror
Religious Views:	Animist

Personal Information

Interests:	rock climbing, outfits (shoes); marathons, decoupage, flora and fauna, diacritic marks, irony; The Monkeys; The Beatles; French films; photography; chick flicks.
Favorite Books:	The Awakening; V. Woolf (even the last two indecipherable ones); Charlotte's Web; The Phantom Toll Booth; W. Cather (even that weird middle chapter in The Professor's House); the poetry of Elizabeth Bishop; T. S. Eliot; the great E. Dickinson; the complete works of Robert Browning (long story); S. Plath; A. Rich; J. Gilbert; S. Olds.
Favorite Quotes:	"Life shrinks or expands in proportion to one's courage."—Anaïs Nin "Courage in women is often mistaken for insanity."—Somebody else
About Me:	My great-great-grandmother starved herself for suffrage. Color me Revolutionary.

EVELYN CHARLOTTE TOWNSEND

New York City, New York, 1985

I am not yet dead, I tell Susan. She knocks on the front door as if I'm dead. She bangs and bangs. I've told her to use her keys for emergencies and so she uses her keys. What's on fire? I'm yelling, but otherwise I'm occupied. I tell her I am writing something. I have decided to call it Eulogy for a Woman Not Yet Dead. I say it goes like this, "She came. She went."

"How's that?" I say.

"Hah hah," she says. Susan feels qualified to judge, she of the full scholarship to Barnard and, back in Michigan, first in her class. She has certain heroes I have never heard of, and occasionally uses words I find absurd, but I like her, this Susan. She's a good egg and far better than the last one the college found for me, the one who smoked and popped her gum. It was Susan's idea that we should take notes on life and read them aloud occasionally, that we should spice it up a bit, this relationship, so that it is not just about feeding and being fed, the caretaker and the taken care of: There is more that women have to offer one another, isn't there?

I say, "On my deathbed, these will be my last words to you: Get a sense of humor."

"It's my job to worry," she says.

"Right, right," I say.

She pushes me into the kitchen to show me what she's brought, sliding me underneath the old wooden butcher block Stephen Pope and I bought at the flea market on Sixth Avenue, with its chiseled initials of persons we never knew but liked to guess the stories of.

"Have you noticed a smell?" I ask her.

"I don't smell anything," she says.

"There's a smell," I say.

I like looking at her as she looks around. She's concerned and young and though she is getting paid, I believe she's my friend. I believe she will actually miss me, this girl who dresses like a boy, mostly, or indistinguishable, her hair crowned with purple, or a black that's close. Several months ago, when she first arrived, she had a stud in her lip that made me itch. Wouldn't she please lose it? I asked, and that she agreed convinces me I am right, I'll be missed.

"Read it," she says, sitting opposite.

"What?" I say.

"The poem, the eulogy," she says.

"I did," I say.

"There's more," she says, uncovering the dish she's brought, gruel or something equally tasteless. It's terrible to grow old, I tell her every other time, there's not a thing cheerful about it. But not today; today I am writing. Today is good. But what was I writing? My hands are on the loose pages though I forget one minute to the next. My fingers point west, I could show her, toward sunset. See how they curve at the knuckle? How does the body do that, bend its own bones?

"Private property," I say.

"I won't tell," she says.

"She came, she went," I read. "She once had a heart; her heart stopped. She loved or did not love. Words she ate like popcorn—"

"That's pretty good," she says, scooping the food onto a plate she's taken from the cabinet. She sets down a glass of the warm water she feels is best for digestion, lining up my pills, five, alongside my plate. She is telling me a story she heard on the television this morning about a dog who learned to dial the telephone. She is saying it's too hot in here, we should open a window. She is describing her dream and how it is virtually indescribable but here goes.

She is here with me because this is a better-paying job than filing, and easier than waiting tables and "whatever," whatever that would be—she has had many jobs, she's told me. "Besides, I like old people," she said, "especially old ladies." She tells me everything, and once she read me a poem of her own, something personal, she said, that I would understand, having lived the life I led. Which life is that? I wanted to ask her.

She grips my bad hand and molds it around the spoon and feeds me as if I am feeding myself. It is bland and tasteless, what they suggest for old people, apparently, somewhat solid though it would slip through cheesecloth. Still, I'm starving, I tell her. I forgot breakfast and I've been working so hard.

"The title's the best," she says.

"It's coming along," I say.

She stands to straighten the mirror that never hangs right. She is cleaning up a bit. I smell the smell, feel a buzz in my ears. I am used to being alone, mostly, and company, even Susan, is difficult. For the last few years, I have remained solely on the first floor, wheeling between the kitchen and the library, the library and the dining room where I now sleep on a cot Susan will remake before heading home, the trompe l'oeil path of my former dressing room, with its trees and fallen leaves, what I picture at night to block out the city sounds that bear down on Gramercy Park, the city too crowded and dangerous in ways I am glad Stephen Pope never lived to see. On certain evenings, I wheel myself into the foyer, unable to sleep, my mind switched back to the beginning and my arrival here. I was a slip of a girl then, and still hungry. Stephen Pope offered me a hand. He said I would find his wife's dressing room at the top of the stairway, first door on the right. He said she had an adjacent bedroom where I could spend the night. He said we would figure out other arrangements tomorrow. I was hard as flint. I might have then smoothed the worn part of his face, or hand, and set us both on a different course. What did I have to prove? Who was even watching?

"It's a beautiful day," Susan says, turning, and against the kitchen window, bright now that she's raised the shade and opened the sash, she drops into her shadow and is gone. People disappear frequently now, as if they are nothing more than a glint of reflection. Come back, I think. And when I look up there Susan is again, as if she never stopped talking. "A walk?" is what she's saying.

"A sit," I say.

"Agreed."

"You got this," she says, putting a letter on the table, an envelope. "They gave it to me at school. It went to the chemistry department. Special delivery," Susan says. She has slit the envelope open, already anticipating my shaky hands. I wonder if it's from a former student, although I receive fewer and fewer of those letters these days. I look at the return address. I cannot read this letter, I say to Susan. It's against my principles.

"Who is she?" Susan wants to know, looking over my shoulder. "Dorothy Townsend Barrett?"

Gramercy Park is locked, a stalled renovation, Susan tells me. New York broke. I can't keep up with the rise and fall of it, the down and up of it, the round and round of it. Stephen Pope believed in Communists, the threat of the Chinese and the Soviet Union, the possibility of the extinction of humankind. Then he believed in nothing. But Stephen Pope is dead and Susan is still here. She has been here several months and is not likely to go anywhere for a while, she promised.

No, I answered the day she first arrived. No other family, no.

"Just you," she said, unwrapping a long scarf, though it was August, and hot.

"Look," she said, pointing to where the wisteria had grown in through the library window, curling around my reading lamp.

"It does it every afternoon," I said.

"Cool," she said. "Nice place."

"Home," I said.

"Your husband?" she said. She leaned into the bookshelves, the photographs there. She must have had Stephen Pope in her hands.

"A friend. My compatriot, of sorts."

"Awesome. I knew you were ahead of your time." She hooked some hair behind her ear, thrice pierced. I am hungry. I wait to see what she's brought. It is difficult for me now, to eat. I depend on others.

I am eighty-four years old, felled by a stroke, sitting on the daybed in what had once been my favorite room, where Stephen Pope and I would, for too many years to count, exchange the news of our days, Stephen Pope speaking of what he had read and I of what I had observed or taught. The beveled shelves of books loomed over us. A fire burned in the grate of the fireplace. The draperies were drawn against the muffled street sounds. Had there been snow? Now I am trying not to shake, trying to make a good impression—Susan a very bright and responsible girl, they had phoned from the college to tell me. Exactly what I was looking for.

"When did he die?" she asked, turning, holding the frame.

"Oh," I said. "Many years ago. He was much older."

"Handsome," she said.

"Was he?"

"Dashing," she said. They always think of you as an idiot, the young, speak to you in that way.

"Put him down," I said, too harshly.

"I'll put him back," she said, and did, then walked over to stand in front of me.

"I'm sorry," she said. "I've never done this before, fed the elderly."

The clock Stephen purchased, the loud-ticking one mounted over the fireplace, with the graceful, Roman numerals, the rusted hands, ticked as if insisting. Time insists, I said once to Stephen Pope.

"You're very pretty," I said.

She smiled and was even prettier. "Thank you, Professor Townsend," she said.

* * *

Susan finds a way into Gramercy Park and pushes me toward the central square and the fountain. The fountain's drained, its granite jack-hammered, something being carved or routed. It is early spring and the pear trees look drawn from fairy tales: skewered clouds. Skewered clouds? Words, either right or wrong, are suddenly sharp as numbers, though numbers I have mostly forgotten, or grown tired of—my students carrying on, I suppose. It only goes so far, your work, I could tell Susan, she of the mountains-to-scale variety. What did I accomplish? Three books. Twenty-seven articles, a handful of covers: *Science*, my first; attributions by other scholars, citations, co-authorships. I never filled in an element on the Periodic Table, I could tell her, though I had often imagined, if I did, what I would name it, what word I could claim as my own when it is often so difficult to speak. Sweet Susan. She has looked up my books in the Barnard library. She liked the title *Factors in Principles* the best, she said. It sounded abstract to her, philosophical. Very French, she said. Very Sartre or de Beauvoir, though the introduction was the only thing she could comprehend, physical chemistry—all of it, science—not her thing.

But wasn't Professor Townsend quite the smart gal? she said.

I knew which edition she meant, which introduction: Van de Horn, rabidly hyperbolic concerning my accomplishments (in quest of the department chair at the time), spewing about the age and odds as if I were some kind of racehorse that had been let too soon out of the starting gate, leading the pack, blinders secure, plunging ahead as my teammates fell behind exhausted, broken of will: theories to theorems and round, again. Still, the publisher liked it, said it would sell more books and wasn't that the point of it?

"What was the point of it?" I say, randomly, and then, "Stephen Pope."

I called him Stephen Pope when he was alive, as if to insist we remain strangers and because I liked the sound.

Susan sets down her book on the bench and stands to tuck Stephen Pope's old plaid blanket more firmly around my legs. She asks if I want my feet up but they're fine down, I tell her.

"Lovely day," she says.

"One hundred percent divine," I say, because it is, and it hasn't been.

"Is it good?" I ask.

"Wordsworth," she says. "My required dose of dead white men."

"Oh," I say.

I stare out at the drained fountain. Pear blossoms ash the stone, then are swept into drifts by the breeze.

"I've brought the letter if you'd like to hear it," Susan says.

"All right," I say. "Go on," I say, as she clears her throat.

"Dear Professor Townsend," Susan reads. "I'm writing to you with the hope that you might be the person I am looking for, sister to Thomas Francis Townsend, my father, who, I'm afraid, died of alcoholism many years ago. It is only recently that I have even learned that my father had a sister. He was not a happy man, nor was he ever given to discuss our family history. I was his only daughter, and a disappointment to him. You may have known about his extraordinary talent in music. I was not blessed with this. I apologize for writing as if you are, indeed, my aunt Evelyn, daughter of my namesake, the suffragette Dorothy Trevor Townsend. I now know something about her, her death by starvation, the boy and girl she left behind, but I have so many questions and am so eager to meet you, if you are the right Evelyn Townsend. I would wish it so, and would be forever grateful if you could please write to me as soon as possible.

"Sincerely, Dorothy Townsend Barrett."

"Wow," says Susan. "That's heavy."

"Put it away," I tell her.

"Are you the right Evelyn?" Susan says.

"Put it away," I tell her. "Please."

* * *

I might doze. I might be wide awake: Mum another glint of reflection, as easily cut from the light as Susan or any of these passersby who hurry along outside the park fence, on the sidewalks, who no more see me here than they know her, dead as she is, dead as she always was, her body as crippled as mine is now, her spine curved into a singular question. I have not been given permission to come to hospital but I am here, slipped through, Nurse busy with Thomas or elsewhere, Michael giving me a lift on his bicycle if I keep quiet about it. I'll keep quiet about it, I tell him. I still look a child and am thin as a switch and given to rudeness. I can be very rude, Mum says, and I must take care to be more polite. I must get my nose out of books. I am old enough to know better, to listen when I'm being spoken to, to be kind, to stop looking down.

I like the color blue, and the news I have read of the aeroplane scheduled soon to arrive, crossing the Channel, driven by the Frenchman Junot, a man of such bravery and daring that the papers have been writing about him for weeks. There will be a parade, apparently, and fireworks.

I push in through the door and slip up the ammonia-smelling stairs, hand on the metal banister squeaking as I count to thirteen, my already unlucky number. I am near to her room. Last week they would let me visit, but Mum's taken a turn for the worse, Grandmother says, and so children are no longer allowed. I have stood beneath the window and called her name, though someone has pushed the window down against the morning rain and, besides, Mum could no longer hear me. They've given her something and she can no longer hear you, Grandmother said last week when I said good-bye. "She's near to gone."

I climb the stairs. Adults only, Grandmother says, and even so, Grandmother stays away, Mum now preferring her solitude, she said, the word closing around Mum as a shell would around a seed, as hard as the steel of a submarine. She sits within it, and you can no more get to her than she can get to you. It is as if she is going somewhere; she has made up her mind. Or maybe she's just waiting for time to pass; for something to be over. She is caught in there, in her solitude, held in the light and pounded steel of it and moving away at great speed.

Someone has shut the window. It is warm in the room. I sit for a while in Grandmother's chair and I look at everything not her, thinking maybe I will see the aeroplane's trail after all, this the day for it, the day for the spectacle, but in truth it is far from here and already landed—the gathered onlookers discussing the mystery, the terror, the eventuality of all things natural to mechanical.

I turn to watch her breathe. I am watching her breathe and then I cannot stand it. I climb into the bed with her, into that place where she is and if I get caught, if I am found here, I am sorry, I will tell them: There is nowhere else to be.

ACKNOWLEDGMENTS

I am grateful to the following editors: Cressida Leyshon at *The New Yorker*, Heidi Pitlor and Stephen King at *Best American Short Stories*, Don Lee and Rosanna Warren at *Ploughshares*, Hannah Tinti at *One Story*, and J. D. McClatchy at *The Yale Review*. I am especially grateful to Nan Graham, and to Eric Simonoff.

Writing a Woman's Life, by Carolyn G. Heilbrun, and *The Feminine Character: History of an Ideology*, by Viola Klein, were invaluable for the writing of this book.

A heartfelt thank you to Carolyn Cooke, and, as always, to Rafael.

Turn the page for a preview of
Kate Walbert's novel

THE
SUNKEN
CATHEDRAL

Available June 2015 from Scribner

III

The mothers, dressed for exercise, gather on the steps of Progressive K–8—Stephanie G. at the center, forty-five, give or take, her hair in short braids, dandelions woven into the bands— Elizabeth sees her and sidesteps but too late.

"Elizabeth!" Stephanie G. calls. "Elizabeth!"

How had she agreed to the idea at all? Now Stephanie G. blocks her path, clearly determined to see the vision fulfilled: Who We Are stories line the hallways of Progressive K–8 like so many snowflake cutouts in winter, each sincere and beautiful and excruciatingly heartbreaking for reasons Elizabeth cannot name and does not want to examine. The idea had grown out of the school's pledge for better communication by way of stronger community, dialoguing through dialogue, something like that, one of those tautologically challenged declarations beloved by their new interim head of school—Dr. Constantine—an elderly woman whose early advocacy of sexual education in pre-K put her on the academic map. If everyone could share their roots, or dig down to their roots, or expose their roots the school might come together in a grand way, or at least in a way that would increase the parent participation in the annual fund drive.

It had all been outlined in an e-mail: IMPORTANT ANNOUNCE-
MENT FROM DR. CONSTANTINE, which Elizabeth opened expecting to
read of another outbreak of nits on a fifth grader's scalp or an
additional plea for vigilance when patrolling the City blocks
after pickup. This, Elizabeth's favorite parental responsibility:
mothers and the occasional bemused father wandering Bleecker
Street in pairs regardless the weather, dressed in bright orange
vests and carrying heavy walkie-talkies, a bit over-the-top, yet
still: vigilance must be maintained, Dr. Constantine stressed,
especially in the event of a What If.*

Last month Elizabeth had patrol duty with a woman
whose son was in first grade, a woman tall and thin with dark,
New York hair and glasses suggesting a love of books or at
least a graduate degree in the humanities. The two had wandered the block greeting other mothers they knew, nodding to
clusters of students and telling them to get along, eyeing any
stray man who seemed not to have a destination in mind, their
hands gripping the walkie-talkies just in case they needed to
call back in to, whom? Dr. Constantine? Central control? The
crackle of static had felt comforting, as was the idea of a direct
link to someone who might allay her more general fears: Dirty
bomb a hoax, the voice would whisper; organic beef as good
as grass-fed.

But this e-mail had a different message:

What's Your Story? it read. We're asking the Progressive

---

*What Ifs were favorites of Dr. Constantine's, who often opened her monthly
Cappuccinos with Constantine by tossing What Ifs to the crowd: What If an
earthquake were to knock out the power grid? What If an outbreak of avian flu
occurred during a blizzard? What If I never do my homework? Elizabeth's son,
Ben, newly thirteen, now liked to throw back at her, What If I refuse to get out
of bed?

K–8 Community to participate in a 3-E endeavor to Enliven, Engage, and Enlighten with Who We Are stories. Everyone has one: Great-Uncle Vic worked as a tailor for Chiang Kai-shek; Grandmother Sanchez escaped from Castro's Cuba. Whatever it is, we want to know! And please, include pictures!

"So, who are we?" Ben asked that night at the dinner table.

"What?" Elizabeth said, distracted by the amount of cheese he had stuffed in his taco.

"Dr. Constantine said we were supposed to remind you," Ben said, negotiating a bite. "I'm reminding you."

"Oh, that," she said, turning to her husband, who scooped the meat with a spoon and whose pale, delicate fingers, long and tapered, looked as if he should be playing a musical instrument. "What?" Pete said. "What are we talking about?"

"We're supposed to write a Who We Are story," Elizabeth said. "You know, where we come from, how we ended up here. They're asking everyone to do it. One of those community things."

Pete looked at her as if not comprehending. She had noticed this more and more about him, these brief synapses—hamster trances, Ben called them—and wondered if it had to do with his not sleeping, or maybe the hours he spent sitting at a desk staring at small numbers moving across a computer screen or on the device held in his palm. Perhaps he was waiting for his wife and son to morph into something else, for the trading feed to begin its loop across the bottom of the page: information, statistics, the rise and fall of the stock exchange; or possibly he hoped the text might offer links to other sites, sites that would explicate his family's deeper, troubling mysteries—his wife's increasing restlessness, his son's unpredictable moods.

"My ancestors were Welsh," Pete said. "You could write about that. The Welsh are interesting."

"I thought Holland," Elizabeth says.

Pete shrugs. "Somebody sailed from Rotterdam before the Revolution, but then there was also something about Wales. Nobody really knows."

"If you were a girl you could be a member of the DAR," Elizabeth says to Ben. "That's kinda cool."

Ben looks from one to the other then takes a tremendous bite of his taco, tomatoes and cheese and lettuce shreds raining down on his plate, and to the side of the plate onto the good tablecloth.

"Promise me you won't take your first date out for tacos," Elizabeth says.

"I promise I won't take my first date out for tacos," Ben says, his mouth full. When did he get so large, so ungainly, so hairy? He is all arms and legs, as if he can't even fit into his chair. They sit on the chairs she and Pete bought in Mexico, right after their wedding. The chairs have rattan seats the cat has destroyed and are grease-stained and worn but when she looks at them she thinks of Pete speaking broken Spanish, attempting to bribe someone at the post office in Oaxaca to mail them freight.

"We could write how we had tacos on our first date," Elizabeth says to Pete, feeling suddenly expansive, young; she might be twenty-eight; she might be walking on that beach in Mexico, the one where they stayed before leaving for Oaxaca, where the chickens and seagulls followed them for crumbs. They were eating galletas; they were leaving a trail in case they got lost. "We could write that when I took the first bite he wondered if he could have a second date, much less spend the rest of his life with me."

"I did wonder that," Pete says.

"First date?" Elizabeth says.

"What did we do?" Pete says.

"Chinese," Elizabeth says.

"Right," Pete says. "I was thinking egg roll."

"Chinatown," Elizabeth says.

"Right, right. You had the spicy braised fish," he says, though she didn't—at the time she refused to eat anything with scales.

"And then we went to hear music," she says.

"Muddy Waters," Pete says.

"Willie Dixon," Elizabeth says. "And ate those little balls with the toothpicks for dessert. They were too sweet. They're always too sweet."

"I moved into your mother's apartment. It was above Sherm's—" Pete says to Ben.

"Sherman's was an upscale diner and all day Sunday you smelled all the delicious—" says Elizabeth.

"Sausage."

"Your father didn't have a dime. We never ate out again," Elizabeth says.

"One time your mother found this stray dog and asked the waiters if they had any leftover sausage—"

"Oh God!"

"For the dog," Pete says. He smiles, remembering.

Ben has his eyes covered, head on the table, or the pretty tablecloth. "Should I be writing this down?" he says.

Two fathers sprint past Stephanie G., their jacket tails flying as if they can't wait to get the hell to their jobs. Certain days the fathers turn out in impressive numbers, walking their young children to school, looking handsome and freshly showered, many in well-cut suits and a few in jeans and bomber jackets, good shoes, and one or two in grungy clothes. The fathers must exercise at different times, maybe earlier in the morning before they have showered, or possibly at night or possibly not at all, though in general the fathers look more physically fit than the mothers and, truth be told, Elizabeth thinks, younger. How could you account for this? How can you possibly reconcile the great inequities of gender—coupled with the perversions of age and the general randomness of everything? Who could you call to complain? Or is it *whom*?

"Elizabeth?" Stephanie G. is saying. "Are you with me?"

"Oh, sorry," Elizabeth says, too quickly. "Yes, of course. Absolutely. What?"

"I was saying we're trying to get one hundred percent participation. It's part of the General Mandate. I saw you signed up for the Environmental Committee, too," she says. "Of course there's no saying you can't do both." Stephanie G. cocks her head to one side. She actually looks cute in braids, Elizabeth thinks. Maybe how she looked as a child, eager, happy, always ready to include the third girl or stand up to the bully. She clerked for a Supreme Court justice until she had her second son—now there are four—worked as the editor of the law review, supported her alcoholic mother, et cetera, et cetera. When she had started putting dandelions in her hair Elizabeth can't quite remember, though it may have been right around the time Stephanie G. cochaired the third-grade flower drive. Those days you would never see her without a potted plant in her hands or a sprig of something behind her ear.

"I mean unless you want to," Stephanie G. says. "If you want to, that would be terrific."

"No, I'm good," Elizabeth says. "That sounds great," she adds, not quite understanding what she's agreed or not agreed to. She had joined the Environmental Committee after the e-mail went out that every parent was expected to serve on a volunteer committee or two, given the lackluster response to the all-volunteer volunteer committees. She had a vision of herself with the rest of the committee in gloves and comfortable boots, the sun streaming down as they tended to the delicate morning glories entwining the chain-link fence that guarded the children from running off the roof playground, or clipped a potted hedgerow or two, possibly, or watered a copse of birch, birch mostly foreign to the City, especially downtown, but for a while she could picture it: the kindergartners tricycling through the birch, their little legs turning the wheels as fast as they could, careering around the roof playground as if they had suddenly found themselves in a magic forest. The birch might even mute the sounds of traffic and attract the wildlife from farther north, near Central Park, the families of squirrel and raccoon and even otter.

"Anyway, there's no rush," Stephanie G. is saying, "though we do hope to get everything in by the end of the year."

"All right," Elizabeth says. "We'll think of something," she says.

"Wonderful!" Stephanie G. says, striding down the steps and disappearing into the band of suitably stretched women. They will run from here a few blocks north, across Fourteenth Street, then up the West Side Highway bike path as far as they can go, some of them, even, sprinting the GW Bridge to the Palisades, these the most determined, the marathoners, the ones who, heads down, feet sneakered, push and push their tired hearts, as that runner once did to warn the Athenians of the Spartans, or maybe it was the other way around.

Turn the page for a preview of
Kate Walbert's novel

THE

GARDENS
OF KYOTO

Available from Scribner

I had a cousin, Randall, killed on Iwo Jima. Have I told you? The last man killed on the island, they said; killed after the fighting had ceased and the rest of the soldiers had already been transported away to hospitals or to bodybags. Killed mopping up. That's what they called it. A mopping-up operation.

I remember Mother sat down at the kitchen table when she read the news. It came in the form of a letter from Randall's father, Great-Uncle Sterling, written in hard dark ink, the letters slanted and angry as if they were aware of the meaning of the words they formed. I was in the kitchen when Mother opened it and I took the letter and read it myself. It said that Randall was presumed dead, though they had no information of the where-abouts of his body; that he had reported to whomever he was intended to report to after the surrender of the Japanese, that he had, from all accounts, disappeared.

I didn't know him too well but had visited him as a young girl. They lived across the bay from Baltimore, outside Sudlersville. No town, really, just a crossroad and a post office and farms hemmed in by cornfields. Theirs was a large brick house set far back from the road, entirely wrong for that landscape, like it had been hauled up from Savannah or Louisville to prove a point. It stood in constant shadow at the end of an oak-lined drive and I remember our first visit, how we drove through that tunnel of oak slowly, the day blustery, cool. Sterling was not what we in those days called jovial. His wife had died years before, leaving him, old enough to be a grandfather, alone to care for his only child. He had long rebuked Mother's invitations but for some reason had scrawled a note in his Christmas card that year—this was before the war, '39 or '40—asking us to join them for Easter dinner.

Mother wore the same Easter hat and spring coat she kept in tissue in the back of the hallway linen closet, but she had sewed each of us a new Easter dress and insisted Daddy wear a clean shirt and tie. For him this was nothing short of sacrifice. Rita said he acted like those clothes might shatter if he breathed.

Daddy turned off the engine and we all sat, listening to the motor ticking. If Mother had lost her determination and suggested we back out then and there, we would have agreed. "Well," she said, smoothing out the lap of her dress. It was what she did to buy time. We girls weren't moving anyway. We were tired enough; it was a long drive from Pennsylvania.

"Wake me up when it's over," Rita said. She always had a line like that. She curled up and thrust her long legs across Betty and me, picking a fight. Betty grabbed her foot and twisted it until Rita shrieked *For the love of Pete!* Mother ignored them, reapplying the lipstick she kept tucked up the sleeve of her spring coat. I looked out the window. I'm not sure about Daddy. No one wanted to make the first move, Betty twisting Rita's foot harder and Rita shrieking *For the love of Pete, get your gosh darn hands off me!* and Mother jerking around and telling Rita to stop using that language and to act her age.

The last reprimand struck Rita to the core. She sat up quickly and yanked the door open.

Did I say oak? It might have been walnut. I believe at that point, standing outside the car, we heard the comforting thwack of a walnut on a tin roof, the sound popping the balloon Rita had inflated, releasing us to walk, like a family, to the front door, where Randall already stood, waiting.

He had some sort of sweet-smelling water brushed into his hair. This I remember. It was the first thing you would have noticed. He also had red hair, red as mine, and freckles over most of his face. He stood there, swallowed by the doorway, his hand out in greeting. His were the most delicate fingers I had ever seen on a boy, though he was nearly a teenager by then. I have wondered since whether he polished his nails, since they were shiny, almost wet. Remember he was a son without a mother, which is a terrible thing to be, and that Great-Uncle Sterling was as hard as his name.

Anyway, Rita and Betty paid him little mind. They followed Mother and Daddy in to find Sterling and we were left, quite suddenly, alone. Randall shrugged as if I had proposed a game of cards and asked if I wanted to see his room. No one seemed much concerned about us, so I said sure. We went down a water-stained hallway he called the Gallery of Maps, after some hallway he had read about in the Vatican lined with frescoes of maps from before the world was round. Anyway, he stood there showing me the various countries, pointing out what he called troublespots.

I can still picture those fingers, tapering some, and the palest white at the tips, as if he had spent too long in the bath.

We continued, passing one of those old-fashioned intercom

contraptions they used to have to ring servants. Randall worked a few of the mysterious oiled levers and then spoke, gravely, into the mouthpiece. "I have nothing to offer but blood, toil, tears, and sweat," he said. Churchill, of course, though at the time I had no idea. I simply stood there waiting, watching as Randall hung up the mouthpiece, shrugged again, and opened a door to a back staircase so narrow we had to turn sideways to make the corner.

"They were smaller in the old days," Randall said, and then, perhaps because I didn't respond, he stopped and turned toward me.

"Who?" I said.

"People," he said.

"Oh," I said, waiting. I had never been in the dark with a boy his age.

"Carry on," he said.

We reached a narrow door and pushed out, onto another landing, continuing down a second, longer hallway. The house seemed comprised of a hundred little boxes, each with tiny doors and passages, eaves to duck under, one-flight stairways to climb. Gloomy, all of it, though Randall didn't appear to notice. He talked all the while of how slaves had traveled through here on the underground railway from Louisiana, and how one family had lived in this house behind a false wall he was still trying to find. He said he knew this not from words but from knowing. He said he saw their ghosts sometimes—there were five of them—a mother and a father and three children, he couldn't tell what. But he'd find their hiding place, he said. He had the instinct.

I'm not sure whether I was more interested in hearing about slaves in secret rooms or hearing about their ghosts. This was Maryland, remember, the east side. At that time, if you took the ferry to Annapolis, the colored sat starboard, the whites port, and docking felt like the flow of two rivers, neither feeding the other. In Pennsylvania colored people were colored people, and one of your grandfather's best friends was a colored doctor named Tate Williams, who everybody called Tate Billy, which always made me laugh, since I'd never heard of a nickname for a surname.

Anyway, Randall finally pushed on what looked like just another of the doors leading to the next stairway and there we were: his room, a big square box filled with books on shelves and stacked high on the floor. Beyond this a line of dormer windows looked out to the oaks, or walnuts. I could hear my sisters' muffled shouts below and went to see, but we were too high up and the windows were filthy, besides. Words were written in the grime. *Copacetic*, I still recall. *Epistemological, belie.*

"What are these?" I said.

"Words to learn," Randall said. He stood behind me.

"Oh," I said. This wasn't at all what I expected. It felt as if I had climbed a mountain only to reach a summit enshrouded in fog. Randall seemed oblivious; he began digging through his stacks of books. I watched him for a while, then spelled out *HELP* on the glass. I asked Randall what he was doing, and he told me to be patient. He was looking for the exact right passage, he said. He planned to teach me the art of "dramatic presentation."

Isn't it funny? I have no recollection of what he finally found. And though I can still hear him telling me they were smaller then, ask me what we recited in the hours before we were called to the table, legs up, in his window seat, our dusty view that of the old trees, their leaves a fuzzy new green of spring, of Easter, and I will say I have no idea. I know I must have read my lines with the teacher's sternness I have never been able to keep from my voice; he with his natural tenderness, as if he were presenting a gift to the very words he read by speaking them aloud. I know that sometimes our knees touched and that we pulled away from one another, or we did not. I wish I had a picture. We must have been beautiful with the weak light coming through those old dormers, our knees up and backs against either side of the window seat, an awkward W, books in our hands.